THE FAULT TREE

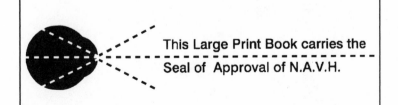

This Large Print Book carries the
Seal of Approval of N.A.V.H.

THE FAULT TREE

LOUISE URE

WHEELER PUBLISHING
A part of Gale, Cengage Learning

GALE
CENGAGE Learning

Detroit • New York • San Francisco • New Haven, Conn • Waterville, Maine • London

GALE
CENGAGE Learning

LIBRARY OF CONGRESS CATALOGING-IN-PUBLICATION DATA

Ure, Louise.
    The fault tree / by Louise Ure.
      p. cm.
    ISBN-13: 978-1-59722-743-8 (hardcover : alk. paper)
    ISBN-10: 1-59722-743-9 (hardcover : alk. paper)
    1. Blind women — Fiction. 2. Murderers — Fiction. 3. Large type books. I. Title.
    PS3621.R4F38 2008b
    813'.6—dc22   2008002689

Published in 2008 by arrangement with St. Martin's Press, LLC.

Printed in the United States of America
1 2 3 4 5 6 7 12 11 10 09 08

To Bruce, as always

ACKNOWLEDGMENTS

I've been especially lucky to have smart friends who are willing to help with my novels. My thanks to Judith Greber, Imma Trillo, and Elaine Flinn for reading and rereading *The Fault Tree* in all its incarnations. And to my expert resources, Mike Smiley, David Arnold, and Brian Washington, for their advice on all things related to aviation, car repair, and emergency medical procedures. Once again, thanks to Anna "Tina" Ortiz and Don Hodges, who answer all my odd legal and forensic questions. It is a better book because of all of you, but the errors are still all mine.

A special thanks to Lee Ure for the inspiration to create both the main character and the solution she finds. Thanks, too, to Cade Deverell, who unwittingly gave me her name. And to Cornelia Read, Sharon Wheeler, and Andi Shechter, the members of the Sad Anoraks band, for their ceaseless en-

7

couragement. To departed friend Barbara Seranella for her wisdom, her inspiration, and her helpful comments after an early read of this novel. And to the late Kathy McAnally, mystery fan extraordinaire, for whom I've created a character named Haley in this work.

I owe a debt of gratitude to the readers, librarians, reviewers, and booksellers who gave my first book, *Forcing Amaryllis,* such a nice welcome to the world. I hope to see many of you again with this new book.

My continuing thanks to my agent, Philip Spitzer, whose passionate support keeps me going. And to Andrew Martin, Michael Homler, and all the fine folks at St. Martin's for embracing *The Fault Tree.*

A Fault Tree analysis is touted as one of the best methods of identifying and graphically displaying the many ways something can go wrong.
— NASA SCIENTIFIC AND TECHNICAL INFORMATION PROGRAM, FEBRUARY 2000

CHAPTER 1

At the end, there was so much blame to spread around that we could all have taken a few shovelfuls home and rolled around in it like pigs in stink. But that's not the way it goes with most of us. Most of us like to think that blame belongs on somebody else's doorstep. And I'm no different.

I can picture the way it was on the day everything went bad just as clearly as if I still had my sight. Of course, I probably made up most of it. You know how it goes: your mouth fills in the details your mind doesn't catch. And then later, when you're looking back over everything that happened, your memory just smoothes out some of the corners, takes away that metal taste of fear, makes you seem a little braver than you really were, and then paints in a rosy-toned sunset.

You're always the hero of your own story. Even if that's not the way it happened at all.

CHAPTER 2

I slammed down the hood on the old Impala. Mrs. Wiggins was just whistling through the graveyard if she thought it was going to last another hundred thousand miles. I wiped the sheen of oil off my hands with a shop rag, then used the same cloth on my forehead and jammed it into the back pocket of my overalls.

By now, nobody expected me to leave when the shop closed. I liked working alone at night. No one around to bump into, no one to misplace my tools, and no other sound than that of an ailing engine. It was a bonus that, by this time of night, Arizona temperatures had usually dipped below ninety and I didn't feel like a freshly baked Frito anymore.

There was no buzzing from the fluorescent lights, but I made sure the switch was in the off position anyway and double-checked the locks on the doors. It was fine with me if the rest of the world thought that Walt's Auto Shop was closed for the day.

I'd been at the garage for six years now. Walt saved all his problem cars for me — the ones that couldn't be fixed just by reading the repair manual or plugging into a diagnostic machine — the ones you had to listen to. And that suited me just fine. I'd rather be around cars than people anyway.

I skinned off the overalls, hung them on a hook marked with a wooden *C* for Cadence, and tugged the tank top and shorts I had worn underneath into a more comfortable position. I found a clean sheet of paper in the drawer, rolled it into the typewriter Walt had resurrected just for me, and typed a note telling Walt what I'd done on the Impala. Flipping up the dial on my watch, I calculated my hours for the invoice and typed that in as a last line. Then, like a thief with a conscience, I walked out through the front of the darkened shop and locked the door behind me.

It was nine-thirty and quiet on the street. The desert air was calm, but heat still radiated from the asphalt and sidewalk. It was going to be another record-baking July in Tucson. I sidestepped around the prickly pear cactus that grew next to the doorway.

"C'mon, Lucy," I said to the cane in my

hand. It was a gift from my cousin Kevin eight years ago when I was blinded, and was made of ironwood, with the rounded shape of a floppy-eared dog's head as a handle. "I put turquoise in for the eyes. Now you have your own Seeing Eye dog," Kevin said, after his arguments to get me to ask for a real Seeing Eye dog had failed. I didn't want anything that relied upon me for food or water, companionship, or a job.

At his urging, I nicknamed it "Lucy" for one of the patron saints of the blind.

It was better than those red-tipped white canes. I don't like people thinking of me as a blind person before they've had a chance to think of me as a person at all.

A lawn sprinkler ratcheted around several yards to my left — probably a last-ditch effort to save that little patch of dry grass in front of the insurance office — and a horn honked down by the Guardian Motel on the corner. Although the air was cooling, Apache cicadas still thrummed in concert from the cottonwood tree down the block. Farther away I heard the dentist's drill whine of a Japanese motorcycle revving through the intersection at Ft. Lowell. Rice burners, Kevin used to call them.

The sound was a reminder of my cousin's Guidelines for Being Able to Move Away

From Home. "There are three tests. First, you have to do a major tune-up, blindfolded, in thirty minutes. Second, you have to recognize the make and model of a motorcycle by the sound of its engine. And third, you have to know the passing record of every quarterback in the NFL."

Kevin Dulcey was seventeen that summer and I was a ten-year-old tomboy who idolized her older cousin and tried to mimic his shoulder shrugs and gliding gait. I would sit quietly beside him as he struggled through algebra homework, and if he'd let me, I'd tag along when he trolled El Con Mall with his friends. My mom called him a cheap babysitter. I called him the best thing that had ever happened to me.

What a joke. I had finally perfected those thirty-minute tune-ups, but of course I didn't need the blindfold now. And I never did find a use for the football stats I'd memorized.

I stopped at the corner and listened for approaching traffic. Nothing. There was a major intersection a quarter of a mile away but not much traffic to worry about on this two-lane cross street. This part of Tucson was mostly residential, with a couple of strip malls, grocery stores, and one-man insurance offices thrown in for good measure.

I heard a cry of distress from some house down the block, but silence followed it. Probably somebody burning dinner. I moved toward the corner. Not many people going not many places on a summertime Tucson night. An engine idled behind me, but the car wasn't moving. I tapped the cane once on the edge of the curb and stepped into the street.

Suddenly, running footsteps stilled the cicadas. I stopped halfway across the street. The runners were behind me, in the direction of that idling engine. I swiveled my head, pivoting left and right like a bat, to triangulate the sound. A moment later two car doors slammed, and I heard high-pitched laughter.

I was head on to the sound. A young voice above the dull rumble. Tight. Higher register. Then the screech of spinning tires. My heart rose to my throat.

How many steps had I taken into the street? The angry-engine roar kept coming. A sound that had caused me nightmares for eight years.

I threw myself sideways and landed with a gasp as the edge of the curb caught my ribs. The cane clattered out of my hand and I cried out, orphaned by the loss of my divining rod.

Rolling into the gutter, I pulled my arms over my head as if they could protect me from three thousand pounds of hurtling metal. The engine revved to a banshee wail and raced toward me.

CHAPTER 3

The old woman on the floor had reached up and wrapped herself around his legs. He pushed Lolly toward the front door but she stumbled, grabbing on to the doorjamb to keep herself upright.

He kicked again, but the old lady held on like Velcro.

Lolly turned back from the door, re-adjusted her grip on the buck knife, and stabbed the old woman again. The woman's grip went suddenly slack, her final breath a wet, sucking sound.

"Oh, God, Lolly. Oh, my God."

It wasn't supposed to happen this way. Lolly had told him about a mattress stuffed with cash and piles of jewelry hidden in the ice cube trays. But none of it had been true. The woman had put up a struggle, and he'd just frozen. Lolly had had to do all the fighting for them. He didn't know that an old lady could scream that loud.

He wiped a sleeve across the doorjamb to blur the prints, grabbed Lolly's hand, and raced to the car, the screen door slapping uselessly against the old woman's arm in their wake.

Lolly — already on that continental divide between fear and hysteria — laughed, then cried out, "Get her! She's seen us!"

He looked up, surprised to see a tall, dark-haired woman in the street only ten or fifteen yards away from the car. He hadn't seen anyone come down the sidewalk and there were no businesses open except for the motel back the other way.

Shit, oh shit. How had it all gone so wrong so fast?

"Quiet. I'll take care of it."

Maybe it wouldn't be a problem. With any luck, the dark-haired lady couldn't see the dead woman from here. And the lighting wasn't great; maybe she wouldn't be able to identify them.

They needed to get away before the woman saw any more. A flick of the headlights to blind her, a stomp on the accelerator, and they'd be outta there.

Twenty feet . . . fifteen . . . ten. "Stand up! Stand up!" The voice that haunted his dreams. He bit his lip when he saw the woman leap toward the curb.

He knew the tires had missed her entirely, but there was a ricochet of sound against the undercarriage, as if he'd hit something solid, like a pipe.

Lolly laughed again. "Guess what?"

"What, Lollipop?" he said, concentrating on the road ahead.

"We got nineteen dollars." She grinned as she pulled the one-dollar bills from the canister, then dumped the remaining coffee grounds out the window.

CHAPTER 4

I tried to stand, but my knees folded. My breath was a whimper. I stayed on all fours until the tremors subsided, then groaned into a sitting position.

Everything hurt. Sharp pieces of gravel were embedded in my hands and forearms, and my head and ribs throbbed from contact with the sidewalk and curb.

Heart pounding, I was adrift in a black sea. I scrambled left and right but couldn't locate the cane. Calm down. You're alive; you know how to take care of yourself. It was a lifetime of moments before I could breathe without that mewling sound.

I stretched out on my back and made dusty desert snow angels. My right heel tapped something wooden ahead of me and I groped the empty air in wide, frantic sweeping motions until I connected with the wooden shaft. Fuck. There were jagged splinters about eighteen inches below the dog's head. Another eighteen inches and those splinters would have been my bones.

Feeling my way back to the shop entrance, I sank to the stoop, inadvertently rubbing up against the prickly pear next to the door. Fuck again. I picked off the beaver-tailed paddle and winced when the long thorns let go. My breathing remained shallow until the fright tapered off and my heart slowed down from its woodpecker pace.

That asshole. I had taken my share of falls and smacked into an untold number of overhanging objects through the years, but this one wasn't my fault. The jerk.

I took a deeper, calming breath and got the street and the buildings realigned in my mind. I had taken this walk almost every day for six years. I could do it without Lucy, but it would be slower going.

Sweeping the amputated dog's-head cane ahead of me like a bomb detector, I crossed the street and limped toward home.

Idiots, that's for damn sure. Maybe they were drunk and didn't have their lights on. Maybe I was the victim of somebody's end-of-day road rage. Didn't matter. I'd still be just as run over if I hadn't jumped.

I reached out with my right arm and confirmed the placement of the arch-shaped mailbox on the corner. Thirty paces farther on I found the concrete bus stop bench. Maybe the streetlights hadn't been working or were too dim. I'd heard a story on the radio earlier in the week about limiting the wattage of streetlights in Tucson so the reflected glare wouldn't affect the telescope at Kitt Peak National Observatory. That'd make for a great headline: "Blind Woman Killed Because She Could See Better Than the Guy Driving the Car."

My street didn't have a sidewalk, but the hard-packed earth next to the curb felt almost as smooth. A fast, short step with the left leg to get the pain over with, then a drag and shuffle with the right to make some progress down the road. I whistled with the ache of each step.

I try not to whine about being blind, but this was one time that I really could have used a pair of working eyes. I would have loved to pass along that license plate. Sons of bitches.

Two blocks later my feet scuffed across the larger pebbles of the Cardozas' front yard. I turned the corner and, three houses down, turned left when I smelled the honeysuckle vine that marked the edge of my driveway. I winced as I dug bloody fingers into the small front pocket of my shorts in search of house keys. "Fuck, fuck, fuck,

fuck," I muttered, a powerless four-letter incantation, as my stiff fingers forced the key into the lock.

I headed into the bathroom and opened the mirror-fronted medicine cabinet, imagining what my reflection would look like: gravel and road rash strewn across my cheeks and chin like the remains of a messy spaghetti dinner. My ribs were raw and the heels of my hands were puffy with scratches. I rifled past a metal box of Band-Aids, a small round tub of ProSoap, and a square, plastic container of floss I'd gotten free from the dentist. On the second shelf, I knocked over a plastic bottle with a screw top.

"Might be just what I'm looking for." I unscrewed the cap and sniffed. No fragrance, no clue to its identity. I usually labeled any new purchase with a Braille marker as soon as I brought it home. I must have forgotten this time, and I hoped that the only bottle of liquid in there that didn't have an odor would be the hydrogen peroxide.

I dipped a finger in and brought it to my lips. Recognizing the familiar bubbling on my tongue, I set the bottle on the counter and groped to find a washcloth and gauze pads.

After I cleaned and dressed the most obvious scrapes, I called Kevin.

"Sorry, Kev, but I think Lucy's going to need repair. I almost got run down tonight. A bad driver in a bad mood." I didn't want him to hear the marrow-chilling fear that still crept through my bones. Silence on the line while we thought of another bad driver we both knew too well.

"Forget the cane," Kevin said. "Are you all right?"

"I'm fine."

He promised to come by the house the next day and told me to tuck the decapitated stick behind the pot of lavender on the front porch, where he could find it if I wasn't home.

I opened all the windows to encourage a breeze and went to bed cursing bad drivers everywhere, including myself.

CHAPTER 5

Detective August Dupree squatted inside the front entrance, next to the old woman's body. The pool of blood had gelled into the shape of Australia just beyond his wing-tipped toes. She lay on her side, one arm stretched through the open doorway in a last-minute plea for attention. The newspaper delivery boy had phoned 911 at seven o'clock this morning, when he'd spotted Mrs. Prentice's body in the doorway.

"Forced entry?" He pointed to the gouges on the lock's striker plate.

"Looks like it," the police officer at the door replied.

Dupree turned to the medical examiner, who knelt next to the body. "Cause of death?" He never knew how to address the guy. Harry, like his first name? Or James, like his last? They both sounded too casual for the death dance he and the medical examiner had to do.

James didn't seem to notice either way. "Multiple stab wounds. She fought back. I'll have a better idea about the weapon after we do the autopsy."

Dupree examined the wounds on her back and chest. Had she surprised someone? Tried to stop a burglary? "Any guess on time of death?"

"Body temperature suggests sometime between eight and midnight last night. Can't be sure with this summer heat. And she was wearing a heavy robe. That would have stalled it even more."

Wanda Prentice had been small but strong. Even at seventy-six, her crepey arms still held the definition of solid muscle beneath the skin. Dupree lifted one outstretched arm. He didn't see anything under the dead woman's nails, but they would bag the hands anyway.

"Starting to come out of rigor," the medical examiner noted. "Might err on the early side of that estimate."

Dupree nodded, rose with a groan, and followed the trail of blood into the kitchen. Although his childhood home had been tidier, the room reminded him of his mother's kitchen back in Louisiana. The refrigerator was new enough to have sharp corners instead of the rounded silhouette he remembered, but all the appliances, along with the furniture in the living room, were firmly fixed in a forty-year-old time warp.

"Find anything?" he asked his partner. The door to the freezer compartment stood open. Ice cube trays, coffee grounds, flour, and dry cereal had been dumped in the sink and scattered on the floor. One kitchen chair was overturned and the tablecloth pulled askew.

Detective Richard Nellis picked up a flower-patterned green and orange apron with gloved hands, placed it in an evidence bag, and stood up. The junior member of the team, he towered over Dupree. "It looks like the fight started in here. And we may be looking for more than one suspect. Can't be sure yet, but I think there are two sets of footprints leading out to the door."

"Does one of them belong to the victim?"

"She had slippers on — lost one during the fight — and there's plenty of blood on them. But no, these look like two different sets of shoes."

Dupree passed through the living room and into the bedroom. It was undisturbed, except that the light bedcovers had been thrown to the side as the woman had risen from the bed. Had she heard the intruders? If so, she probably hadn't trusted her own senses, since she'd stopped to put on a robe and slippers and hadn't been worried enough to call the police. Or maybe she had been expecting someone.

He wandered back into the living room and picked up a washed-out framed photo of a younger Wanda Prentice on a fly-fishing trip with a bearded man who had his arm around her waist. Her smile, or maybe the sunlight, made her eyes scrunch into slits.

There were three full shelves of fairy tales and nursery stories, the books arranged by height. A grandchild? Or had she entertained a gaggle of children here at the house? The spines of all the books were etched with the white creases of repeated readings.

He pulled open the center drawer of a small desk next to the television. A checkbook, a bundle of seasonally appropriate greeting cards, a plastic bag full of rubber bands and another of paper clips. A well-organized woman. One used to taking care of herself after years alone.

The drawer on the right held notepads, bills, and an address book. He flipped it open to *P*, looking for any family members. There were more cross outs than current listings. "Joe Prentice" might have been a brother. His listings had started as "Joe and

Barbara," then followed Joe alone after 1985. She'd crossed out and rewritten his address five times, noting the year with each change. His latest address had been crossed out with the addendum, "Died, April 2, 1998."

The only Prentice with a current address (well, current as of two years ago) was Priscilla, who lived north of Tucson in a tiny residential community in the shadow of the Catalina Mountains.

He placed the book, Mrs. Prentice's current bills, and what looked like recent letters in an evidence bag and called to Nellis, "Let's canvass the neighborhood before everybody leaves for work. We can finish here later." Nellis joined him at the front door and they edged past the forensic team dusting the door and threshold for prints.

"She didn't go easy," Dupree said, swatting at the flies that had come to gather at the celebration of blood.

CHAPTER 6

That morning, at the very back of the bottom dresser drawer, I found the heavy-rimmed Ray Charles sunglasses and the telescoping red-tipped cane the rehab center had given me when I was first blinded eight years ago. The cane was lightweight and insubstantial in my hands, a magic wand with very little magic left.

I made chorizo and scrambled eggs for breakfast, then stood under the hot water in the shower until my skin cried uncle.

I had promised that I'd have the Lugosis' pickup truck ready by noon. If I got to work this early, I sure as hell wasn't going to stay till nine o'clock again, not with the aches and pains that had already taken root. I fingered the scrape on my chin. Still sensitive but no longer bloody.

It was cool on the porch, not even ninety yet. I leaned the stubbed end of the dog's-head cane against the terra-cotta pot in the

31

corner as I'd promised Kevin, thinking again about the morning's planned work. The truck was misfiring and it needed new brakes, especially with the way their teenage son drove.

The tenderness under my eye and across my cheekbone had probably developed into a bruise by now. Sunglasses would hide some of that but would also make me look like I was on the ragged end of some boyfriend's beer punch.

I tried for long, even strides to stretch out the kinks and soreness from last night's swan dive across the street, the cane swinging and tapping ahead of me like a town crier.

The block was a bustle of activity when I arrived: dogs barking, tense conversations in male voices at the street corner, and the *thump-thump* of a helicopter in the distance. A couple of conversations stopped when I neared the speakers, but I'm used to that. *Would the blind lady be offended if we notice her disability? Would our talking distract her and make her trip?* Nobody stopped me as I tapped my way to the front door of the shop.

I crossed the first lube bay and headed toward the office, where I heard the squeak of Walt's swivel chair. "What's happening out front?"

"Dunno. Just got here myself, but I came in the back way. You got a new cane?"

He hadn't noticed the bruises. "Almost got myself run over last night. Smashed Lucy."

"That so?" Walt's voice was faint, as if he was busy with something on the desk and wasn't looking at me. "Tsk, tsk, tsk." Offered in a distracted cluck that suggested he hadn't heard a word I'd said.

I smothered a smile, grabbed my coveralls from the hook, and turned away from him to step into them. Six years ago, Walt had laughed when I'd asked him for a job. But at least he'd listened that time, even if he'd treated my inquiry like a joke. "I'm going to hire a female auto mechanic? And a blind one at that?" He shared the joke with the rest of the shop. "You hear that, Turbo? This lady here wants your job."

Two young male voices had laughed, then one of them — most likely not Turbo — said, "I'd work with her. She's probably better than Turbo and she's a damn sight easier on the eyes." He swallowed the last word. The shop was quiet.

"Back atcha." I smiled in his direction. I was just as likely as the next person to use sight-oriented words. *Look at this. Here's how I see it. A sight for sore eyes.* And I knew

33

that if I were going to work with these guys, they'd have to quit watching their language, quit tripping over themselves to get out of the blind lady's way.

This morning the shop was already humming. The *click-click* of tightening lug nuts to my left. The whir of loosening other lug nuts at the back of the shop. Danny gave Turbo a bad time about which end of the wrench to use. Turbo suggested a place to put it. Somebody revved an engine in the far-left bay and pegged it at about five thousand RPM.

I shrugged into the uniform, double-checked the block print letters over the pocket, and zipped it up. Everybody else's name badge was sewn in cursive letters. It was easy to find mine.

The first pair of coveralls had been Walt's welcome present when I started work there. "I had to get the badge sewn special," he said. "The suppliers didn't have any that said 'Cadence.' " He shouldn't have bothered. Nobody at the shop used my real name anymore.

"Mornin', Stick," Turbo called from my left. "What's with the Stevie Wonder look?"

I offered him a raised middle finger and headed for the old pickup I had promised for noon. I folded the cane and put it and the sunglasses on top of my tool kit. Reaching behind the truck's grille, I yanked the release and lifted the hood.

By now, Danny and Turbo were both comfortable asking me to use my ears and fingers as diagnostic tools. And they didn't watch their language anymore.

"Oh, yeah?" Turbo replied to my upraised finger. "Hey, you want help setting the timing?"

"No, I'll just play it by ear."

I loosened the bolt that held the distributor in place, then moved around to the driver's seat and reached past the steering column to the ignition. Like an old man on a bean tostada diet, it started up with the round, flatulent pop of a misfire. I set the emergency brake, put the gear in neutral, and returned to the front of the truck.

Keeping my hands well away from the spinning fan blades, I pushed down the carburetor linkage until it was revving at about three thousand RPM. I made minute adjustments to the distributor, wrenching it left, left again, and then a little tweak to the right until I heard that perfect pitch and harmony of a well-tuned engine.

"Sure you don't want me to check it with the timing light?" Turbo asked, offering to verify that the strobe flash matched up to a

35

painted stripe on the pulley.

"I think I've got it. But I'd appreciate it if you'd take it for a test drive when I'm done." The Tucson PD would frown on my style of driving.

"Will do."

"Thanks. Let me know if you need my Ferrari fingers. And I don't mean just the middle one." It was a running joke. You need really long, thin fingers to reach the back spark plug on Ferraris, and my hands fit the bill. Long-fingered work was one way I could pay the guys back for the "sight" work they helped me with. Of course, we never got fancy Italian race cars in the shop — Walt's customers were mostly the Ford truck and dented-Camry crowd — but I still joked about filing my nails into Phillips head and regular screwdriver shapes.

I had done the rest of the tune-up yesterday and replaced all the fluids. Testing the engine again proved that the misfire was gone. I was ready to get started on the brakes. I rolled the jack under the rear axle, found the sweet spot, and started pumping.

Footsteps. Then a clipped voice carried from across the shop.

"I'm Detective Nellis and this is Detective Dupree." I heard the soft slap of his wallet — maybe his badge holder — closing. "Can you help us with some information?"

"Sure." Walt's footsteps crossed the shop to meet the detective.

"What time did you close last night?" He was carrying more weight than his lungs would have liked and his voice had the rasp of a longtime smoker.

"Six o'clock, thereabouts."

"You see anything unusual in the neighborhood?"

"Why? What happened?"

"Mrs. Prentice, your neighbor down the street, was killed in her home last night. Like to know if you saw anything."

"Nothing. What time did it happen?" Everyone in the shop had stopped to listen.

"Sometime between eight and midnight."

"Nah, we were long gone." Walt paused, then his voice boomed in my direction. "Stick, you were here for a while last night. Did you see anything?"

He had already forgotten my story of the demonic car, and that was fine with me. But now the police thought they might have lucked into a witness, and that wasn't fine.

Two sets of footsteps approached, one with hard-soled shoes and one with squeaky gum rubber. Nellis, the one who had spoken to Walt, was the smoker with the hard-soled shoes. From the angle his voice was coming from, I guessed his height at about six three. Couldn't tell about his partner yet.

"Miss, were you here, did you see —" His voice shorted out midsentence. Must have just noticed the red-tipped cane on the tool-box.

I tilted my head up toward his face. "No, I'm sorry, I didn't see anything."

"What time did you leave last night?"

"About nine-thirty." I turned back to the truck and pulled new brake pads from their boxes.

"Thanks anyway." Their footsteps crossed the garage.

"Wait a minute." I stopped their retreat. "You said the name was Prentice. Which house is that?"

"Four houses to the south. This side of the street."

"Does it have a line of bricks — just one brick high — around the yard?" That was right about where I'd heard that idling engine.

"That's it."

"Thanks. Sorry I can't help you." They wrote down my name, address, and phone number, and walked back to the shop entrance.

I moved a jack stand into position under the truck, wiped the sweat off my face with a clean shop rag, and called out to Walt, "How about turning the fan on out here, boss?"

I hadn't known Mrs. Prentice's name, but we'd become friendly through the years. She'd call out if I passed by while she was watering the plants on her front porch. And I could tell by the smell that she made a mean meatloaf.

I was sorry she'd been killed, but those voices I heard and my near accident probably had nothing to do with her death. The location of that idling car was right, but, hell, those people were laughing.

And even if that car did have something to do with her murder, it wasn't my business. I didn't want to be responsible for anybody else. I had already shown I couldn't be trusted with that.

CHAPTER 7

Dupree finished the canvass of the neighborhood without finding any good witnesses. He mopped his neck with a pale yellow handkerchief. There must have been plenty of traffic last night, but no one driving past had noticed the open screen door and the woman's body just inside. And there would have been few people on foot after eight or nine.

"Want to do next of kin?" Nellis asked. "I found this in with the letters and bills you picked up at the house." He handed Dupree a birthday card. One of Hallmark's cheapest, the front of the card showed pastel-colored robins carrying a banner that said "Happy Bird-day Grandma!" It was signed, "XOXO, Priscilla."

Dupree checked the return address on the envelope. "Might as well." He hated doing the family notifications. There was either an immediate denial of the possibility of death

("But I just saw her yesterday!") or a sucking vacuum and emptiness at the thought of being left alone. And Dupree wasn't far away from the day that his own daughters would have children sending him cards.

They cranked up the air conditioner and traveled twenty miles north on Highway 77. Nellis pulled out a pack of unfiltered cigarettes and dug into his pocket for a lighter.

"I thought you were quitting," Dupree said.

"I am. Quitting but not quit yet. I'm down to five a day."

"Good. Then you can save that one for when you're not in the car with me."

Nellis grimaced and tucked the pack back into his pocket. "You ever been out this way before?" he asked, a few miles down the road.

"Not that I recall." Dupree had lived in Tucson for ten years, but there were still neighborhoods and small outlying communities that were new to him. And, given the rate of new building and development in town, there always would be.

Catalina was a small residential community of eight thousand — a little older and sadder than the closer-in developments in the foothills. The strip malls looked like they'd taken the rejects from the offered

41

franchises, and the houses were neat, but scrubbed down to the bones by decades of sun, heat, and dust devils.

Priscilla Prentice's house backed onto Twentyseven Wash, a shallow, dry riverbed that ran north to south through town. A paloverde tree screamed for water in the dusty front yard.

"You ever heard the name Wanda Prentice before today?" Nellis asked as they approached the front door.

"No. Why?"

"I remember the name from somewhere." Nellis knocked on the door.

"Are you Priscilla Prentice?" Dupree asked when the bouffant blonde answered. He wondered if you had to be twenty-something to live on Twentyseven Wash.

"It's Strout now."

"Are you related to Wanda Prentice, of Tucson?"

"That's my grandmother. Why? What's wrong?" She had bands of blue and purple shadow arching over her eyes like some kind of tropical bird.

He told her the news, then followed her inside and took a seat in the living room. Nellis stood behind him.

Priscilla Strout wore short, tight cut-off jeans, a man's cotton shirt tied at the waist, and high heels. She had an intricate gold ring with a large, square yellow stone on her right hand and a plain silver band on her left.

She tucked one leg under her thigh, scratched her leg where her shorts ended and the couch's itchy brown upholstery met her skin, and pulled a fresh cigarette from the pack, even though she already had one going in the ashtray.

There were no tears. No display of unspoken regret. Strout wasn't showing any of the concern or grief that Dupree expected from the closest relative of a murder victim. But grief showed up differently in some people, or maybe she'd never been close to her grandmother.

He glanced at his partner, who was admiring the framed paint-by-numbers landscape that hung on the far wall. Nellis had grown up in Tucson but couldn't stand the heat. His short-sleeved shirt was already ringed with dark sweat stains. Nellis eyed the woman's cigarette and patted his pockets.

Dupree tugged his cuffs back into position. Arizona heat couldn't hold a candle to the wet, sucking summers he remembered from growing up in Louisiana. Dry heat? That's a vacation. Hell, he was happy with any day that the temperature was lower than his LDL cholesterol level.

Only ten o'clock, but the Strouts' apartment was already in those cholesterol-matching triple digits. The furnishings weren't helping. Someone had selected the heaviest, darkest plaid available for the boxy couch and matching armchairs. A dark brown coffee table, scarred by wet glass rings and nicks, graced the center of the room, and a feeble window air conditioner farted a semicool stream of air, flapping three finger-shaped plastic banners in front of the vents in celebration. The television, old enough to have rabbit ear antennas, was tuned to a morning talk show, but the volume was low.

"I call her every day. Well, almost every day," Priscilla Strout said. She stubbed out the cigarette that lay smoldering in the ashtray and ignited the second one.

Dupree jotted a note, letting her know he was paying attention. At this point he had nothing important to write down, but he always started with a sketch, just to jog his memory. He'd perfected the technique over years of drawing caricatures of both friends and enemies alike. A half dozen lines and he could capture the essence of a person. He rarely had to even look at the page while he worked.

He drew in the arcing lines of her bottle-blond hair. How could he show all the cosmetics? There was more makeup here than you'd find at a liars' convention. He added raccoon eyes.

"Maybe you can give me some background on your grandmother, Mrs. Strout."

"Call me Priss, please. But you gotta' leave a little gap between the words, you know what I mean?"

He raised an eyebrow.

"I mean my first name and my last. If you run 'em together, PrissStrout, real fast like that? I sound like some kind of fish."

"Mrs. Strout, I'm sure —"

"And it's just as bad if you use 'Missus' instead of Priss. I mean, what's a girl to do? I started out as a Prentice. Priscilla Prentice, that's not too bad. I mean, you don't get to pick your last name and I got lucky. Well, I guess you can pick your last name, cause Strout was Arlen's name and all, and I married him, but I sure didn't think about sounding like a fish when I did it."

Dupree added to the bubble hairdo in his drawing. "I'll remember to —"

"Just a little gap. Not a whole breath or anything." Priscilla demonstrated the proper technique.

Dupree glanced back at Nellis, who

squinted and patted his shirt pocket again.

"Please, Mrs. Strout."

She took a quick hit off the cigarette and waved in the direction of the kitchen doorway where her husband, Arlen, leaned against the wall. He was short and wiry, a baseball player's physique. His hair was greasy and stuck out in a cowlick in the back.

"When did you last see your grandmother?" Dupree said.

"Did she leave us anything in the will?" Arlen asked.

Dupree and Nellis exchanged glances.

"Priss got nothing from the old bag but a lousy card on her birthday, but I hear she was loaded," the husband continued.

"Where'd you hear that?" Dupree asked.

Arlen searched the ceiling for an answer. "Dunno. Just around. Must have been something Priss's mom said once."

"We don't have the details about a will yet," Dupree said, then turned back to Priscilla. "Do you know who your grandmother's lawyer was, Mrs. Strout? Or if there are any other family members we should contact?"

"I don't know if she even had a lawyer. And there may be some second cousins around someplace, but nobody else. My father was Grandma's son, and he died almost ten years ago. My mom passed just last year. Cancer." She waved her cigarette in a half circle, a recognition of the author of her mother's illness.

"Were you close to your grandmother?"

She seemed stunned by the question. "Sure. I mean, naturally. But I grew up in Tacoma — we only moved down here when my mom found out about the cancer — so I've only been around her the last couple of years."

"When did you last see her?"

"When was it, Arlen? Last week? Two weeks ago?" She twirled a lock of blond hair around her finger.

Arlen's face grew red. Was that concentration or guilt? "I dunno. One or the other."

Dupree rose to leave and handed the young woman his business card. "I'm sorry about your grandmother. Call me at this number tomorrow and I'll be able to tell you when you can claim the body."

"Claim the body! What am I going to do with it?"

"The city can take care of burial —"

"We're not spending our money to bury her, that's for damn sure," Arlen said. He took the business card from his wife and tossed it on the coffee table.

When they were outside, Dupree took off his jacket, folded it, and placed it in the backseat of the unmarked car. "You see that ring she was wearing? That look to you like something a twenty-two-year-old would pick out?"

"More like something a grandmother might have given her. I wonder if she's told her husband the whole truth. Maybe she's been getting more from her grandmother than she's telling Arlen."

"First, let's find out if Mrs. Prentice really had any money to give. And where those two were last night. That Barbie doll in there might have just gotten tired of waiting for her grandmother to die."

"Like they say: *cherchez* the family," Nellis said.

"That's not what they say."

"Well, *cherchez* that white trash Barbie, anyway."

CHAPTER 8

He'd dropped Lolly off at her place last night, his hands still shaking and breath coming in ragged pants. They'd sat in the van — forehead to forehead, fingers entwined in each other's hair — until the risk of being seen together became too great.

He almost lost it again when she got out of the car. He wanted to call her back. Tell her that they could leave tonight, with nothing but nineteen dollars in their pockets. They'd find a way.

"Lolly!" he'd whispered as she approached her house, but she didn't hear him. The door clicked shut behind her.

He put the van in drive and coasted to the end of the cul-de-sac to turn around. There were still no lights on in Lolly's house when he passed by again.

When he got home, he turned on the old TV and flipped the channel knob until he got a late news program. Had they found

Mrs. Prentice yet? Were they talking about a manhunt and witnesses? Nothing, so far.

He'd snugged the van up against the side of the house and covered it with an old gray tarp. It looked like a giant loaf of bread sitting out there, but at least it couldn't easily be seen from the street.

The TV news had moved on to sports, and the reporter was predicting another losing season for the Cardinals. He tuned out the story, caught up in the echoes of the night's violence.

What the fuck had they done? In a split second he'd gone from being a kid with an anything-is-possible future to this. A thief. A life taker. And for what? Nineteen dollars.

They should have run away when Mrs. Prentice woke up.

He cradled a pillow in his arms, then punched it until his arm ached.

He shut off the TV and the house settled into silence. He'd sublet the place from an old high school friend months ago. Nobody but his buddy and Lolly knew he was there. Thin walled and tin roofed, with acres of creosote-choked desert between him and the nearest neighbor, the house was the perfect hideaway. No tourists or fancy buildings out here. Just rusty old vehicles and worthless land. Everybody on the shitty side of town had something to hide.

But the house was a castle when Lolly was there, their special place together. They could shut out the noise and forget the slights, the disappointments, and the rest of the world that wanted to keep them apart.

He needed her here now.

CHAPTER 9

When they reached TPD headquarters, Dupree ignored the stairs and took the elevator up to the third floor, where he and Nellis shared two desks shoved together against the west wall.

"Any news while we were at the Strouts'?"

"Nothing," Nellis replied, flipping through printouts and phone messages.

Dupree shook his head, wishing that he didn't have to wait another ten years before retirement. "I'm forty-two going on sixty-two," he'd told Gloria last week as he eyed his chocolate skin and wiry gray sideburns in the mirror. He knew where the gray was coming from; it was too many years of bludgeoned babies and dead women in the desert.

"Any luck?" Sergeant Richardson asked, approaching their conjoined desks with a loaded clipboard in his hand. Richardson headed the seven-member Homicide detail.

"We made the next-of-kin notification," Dupree said. "A granddaughter, out in Catalina."

"She have anything to give you?"

"Nothing yet. I don't think she was close to her grandmother. Or if she was, she didn't like her very much."

"Why do you say that?"

"She wasn't interested in any funeral services. And the husband kept asking about a will," Nellis said.

"Is she a suspect?"

"We haven't ruled her out," Dupree said. "If we find out that she was seen there yesterday, or if there's a history of elder abuse —"

"We should be so lucky," Nellis offered.

Dupree unbuttoned the cuffs of his striped shirt — a present from Gloria in a shade too close to lavender; he would never have picked it himself — and rolled the sleeves up two turns. "I want to get a better handle on those two. Run 'em through the system."

Nellis scooted his chair in front of the keyboard and typed in both Priscilla and Arlen's names.

"Nothing on the husband, but she got probation on a shoplifting charge two years ago."

"Not much of a résumé for a killer. Okay,

we do Mrs. Prentice first. Who she did business with, where she banked, who knew her, who came by the house."

"I want to stay with this fish girl, Priss Strout," Nellis said.

"Got something against blondes?"

"Naw. Just haven't met a woman yet who'd tell you the truth without a fight first."

"No wonder you're still single." Nellis had been dumped by a waitress named Carole Martini last month and was still bitching about it.

The phone interrupted Nellis's reply. He sprang to answer it, then covered the mouthpiece as he relayed the information to Dupree. "It's the lab. Aside from those footprints, they've got nothing. Fingerprints in the kitchen and around the door were all smudged."

Dupree grimaced. Damn. Twelve hours gone and nothing to show for it.

Dupree was usually the more optimistic of the two, to the point where Nellis accused him of being a downright Pollyanna sometimes. Okay, so he'd been taught to see the rosy side of things. His mother had even cross-stitched her favorite saying on a big square of unbleached muslin and hung it in the dining room: *Happiness is having every-*

thing you want. And you can have everything you want if you don't want anything you can't have. What he wanted right now was a solid lead on Wanda Prentice's murder.

Nellis ended the call with the Crime Scene team.

"Any good witness statements? Anybody see anything?" Dupree asked.

Nellis gnawed a pencil stub and eyed the pack of cigarettes on the corner of the desk. "Just the manager of the Guardian Motel on the corner. He didn't see anything. But he's given us the names and addresses of the five people who had checked in. Of course, given the nature of that place, the names may not be good."

Dupree pictured the one-story, gray cinder-block motel with the lighted sign promising "Free HBO." Unfortunately the "B" had dropped off, leaving the message unintentionally prurient in its offer to provide "Free H O."

"I want to get that blind lady at the garage — what's her name — Cadence Moran, in here." Dupree had a hunch about her. And sometimes a hunch was worth a whole bucket of fact-finding.

Nellis barked a laugh. "You know something the rest of us don't? Unless she's psychic, she sure didn't see anything."

Dupree thought back to Miz Rogers —
the "blind witch," his brother called her —
who had lived in the little clapboard house
at the end of the road when he was growing
up. She couldn't see, but she sure knew a
lot about what was going on around her.

CHAPTER 10

I don't drink anymore, but that night I wanted one.

The shop had been buzzing with details of the murder all day.

"Pools of blood," Turbo had relayed.

"I heard she was stabbed a hundred times," Danny said without crediting a source.

Hyperbole aside, their comments still triggered the poisonous image of Nicole's rag doll body hanging halfway through the windshield. That was my last vision before my world went dark.

I decided to drink by proxy, so I dialed my ride.

"Juanita? Can you give me a lift to my mom's house?"

"Sure. Fifteen minutes."

Juanita may have inherited her height from her African-American father, but she got her accent and verbal venom from her

Mexican mother.

When she asked about the new cane and the bruises on my face, I downplayed the accident, saying only that I'd fallen and broken Lucy. Satisfied with that explanation, Juanita returned to the complaint she'd had in high gear when I got in the car, railing against the Arizona authorities about the motor vehicle registration process.

"Do you know they only have four — count 'em, four — inspection stations for this whole damn city? Over a half million people here and we've got to get into this conga line for three hours in the sun, waiting to have the car inspected? I had to take the whole damn day off work for this!" I could guess what a spectacle she made while waiting in line. A desert-brown Amazon with a black belt in verbal abuse.

Her full name was Duchess Juanita Greene and her brothers were Chance, Rooster, Books, and Cahill. "Thank God it was only a John Wayne obsession. Our parents could have been Charlton Heston fans." I pictured latte-hued boys named El Cid, Moses, and Michelangelo.

We weren't the most likely of friends in high school. Juanita was the smart kid who loved science and math; I looked forward to shop class. But the friendship was cemented one quiet, gray Friday when I pulled Johnny Deare off Juanita in a corner of the sports field where two chain-link fences met. Her blouse was ripped and his fingernails had left wet, red scratches down her chest. "What are you, deaf?" I bellowed. "You didn't hear her say no?"

Juanita had turned her love of chemistry and physics into a job as a latent print specialist for the Tucson Police Department's Crime Lab.

She'd been my friend before I was blinded and stayed that way afterward. Now Juanita dropped by at least once a week to run errands, drive me to appointments, and read my bills and letters out loud. I kept her Toyota gassed up and in good running condition. We both thought we were getting the better end of the deal.

"I've got some shopping to do at the mall," Juanita said. "Just give me a call when you're ready to go home."

I took a deep breath, pulled my shoulders back, and steeled myself for a visit with my mother.

"Come in, come in," Momma trilled. "You want something to drink, Cadence?" I smelled hair spray and the acrid juniper scent of cheap gin as it poured from the shaker. I crossed the room and bent down to kiss her cheek. Her hair was as stiff and hard shelled as a wasp nest.

"Just a little martooni to straighten out the day?" she said.

When I was growing up it was my job to refresh the pitcher when I got home from school. Gin was the perfume of motherhood.

I sat broom straight in the armchair across from the couch. By this time of night Momma was usually listing to the left, propped up on loose couch cushions, twirling the strap to a high-heeled sandal around a pinkie finger. Always sandals, of course, since she kept her toenails the same shape, length, and color as her fingernails, like little pink daggers on her feet. Doris Day with a substance abuse problem.

Only Aunt Caroline, Kevin's mother, still had patience with her sister. "She's just weak willed, Cadence. You have to forgive her for that."

Momma didn't seem to have noticed either the gravel damage on my face or the new cane.

Something with the swallowed consonants of Portuguese played softly on the stereo: my mother's version of urban-desert chic. I heard the hum of a dimmer switch set low. She must have needed the forgiveness of mood lighting tonight.

"You really need to start taking care of yourself, Cadence," she said between sips. "Get the grease out from under your nails. A little makeup wouldn't hurt. I'll bet you could still get a guy . . ."

Even if you're blind, she usually said. Even if you're less than whole. She should have been more worried about my own lack of desire to be with a man. For years after the accident I had allowed myself no pleasure. No belly laughs, no sweetness on the tongue, no sexual release. Even now, love-making was a solitary pleasure for me. An aria, not a duet. An animal release of tension but never something to be shared. I couldn't trust myself to care that much about someone again.

I got up to get a glass of water and turn down the glacial setting of the air conditioner.

The last time I had seen my image was eight years ago. At that time I was a trim twenty-three-year-old with short, wispy black hair, Arizona-burnished skin, and eyes a little too far apart for my face.

I wondered how my looks had changed. My weight was probably the same, as I was still buying the same size jeans. And I still wore my hair short. I wondered if there was

61

any gray in it yet and if the scars alongside my mouth now looked like frown furrows instead of the result of an accident.

"Did you hear about that murder in your neighborhood?" Momma said. "You should see the pictures of that lady. Sweetest thing. Butter wouldn't melt." She made a sucking sound to get the last drops of gin. "But I'll bet they used old photos. Bet she doesn't look like that now."

I swallowed hard. Almost twenty-four hours gone now. The radio said the police had no leads.

Could I really have heard the aftermath of a killing? At the shop, the cops had said she had died sometime between eight and midnight, so the timing was right. And so was the direction. And I had heard that strangled cry when I first walked out of the shop. Was that the precise moment that Mrs. Prentice ceased to exist?

But a minute later, there was also laughter. Would a murderer have laughed? Oh, God, I hoped not. And I couldn't tell the police anything that would help them find the car anyway.

". . . and that bitch next door keeps complaining about my music . . ."

What did I know for sure? The car had been idling rough. It sounded like it was out of tune. What else?

". . . she couldn't get a man's attention if she was buck naked with a hundred-dollar bill in her mouth . . ."

There had been another smell. Sweet, almondlike. There was no breeze that night so it must have come from somewhere close by. What was that smell? I knew it but couldn't place it.

". . . and whose fault is that? They're the ones who sent me the damn credit card and now they've got the gall to complain about . . ."

Antifreeze! That's it. Sweet, like almond candy. Smells so good that dogs lap it up and die, I'd heard one animal lover say. So maybe the car had a leak. Or maybe some other car that had passed by had dripped antifreeze.

Great, that will do the cops a world of good. A car that needs a tune-up and might be leaking antifreeze was in the neighborhood at some point during the four-hour window when the woman had been killed.

". . . it's not my fault that your father didn't leave us any money when he sashayed out the door . . ."

I tuned back in to Momma's monologue just in time for her favorite word: *fault.* Whose fault was it that she dropped the glass? "Look what you made me do!" Whose fault was it that her new beau with all the money never called back? "Cadence, what did you say to him? This is all your fault!"

Then she would send me to the Tree. It was a graceful old eucalyptus in the back-yard, once struck by lightning so the trunk was cleaved in two. Over the years the two halves had twined back together until they looked like lovers dancing, one with her back arched in a tango dip, the other with an arm held tight to his partner's waist.

"You'll stand there until you're ready to say you're sorry." I spent hours with my forehead resting against the cool, papery bark, my fingernails carving memory lines in the newly naked wood. Stood there until I felt that I had grown into its flesh, until my skin feathered and curled like the crust of the tree, and my feet took root alongside it.

I called it the Fault Tree.

"Momma, I've got to be going." I called Juanita from the kitchen phone and went outside to wait for her. She was only five minutes away and arrived with a squeal of brakes.

"You want to bring your car into Walt's over the weekend? I can take a look at those brakes. Walt won't mind if we use the shop outside of business hours."

"There's an unmarked cop car in your driveway," Juanita interrupted as we rounded the last corner before my house. "I'd recognize one of those anywhere. Hmmm, it looks like Rich Nellis, from Robbery. Or is he Homicide now? I worked a hijack case with him last year. Wonder what he wants."

"I think I know what it's about."

CHAPTER 11

Dupree answered the phone on the first ring.

"August, is that you? It's Juanita from the Crime Lab." Behind Juanita's voice he heard Willie Nelson's exhortation about not making cowboying a career.

"Hey there, girl. Hope you're not working this late."

"No, I just got home from helping a friend. But I could say the same to you. What are you still doing there?"

"Waiting for Nellis to get back here with a witness."

There was a pause on the line, then Juanita said, "That's what I was calling about. I just saw him at my friend's house. What's going on?"

Dupree knew Juanita Greene and liked her, but he didn't want to give away much information this early in the game. Who knows? Although it seemed unlikely, Cadence Moran might have had something to do with the killing. Or she might be protecting someone else who was there.

"Why don't you just ask her?"

"Come on. She's an old friend and she's blind. I just want to make sure she doesn't need any help."

"Gear down, Juanita. She might have been in the area when a senior citizen was killed last night. We're just double checking to see if she noticed anything."

"She notices *everything,* August. Last week she noticed that I'd eaten asparagus the night before because my sweat still smelled like it."

Well, that was a vote for her accuracy as a witness.

"What did you find at the murder scene?" Juanita continued.

"Not much. Two sets of footprints in the blood trail. No witnesses."

"Do you have anything for us Latent Print folks?"

"Somebody from the lab has gone over the scene. Don't remember his name. He didn't find any clear prints and we don't have anything else for the lab to test yet."

"I'll take another look at the house for you, if you want."

Dupree smiled. They had worked some

tough cases together over the years, like the one with the cop who shot his girlfriend and then used his knowledge of police and forensic techniques to cover his tracks. Juanita had come up with the evidence to convict him when others insisted they'd already looked everywhere.

"You do that."

CHAPTER 12

"There are three steps up in front of you," Nellis advised me just a beat too late as I tripped over the first one.

"It'll be easier if I use my stick." I brushed his meaty hand off my arm.

If my sense of the twists and turns on our drive was right, we were probably at the Tucson Police Headquarters on South Stone. When I was young, I had thought the building was a bank because of the walk-up "teller window" just outside the front doors, where they checked your ID. I managed to navigate the remaining steps and cross the lobby to the elevator. Nellis pinged the button to call the car to our floor.

"This is us. Third floor," he bellowed a few moments later. Ah, one of those folks who think that being blind affects your hearing. I preceded him into the hallway.

"Would you like a cup of coffee?" Shouted, like an American abroad who hopes that volume can replace vocabulary.

"No, thanks, I'm fine." Nellis gave me a too-strong push on the elbow. In the distance, a man's voice said, "Bye, Juanita," and he hung up a phone. Then soft-soled shoes gummed across the floor toward us.

"We'd like to go over the details from last night," Nellis continued at maximum volume.

I waited a beat. "I'm not deaf, Detective. Just blind."

I could almost hear Nellis's face turn red. His partner, the soft-soled-shoe wearer, rode in to save the day.

"I'm August Dupree." A voice as smooth as Nellis's was harsh. The butterscotch sound of the Deep South. He wore an aftershave that smelled earthy, like something root-bound and solid. He may have been black, I couldn't tell. "Let's go in here." Dupree put two fingers on my back and, with gentle pressure, suggested rather than led me into a small interview room. Three steps in each direction to reach the corners.

"I just got off the phone with Juanita Greene," he said. There was affection in his voice.

"She'd make a good mother hen." I should have known Juanita would follow up on the detective's presence at my house.

"That shiner looks painful," Dupree said. "Did you have a doctor check you out?"

"No. I'm a little stiff, but it probably looks worse than it feels." I'd left the sunglasses at home. The detectives could see the gravel rash and black eye in all their splendor.

"Can you tell us exactly what happened when you left the shop? Your boss phoned to say he remembered you had a close call crossing the street. Anything at all you remember might help," Dupree said.

Damn Walt for his recovered memory. It seemed to pop up at the most inconvenient times. But in some ways, I was grateful for their scrutiny. In the last twenty-four hours I hadn't been able to convince myself that I hadn't overheard a murder.

I told them about the near accident and about my broken cane. "I have no idea if it has anything to do with Mrs. Prentice. It's just as likely I stepped in front of a driver that didn't see me."

"But you heard a muffled scream, and then a few moments later you were almost run over by a car that had been idling in front of Wanda Prentice's house." This from Dupree, questions phrased as statements as if the story would make more sense that way.

I replayed the sounds in my head. "Well, a car that was near Mrs. Prentice's house, anyway."

"When you first heard that scream, what did you think was going on? What was your initial impression?"

"I didn't automatically think *crime,* if that's what you mean. I would have reported that." Right. I knew I would have convinced myself it wasn't serious, it wasn't any of my business, and just walked away.

"I didn't have long to think about it at all. There was the scream, then running footsteps a few seconds later, then two car doors closing. I heard voices, laughter. Then the car came racing at me. I guess if I thought about it at all it just seemed to be some bad driver. You know. No patience and in a hurry to get someplace."

The larger detective was taking notes, his scratchy pencil keeping pace with my words.

"Anything else? What about the car? The driver?" the Southern accent asked.

"I don't know how I can help you. I've been thinking about it. The engine was rough. I smelled antifreeze . . ."

"Antifreeze?"

"Yeah. A sweet smell. Maybe the car had a leak." I shook my head. "Maybe it was some other car. I mean, there are a lot of cars in town with bad hoses or a radiator leak . . ."

"Doesn't mean it wasn't associated with the killing," Dupree said. His partner didn't seem to have as much faith in my story. His silence came across as disinterest rather than close attention.

I told them about hearing two voices before the car accelerated.

"Are you sure you didn't hear a woman's voice? Maybe a woman with a man?" Nellis this time. They must have two suspects in mind.

"I can't be sure. One was definitely a higher voice, but I'm not sure it was a woman. Whoever it was, they were laughing."

They made me go over the story three more times and it didn't get any clearer. Dupree told me that I'd been a big help. I knew better.

On the way back to the car I heard the rustle and shuffle of a small crowd just outside the building. A young woman's voice broke through the rest, brittle and aggressive.

"Detective, do you have any leads in the death of Wanda Prentice? Is this lady a witness?"

"No comment," the big detective said as he steered me toward the car. I had my cane telescoped down to the size of a conductor's baton and tucked under my arm. This time I didn't mind him towing me by the elbow. Camera shutters clicked like handcuffs as we passed by.

CHAPTER 13

The phone woke me far earlier than I had intended to get up.

"Cadence! You're famous!" my mother gushed. "There's a picture of you on the front page of the *Daily Star.*"

She sounded like she'd just won the lottery.

"It says — here, let me read it to you — 'an unidentified witness to the murder of seventy-six-year-old Wanda Prentice is helping police with their investigation. Prentice was best known as the creator and star of *Wanda's Story Hour,* a locally produced children's program, which ran on KGUN television from 1955 to 1967.' I didn't know she was a celebrity. And you didn't tell me you knew anything about this. Why do I have to read about it in the newspaper? What kind of daughter are you?" Her euphoria soured with complaint.

"Sorry, Momma." Sometimes it didn't

take a long vigil at the Fault Tree for me to play my part. I would just say the words; I didn't have to mean them.

I tried to settle back into sleep, but after fifteen minutes realized it was useless. I splashed my face with cold water and scuffed into the kitchen to make coffee.

At least I knew now why there had been so many reporters at the police station. I was too young to have watched *Wanda's Story Hour,* but it had been famous enough to still be part of the local lexicon when I was a kid.

Damn reporters. At least they hadn't given my name. But now Wanda Prentice's family was going to believe I could help them. I knew I couldn't, and I knew I wasn't brave enough to even try.

When the coffeemaker wheezed to a stop, I poured half a cup, dialed the operator, and asked for the number at police headquarters. It took two transfers to get me to sweet-talking Detective Dupree.

"I'm not a witness to anything, damn it! Call that reporter and tell her that."

"I apologize, Ms. Moran. She ran the story without asking for confirmation. It's just that we all want to catch this killer. If there is anything else you remember that might help us . . ."

I hung up without saying good-bye. I didn't like the reporter thrusting me into the limelight. Even worse was the nagging feeling that I should have done more when I heard that scream.

Eight years ago I found out that I couldn't be trusted. Not with my own well-being and certainly not with anybody else's. Eight years since I'd felt brave or invincible. And look how that turned out.

I had only had one beer that night, so I wasn't drunk, but I knew I hadn't been exactly sharp either. I was in a hurry and distracted. I lost Nicole that night along with my eyes. But I never forgot whose fault it was.

It was mine.

CHAPTER 14

He jerked awake, the nightmare still fresh. Images from the old woman's house filled him like a strobe-lit slideshow. He mentally traced each moment, hoping somehow he could change the outcome this time.

It had been tough starting the van this week, so he had left it idling at the curb in front of Mrs. Prentice's house. They needed only a few minutes inside, and it would be safe enough in that neighborhood.

He'd opened the screen door slowly so it wouldn't squeak and used his buck knife on the cheesy little lock she had on the front door. They'd headed straight for the kitchen. Lolly had been egging him on for a week, detailing specific information about where the money and jewels were stashed.

There was nothing, of course. The ice cube trays held ice. And Lolly had made a racket shaking two boxes of dried-up bran flakes into the sink.

Lolly had wanted to look in the bedroom, saying the mattress must hold the real treasures, but he'd pulled her away. They needed cash, not a confrontation. But their voices must have awakened Mrs. Prentice. Lolly had just found that wad of bills in the coffee canister when the old woman stumbled in, her eyes still crusted with sleep.

"What are you doing in my house?" A frail, high-pitched voice but not frightened.

He'd backpedaled, arms straight out, offering her the coffee canister in one hand or the buck knife in the other.

Lolly's reaction had been different. As the old woman grabbed at the canister, Lolly wrestled the knife from his hand and plunged it into the old woman's back. Again. And again. Her scream registered anger and surprise as much as pain.

Everything slowed down. He could hear Mrs. Prentice's ragged breath. A drip from the faucet. His future tumbling away. Someone might have heard the noise. He pushed Lolly toward the front door, metal canister still clutched in his hands. They had to get away.

But the old woman came after them, glued herself to him like original sin, and Lolly had stabbed her again.

A scream rose in his throat, and he'd had

to push it back down. Focus on getting Lolly out the door.

"Come on, Lolly." Whispered. Urgent.

She was his Lolly — Lollipop — never her real name, even in times of crisis. That other name was the one her old man used.

That had been two days ago but it felt like a heartbeat. He left the van under its tarp and headed out on foot. If he cut across the desert instead of following the road, it was only three-quarters of a mile to the 7-Eleven. No reason to risk a cop seeing his plates.

He bought a bottle of cold water along with the newspaper. A photo of the dead woman was on the front page, along with the picture of a dark-haired woman leaving police headquarters. He recognized that second woman too. Tall and lean. Younger than his parents. And standing stiff as a pole, like she was out there directing traffic. She looked straight at the camera and held her lips in a thin tight line, just the way she'd looked at him in the street.

The paper said she was a witness to the killing, but what could she have seen? The street had been pretty dark until he turned on his headlights. She might be able to tell them what kind of car to look for, but there were lots of light brown vans out there.

Could she have read any numbers from the license plate?

She had definitely seen them come running from Mrs. Prentice's house. That was a problem.

He needed to talk to Lolly. About how much he loved her. About what she'd done. And how he almost threw up every time he thought about it.

He'd have to get rid of the car.

And find a way to convince the witness that she hadn't seen anything at all.

CHAPTER 15

"Who was that?" Nellis asked.

"Cadence Moran. She's got a bone to pick with us about having her picture in the paper." Dupree ran his fingers through thin black curls, wondering again if he'd have his father's oxbow hairline by the time he was forty-five.

"She should be thanking us. It might get her a date."

Dupree let the words pass without comment. "She's right about one thing. What if this guy's worried about a witness?"

"They didn't give her name or address; she should be fine. How'd the reporters find out about her, anyway?"

"Dumb luck," Dupree said. "Richardson gave a press conference and said we'd be interviewing all potential witnesses. You know, the standard line. But there have been a couple of reporters hanging out in the lobby and the parking lot ever since." He returned to his perusal of Wanda Prentice's credit card bills.

"Hey, I remember where I heard Wanda Prentice's name before," Nellis said. "I never saw her show, but when I was a little kid and I'd ask for one more story at bedtime, my dad would always say, 'Who do you think I am, Wanda Prentice?' I thought it was just one of those lines you heard and repeated, you know? Like 'What am I, chopped liver?' You getting anything from those bills?"

"Nothing out of line. Groceries, utilities, newspaper subscription, pharmacy. Let's see what her bank records have to say." He grabbed his coat and followed Nellis to the elevator.

The Wells Fargo at Grant and Richey was the bank branch identified on Wanda Prentice's checks. The detectives took the dead woman's ATM card, checkbook, and most recent statement with them.

There wasn't a stick's worth of shade in the parking lot, so Dupree backed the car into an available space on the east side of the lot. That way, the front seats wouldn't be in the direct line of sun fire.

"I recognize her," the assistant manager, Rocky Trillo, said when Dupree showed him Wanda Prentice's photo. "She's a nice lady.

Refuses to use the ATMs or the drive-thru window. She always comes to the counter."

He escorted the detectives to a desk with a computer terminal and entered Wanda Prentice's account information. As usual, Dupree began a quick sketch as the banker looked up the data. A square face, easy grin. He couldn't capture the brightness of the banker's blue eyes with a pencil, so he indicated their gleam with a refractive-looking square drawn onto the iris, like Brenda Starr always had in the old comics.

The banker turned the monitor toward the detectives. "See? She withdraws fifty dollars in cash every week. And her balance in savings hasn't changed. She's still got a little over a hundred thousand in that account. I can't tell you how many times I tried to get her into CDs or bonds, rather than have that money sit there earning a measly three percent interest."

Dupree raised his eyebrows in his partner's direction. They both knew of crimes that had been committed for a lot less than a hundred grand. "Is there any unusual activity in the last six months or so?"

The banker's chair squeaked as he turned back to the computer. "Nothing on the savings. And nothing I can see in checking, either. Her rents come in every month. No significant changes in her utilities or credit card payments."

"What kind of rents are you talking about?" Nellis asked.

"She has some rental property across town. A duplex, I think she told me."

"Can you get us that address?"

"Sure." He typed in the codes that would reveal the checks deposited to the account.

"Two tenants, Harmon and Garafulo. Here's the address." He jotted the names and an east side address on a piece of bank stationery and handed it to Nellis.

"What else can you tell us about her? Did she have a safety-deposit box?"

"No safety-deposit box, but I see here that she changed her contact information a year ago. She used to list Phyllis Prentice as her next of kin. Now it's shown as Priscilla Strout."

Of course, she'd changed it when Priscilla's mother died. Would the promotion to next of kin have been enough to give Priscilla Strout ideas about getting her hands on all that cash?

"They may know already," Trillo continued, "since her murder has been in the papers and all. But have you talked to anybody at the Desert Museum?"

"Why?" Dupree knew about the twenty-some-acre museum west of town, but they hadn't found any literature or paperwork about it in Wanda Prentice's house.

"She was a volunteer docent out there. It was just about the only thing she talked about. The raptor cage was her specialty."

CHAPTER 16

I still "see" everything. It's not easy to forget twenty-three years of colors and perspective. When I hear a bird or feel a breeze, I still see that feathered red wing or the hillside covered in new-grass green. I even see the letters I used to know, when my fingers scroll across Braille dots.

But some images are frozen forever at the time I last saw them. Kevin's face, for example, will always have that just-under-thirty boyish grin and no gray hair. I don't think of him with the sadness of losing a child in his eyes.

New friends, if they become good enough friends, let me see their faces with my fingers. Juanita is one of those friends. I had asked to see what she looked like now, so many years after the scrawny, doe-eyed Juanita I remembered from high school.

"Oh, I'm a real bombshell now," she laughed. "Bazooms out to here, sexiest damn thing you ever saw."

My fingers had tap-danced over her forehead and across her cheekbones. You could read the blend of black and Latino heritage in her face. She was almost as tall as me and had a strong nose, pronounced cheekbones, and a generous mouth. Her hair was as short as mine, and she tucked it behind her ears.

She came by on Saturday morning, just two hours after the call from my mother, and I told her about the scream and the car on the night Wanda Prentice was killed.

"I know. I called Rich Nellis's partner, August Dupree, last night after I dropped you off. Were you able to help them with anything?"

"Nothing much." I explained about the almost hit-and-run, the antifreeze, and the out-of-tune engine.

"You should have told me about the accident, Cade."

"I didn't think it was much more than my own stupid mistake." One in a list of hundreds that I could read like prayer beads if I got started.

"I told August I'd take another look at the crime scene," she said. "See if maybe there's something we didn't spot the first time. Want to go down to the lab with me? I need to go over their findings and photos, see what else we might try."

"Sure." My ribs were still sore and my palms scabbed with gravelly scratches, but I thought I'd be better off moving than having my muscles lock up with the pain. I grabbed a lightweight vest in case the forensics lab had the thermostat set as icy cold as my mother's house.

"You look like shit," Juanita offered as I groaned into the passenger seat.

"I feel like shit too." Based on her reaction and that of the detectives, I knew that my aches and pains had blossomed into living color.

"I've got a good one for you," Juanita said, fastening her seat belt. Juanita took great pleasure in relaying the unintentional puns and bad grammar she spotted on signs and ads.

"Slow Children at Play."

"Huh?"

"Yep. Now there's a road sign just crying out for punctuation. And I got this great list of animal groups."

"Animal groups?"

"You know. Like a pride of lions. A gaggle of geese."

"A murder of crows."

"Yep. But how about a smack of jellyfish?

Or a shrewdness of apes? A rumba of rattle-snakes?"

I silently disagreed with the rattlesnake description as she continued the list. It would definitely have been a cha-cha of rattlesnakes.

The Crime Lab was in the Police Department headquarters on South Stone, the same place I'd gone with Nellis last night. We reached her office without incident, which is unusual for Juanita's automotive skills. She's a graduate of the "point it and punch it" school of driving.

We took the elevator to the second floor, then used a card key to get into the Crime Lab in the south wing. I was glad I'd brought the vest. I followed her through the maze of desks and work areas like a rat on the trail of aged cheddar.

"Gene? I knew I'd find you here on a weekend," Juanita said to someone at the far end of the building.

Almost two dozen criminalists worked at the lab, some on computer forensics or latent prints or DNA, others on chemical analysis and bullet comparisons. I'd met Gene Howard before; he was one of the DNA specialists.

"I've got so much shit to do for upcoming trials that I could be in here every weekend and still not make a dent," he said. "Remember that bank robbery on Prince Road? Guy dropped a Kleenex at the scene and it's got great DNA, but it's not from the guy they're holding."

"Not good news for us, but it's good for somebody. You remember Cadence, don't you?" Howard allowed as how he recognized me.

"Where have we got the stuff from the Prentice murder case?" Juanita asked.

"Prentice? Brodie's got them. But he said there's no clear prints so far."

"Can't hurt to look again, huh?"

"Course not." I heard the disapproval in his voice. I didn't know who this Brodie was, but Gene Howard clearly thought he didn't need to have his work checked.

Juanita must have sensed the same thing. "Brodie won't mind. And I don't really think I'll find anything either. I'm just doing a favor for one of the cops."

I followed Howard across the room, running my hand along a bank of filing cabinets that seemed to stretch as far as the Great Wall of China. He stopped and opened a drawer at waist level. There was a metal-on-metal complaint as he finger-flipped through the hanging folders.

"Here it is. See for yourself."

Juanita and I, with Howard in tow, retreated to a wide table in the center of the room.

"What did I tell you?" he said. "Brodie tested the door handle, the door itself, everything in the kitchen . . ." His voice trailed off.

"Nothing?"

"The only clear prints belong to the victim."

"What about the blood?" Juanita asked.

"We haven't run DNA yet, but it's all O positive, just like the victim."

When Howard went back to his office, Juanita began her inspection. "Let's see if there's any latent print magic we can work here." She slapped down crime scene photographs like a desperate game of solitaire, then proceeded to "uh-huh" and "hmmm" through what I thought must be the fingerprint analysis they'd done.

Funny that her work was to find evidence that you often couldn't see. At least I could listen to a fan belt or a misfiring engine for a clue. She couldn't count on even that sense.

"Brodie did a good job," she said a few minutes later. "There's powder all over the place. Doesn't look like there's anything to be found."

"Tell me about the room. About the house. What's on the floor or in the front yard? Are there curtains?" I needed to *see* the place she'd been killed.

"I'll do you one better. Let's go back and both of us see the house for ourselves."

Did I really want to go to Wanda Prentice's house? To take in that blended smell of coppery blood and day-old meatloaf? To know that a sweet woman who used to read to children and who called out to a stranger in passing also used a lilac-scented perfume and left a ring in her bathtub? I knew that I had to, even though it wouldn't make up for letting her die that night. Would she be alive now if I'd phoned the police after the car screeched away?

Juanita phoned Detective Dupree. He said he'd send an officer to the house with the key. We drove back to Mrs. Prentice's house, arriving before the patrolman did. I found the opening in the shallow brick wall and tapped up the front walk.

"What's it look like?" I asked.

"Red brick. The screen door has some ornamental wrought-iron design on it. Heavy curtains in the front window. They're open about an inch and —"

"So someone could have looked in. Checked to see if she was home. Maybe asleep on the couch."

"It's got bushes and mulch under the window. So, no footprints. Yeah, I suppose somebody could have looked in. Brodie didn't dust here."

"She's got rosebushes here, right?" They had a particularly strong scent. "If somebody was going to get close enough to look in the window without getting scratched, he'd have to lean way over. And that means he had to brace himself on something."

Juanita retreated to the car to get her testing kit, then unscrewed the lid to one of her powders. I waited in silence while she dusted.

"Oh, my, yes."

"What is it?"

"There are prints there, all right, but not fingerprints. More like parentheses marks where somebody cupped his hands around his eyes to look in. And an oily spot right in the middle. Probably where his nose made contact with the window."

"How can you know that it wasn't some curious neighbor looking in after the murder?"

"We can't tell when prints were left. That's why you dust everything. If we ever catch the guy, we can compare the edges of his hands to these prints. Just as distinctive as fingerprints. And I'll take a sample from this smudge too. See if our DNA folks can get anything from it."

She continued to test other likely spots around the window. "We don't know how far he had to lean over, but based on the height of that nose print, I'd say he's at least five ten. That'll help."

A car pulled to the curb behind us. "Ready to go inside?" she asked.

The patrolman must have been a friend. He asked about Juanita's brother Chance and said they'd have to plan to get together. She laughed and agreed.

Juanita positioned me in the doorway and said, "Keep your back against the wood and step sideways." There must have been blood or fingerprint powder there that she wanted me to avoid. I sidled into the house.

The coppery smell was there all right, and the smell of feces. Mrs. Prentice must have soiled herself in her fright or at the moment she lost her life. The house was still, as dead as its former occupant.

"Let's start in the kitchen," Juanita said, guiding me into the next room.

"What does it look like?"

"Café curtains on the window over the sink. It's a pattern with orange blossoms. The kitchen table is behind you, round, covered with a yellow tablecloth. Four chairs, all with arms, but one of them is knocked over. This whole place looks like it'd be right at home in 1965."

"Back at the lab, did you say something about ice cube trays?"

"Yeah, it looks like the burglars searched the cabinets and the refrigerator, maybe thinking she had prescription meds or money stashed there. They've spilled stuff all over."

My next footstep crunched into something that felt like cornflakes.

"Tell me everything you see." The mingled odors of fresh coffee beans, olive oil, and vanilla painted a partial olfactory picture, but I needed to see all of it.

"The report said they pulled almost everything out of the freezer. Bacon, ice cube trays, those little pearl onions, spinach. Dumped it all in the sink. They've taken all those to the lab in case there were prints on them. The cupboards and floor are still in pretty bad shape, though. There's cornmeal, flour, coffee, bran flakes, and a cereal box on the floor. It looks like she kept the cornmeal and flour in these plastic containers."

Something was missing. "What did she keep her coffee in? A bag? A can?"

"I don't see anything. Maybe it's in the garbage." She pulled open a cupboard door, rummaged around, then closed the door again. "Let me check the evidence list. Nope. Not there either."

"Maybe Mrs. Prentice really was hiding money, and that's where she kept it."

It didn't seem logical that an elderly woman in a middle-class neighborhood would have piles of cash or jewelry buried in the groceries, but I couldn't imagine any other reason to trash a kitchen like this and not touch the rest of the house.

"Either that or she buys one hell of a blend," Juanita said.

Chapter 17

The Arizona-Sonora Desert Museum was more of a zoo and botanical garden than it was a traditional museum. Nestled against the saguaro-studded slopes of the Tucson Mountains, it covered twenty-one acres of land west of Gates Pass, with over two miles of walking paths where visitors could come eye to eye with tarantulas, kit foxes, and red-tailed hawks.

Dupree's favorite part was still Prairie Dog Town, a patch of sandy soil surrounded by a waist-high wall and studded with a warren of small holes the prairie dogs dug for concealment. It looked like a life-size version of a Whack-A-Mole game, with the bright-eyed rodents popping up and ducking down in alternating waves of curiosity and fear.

It took them almost a half hour to get across town, through Gates Pass, and across the valley floor to the museum. Dupree had to circle the lot twice — he wasn't about to park in a fire lane — before he found a free space. He shook his head, marveling at the endurance of tourists who insisted on coming to the museum during the hottest part of the day. Most of the animals inside had the good sense to stay hidden from the sun. Why couldn't the visitors do the same?

"We were so sad to hear about Wanda," the elderly man at the ticket window said. "She was like family to us."

"Is there anyone here that she was especially close to?" Dupree asked. They hadn't found any neighbors she spent much time with, and Priscilla seemed to be the only family member. Calls to Channel 9's KGUN TV station had only turned up an intern who was willing to compile a tape of the old *Wanda's Story Hour* programs for their review.

"You should talk to Marjorie Lamar. She usually works with the raptors, like Wanda did, but I think she's doing hummingbirds and butterflies today. We're shorthanded. Why don't you wait in the gift shop and I'll see if we can track her down." He motioned the detectives through the turnstile and to the left.

Nellis browsed the gift shop's selection of

prickly pear marmalade and jalapeño jelly while Dupree looked at the silver and turquoise jewelry. At one point Dupree almost laughed, watching an eight-year-old boy who thought he'd disguised the theft of a rock and mineral collection under his T-shirt. The flat display box was the size of a hardback book and gave the child the look of an armor-plated warrior.

"Can I see that?" Dupree asked, pointing to the sharp corners that stuck through the child's shirt. The boy's face reddened, but he pulled the box from its hiding place. Dupree fingered the tiny samples of turquoise, fool's gold, mica, and agate that were neatly glued into place and labeled as though they were as valuable as pieces of shooting star. He glanced up at the boy's mother, whose aggressive approach suggested that she thought her son was being mauled by a predator. Dupree showed her his badge.

"Maybe your mom will buy it for you." The mother pulled the box from Dupree in a huff. Dupree wondered if he could talk Nellis into a walk around to the other side of the museum where the prairie dogs were.

A strident voice interrupted his thoughts. "Detective? I'm Marjorie Lamar." She was a stocky woman, with no discernible waistline and thick ankles that filled her lace-up shoes to overflowing. Her iron-gray hair was cut Galahad straight and ended where it met her collar.

Dupree motioned Nellis to join them. "Is there somewhere we could talk?"

Lamar led them to the coffee bar next to the gift shop. "Wanda and I have been friends for more than ten years. Most of the women who volunteer here — Wanda called them the Gray Brigade — only want to work with children's groups, or in the orientation room. Wanda said she'd already spent a dozen years with children's groups and was ready for something else. She was tiny but she was strong. Strong enough to work with the hawks and the vultures, even though they don't really let us docents handle the birds. Animals didn't have to be cute for Wanda to love them."

"Can you think of anyone who might have wanted to kill her?" Nellis asked.

"Nobody. But what does it take these days? You read about somebody getting killed because he honked at another driver or because she's wearing the wrong color." She curled her lip, then washed the taste of the words out of her mouth with a long drink of iced tea.

"Did she ever talk about her personal

life?" Dupree asked. He made her eyes look sadder in the sketch he had started in his notebook.

"We both did. Since our husbands died, neither one of us really had anybody to talk to. And we were together here at least four days a week."

"What was her relationship like with her granddaughter?"

"Priscilla? She never did trust her much. She hadn't spent much time with her until a couple of years ago when Priscilla and her mom moved here from someplace in the Northwest. And Priscilla didn't come by often, but when she did, things seemed to go missing."

"Like what?"

"You know, twenty dollars here and there. A silver teaspoon. I think Wanda was still trying to find a ring that might have been misplaced, but it could have been stolen too."

"What kind of ring?" Dupree asked.

"A big yellowish stone — topaz or something. I only saw it a couple of times. It had lots of curlicues around the side."

It sounded like the ring on Priscilla Strout's finger.

"What did she think of Priscilla's husband?"

"I don't remember her saying anything about him. Just about being disappointed in the girl. She's bright but never tried to make anything of herself."

Dupree wasn't sure he agreed with that bright assessment but thought there was merit to the rest of the statement. "And you can't think of any enemies, anyone who would have profited by her death?"

"No one except her granddaughter. I don't mean she was an enemy, just that Wanda wasn't close to her. But Wanda changed her will a couple of months ago and named Priscilla and the museum as the only beneficiaries. So I guess she was close enough that she wanted to leave the girl something."

They hadn't found a will in the Prentice house. "Do you know where she kept it?"

"We got them done together at the Senior Center and gave each other a copy. I've got it in my locker. I'll get it for you." She rose to retrieve the document.

"Oh, and I just remembered. She had a hell of a fight with a pharmacist last week. Real blood pressure–raising stuff. She said she had proof he was bilking Medicare."

"You said she changed her will," Dupree said when Marjorie Lamar returned. "Who was to be the beneficiary before Priscilla was named?"

"The Desert Museum, of course. And me."

CHAPTER 18

Juanita returned the house key to the waiting patrolman. She planned a whole celebration menu on the ride home, claiming that Detective Dupree would owe us a steak dinner for this new evidence.

She dropped me off at the house, declining my offer to check her brakes. Since it was my day off and I was still too much on edge to be alone, I called Kevin to suggest dinner. If he did the grocery shopping, that is.

My cousin and I had come to an uneasy truce not long after the accident: he never mentioned Nicole; I never let her slip from my mind.

"I'll have the girls with me," he said when I called. "Emily's going to a friend's bachelorette party tonight. Do you mind cooking for all of us?"

A tremor of anxiety ran up my spine when he mentioned his two younger daughters,

Bernadette and Teresa. Kevin hardly ever brought them by.

"I'd love to."

I read off the list of ingredients for an easy boiled dinner. Probably too heavy a meal in this heat, but it was simple.

Their arrival that afternoon was punctuated by little girl squeals of delight. Teresa was seven and Bernadette five. They filled the front yard with as much noise as a flock of parrots. The girls had never known their big sister, but I felt her presence like a shadow behind them.

Kevin took their coloring books to the living room and tuned the television to a cartoon program. His hands carried the waxy smell of crayons when he came back into the kitchen. The air was still, and I opened the kitchen window to get a cross breeze blowing.

I quartered potatoes, cabbage, and carrots, then ran my fingers over the Braille labels on the jars. I found the bay leaves in the first row of small bottles and picked out two leaves for the pot.

Kevin opened one of the beers he had bought along with the groceries and leaned back in the kitchen chair until it creaked. He yawned and the heels of his boots thunked on the seat of the chair next to him.

"You sound tired, Kev. Is everything okay?"

"Yeah, it's fine. Work's going okay. I got a raise last week. And we got this little Learjet in to do an engine overhaul. It's a beauty."

Kevin still repaired his own car, but all the rest of his mechanical work was now done on private planes and executive jets. I remembered the first time Kevin took me flying in his boss's old Cessna. It was better than any drug I ever tried in my sighted days. A true unleashing of the spirit. I reveled in the surge of acceleration down the runway, my back plastered to the seat, the thrum of the propeller seeking purchase on the air. Then the joyous rush of the climb. It was almost sexual.

Kevin had taken my hands to show me the location of the dials and controls. Oil gauge. Radio. Ailerons. Fuel mixture. Stick. There was a Plexiglas overlay covering the instrument panel, but he led my finger to each of the dials and described what they looked like.

The Cessna seemed primitive compared to the cars I worked on. Airplanes don't even have reverse. On the other hand it was also simplistically beautiful — thin sheets of metal and Plexiglas as the only things between you and the heavens.

Now I requested an airplane ride every year as a birthday present.

"Everything's okay at home?" I asked.

"Oh, that part's absolutely fine. Em's pregnant again, did I tell you already?"

My heart stuttered. "No, that's great. Congratulations. Another girl, you think?"

He took a long swallow of beer. "Don't know yet. Emily would be happy with a whole tribe of girls, but me? I don't know. I'd kind of like a son." He sighed. "Everything's fine. I guess I'm just tired."

I felt bad about asking him to add one more thing to his already full day. I'd not only had him do the grocery shopping, but he'd spent the better part of the day repairing my cane in his home workshop.

"Thanks again for repairing Lucy. I'd really miss her if I had to get another one."

"No problem. It's even stronger now. I fit a new bottom piece to the head and hollowed it out to take a steel shaft down the middle. Just make sure you tell them at airports or they'll think you're carrying a weapon on board."

"Oh, yeah. A blind terrorist. That would be really effective. I'd have to ask directions to the cockpit."

I filled him in on my conversations with the police and heard the reflected concern in his voice. "Do you want me to come pick you up after work for a while? I don't think you ought to be walking home if there's some killer around."

"I can't start using you as a taxi service; I'd never get comfortable out by myself again. And I don't think I'm in any danger. Juanita said the cops think it was a robbery gone bad. I'll make sure I keep the doors locked." I didn't have the luxury of being afraid of the dark.

Kevin called the girls in to dinner, and they talked in whispers while I located each portion on the plate with my finger. I wish I could have found my courage as easily.

CHAPTER 19

Wanda Prentice's will was exactly as Marjorie Lamar had described it.

"Priscilla was going to come into some money," Dupree said, refolding the pages. "Someplace between one and two hundred thousand, depending upon the value of that house and the duplex."

"Sounds like a motive to me. And that means Marjorie Lamar had the same motive."

"Yeah, if she was the only one with a copy of this new will, she could have waited until the old one surfaced and turned her friendship with Wanda Prentice into some real money."

"But she's the one who told us about the new will," Nellis argued.

"That's a point in her favor. But let's check out her finances anyway. See how much happier a couple hundred thousand dollars would have made her."

Dupree flipped through the stack of pharmacy receipts and medication warnings they'd taken from Wanda Prentice's house. She'd been in pretty good shape for a seventy-six-year-old. Blood pressure medicine. A prescription-strength cream for arthritis aches and pains. "She used two separate pharmacies, but the receipt from last week comes from the Best Aid Pharmacy on Swan. If Mrs. Lamar is right about the date of the fight, this is the place. Can you make out the name of the pharmacist — right here?" He handed Nellis the receipt and pointed to the scrawled initials next to the prescription number.

Nellis squinted at the signature. "Nope. Some of these guys need to take a handwriting course." He started to hand back the receipt, then stopped. "Wait a minute. He's charged her a hundred and thirty bucks for this."

"So?"

"Come on. She's a senior citizen. She at least has Medicare. Probably some supplementary insurance. There's no way she'd be paying a hundred and thirty bucks for this."

"Maybe that's what the fight was about."

"Let's go ask him."

The waiting area at the pharmacy looked

like a scene from *Beetlejuice.* Three cadaverlike seniors slouched on a plastic burgundy bench. Four more shuffled their feet and gazed at the floor, forming a Maginot line of stolid patience at the counter. A mechanical voice droned its message over a scratchy loudspeaker. "Number eighty-four, your prescription is ready. Number eighty-four." No one moved forward with proof of the winning ticket. The man in front of Dupree held ticket number 112.

Dupree excused himself to the customers in line and approached the white-smocked Asian woman behind the cash register. The pharmacy section was built two steps above the rest of the drugstore, so that Dupree had to look up to her.

"Tucson Police Department. I'd like to speak to your manager, please." Saturday was a big day for getting prescriptions filled; he hoped the manager was in.

They waited almost ten minutes, watching what appeared to be a heated, whispered conversation between a short, dark-haired man and his tall, thin coworker behind the pharmacy window. The dark-haired man ended the conversation with a jabbed finger in the other man's chest, then came out a side door to join the detectives.

"John Stephanos," he said, rolling his cuffs

back into place but not offering a hand. "Make it snappy. I have to pick up my girlfriend and her kid." His hair was slicked back Elvis-style, glued in place with some shine-inducing pomade. The style went well with the full-lipped sneer.

Dupree started the sketch in his notebook with just the lips. It was all he would need to remind him of this interview.

"Do you recognize this woman?" Nellis asked, showing Stephanos a picture of Wanda Prentice.

"Yeah, sure. What did she say about me? She was causing a scene. We're not going to do business with someone like that again." He fiddled a dangling cuff link into its buttonhole.

"What kind of scene?" Dupree asked.

"She thought we were overcharging her, but she was wrong. And she wouldn't let it go. She got loud. Got all the other customers involved." He ran his hand along the side of his hair, confirming its placement. "I had to have her removed from the store."

It looked like they'd found their contentious pharmacist.

"How'd she take that?" Nellis asked.

"Oh, she was screaming about senior citizen rights and how she was going to sic the authorities on me. I guess that's you guys, right?"

"So you didn't overcharge her? Maybe charge a branded price for a generic prescription?"

"Of course not. Look, I really don't have time for this right now."

"We all have someplace else we'd like to be, Mr. Stephanos. Including these people in line." Dupree motioned to the seniors who were following the verbal volley like tennis fans. Several nodded and smiled at Dupree's recognition. The three pharmacists behind the shoulder-high glass barrier scurried back to work.

"It looks like she was right to have a beef with the guy," Nellis said when they were back in the car.

"Let's find out a little more about Mr. Stephanos and how he likes to do business. Overcharging? Medicare fraud? There's a whole lot of money involved in those prescriptions."

And money was always a good motive for murder.

CHAPTER 20

On the day I lost my sight, I was working in the plus-size department at J. C. Penney. Even after more than ten years of tinkering with lawn mowers and car engines with Kevin, and two years of being the only girl in shop class, I couldn't get a job as a mechanic. "You'd do very well in retail," my high school counselor had suggested. Retail: the holding tank of dreams for girls with only a high school education.

They didn't even put me in automotive supplies.

We had a family barbecue that afternoon. Momma had consumed a whole pitcher of martinis before the first hot dogs went on the grill. Aunt Caroline watched apprehensively but didn't say anything. "Don't rock the boat," was always her best advice.

Kevin had married five years earlier and his wife, Emily, showed none of the strain and fatigue I expected with the rearing of a three-year-old. She laughed easily and her eyes shone with pride as she watched Nicole's antics at grabbing a dandelion, hugging our almost-toothless golden retriever, or investigating an abandoned anthill.

Kevin was the first to spot the old dinette set Momma had shoved under the oleander bushes against the back fence. It was blond wood, maple maybe, with one broken leg and a top big enough for a family of four.

"Oh, the top has gotten so scarred, and now that the leg broke, I'm just going to throw it out," Momma said.

Kevin glanced at Emily for confirmation. "If you don't want it, would you mind if we take it? I could shorten the other legs and it would make a great play table for Nicole."

"Help yourself." She gestured with an empty glass. "But you've got to take the chairs too, and it's got to be out of here today. I can't bear to look at it even one more day."

When the sun set, Caroline and my uncle Twill were the first to leave. Kevin, Emily, and I stayed another few minutes, enjoying the ghost of a breeze that rustled through the tamarisks. When it was full dark, we started loading the dinette set into his car.

His Toyota was hardly big enough for the

table, even after we'd unscrewed the legs and moved the rear seats all the way forward. We stacked two chairs in the back and tied rope to the trunk lid so it wouldn't bang. Two more chairs were roped to the roof of the sedan.

"We look like the Clampetts," Kevin said.

"At least the Clampetts had enough room to tie Granny and the rocking chair on top." I pointed to Nicole's car seat, which had been taken out to make room for the table.

Momma called from the house, "Cadence, honey, come back in here and rub my feet, will you? I've had such a day!"

I turned back to Kevin. "Don't worry. I'll follow you home with Nicole in my car."

Kevin had moved into a new development on the far east side of town. Façade Estates, he called it, because the homes looked great from the street, but you could see the shoddy construction once you got up close. A drive in the cool evening air would be good for me and keep me from having to listen again to Momma's recriminations about my lack of opportunities and how unfair life was to have left her without someone to take care of her.

I pushed the passenger seat of my old Karmann Ghia all the way back and attached the child seat through the lap belt. Nicole was already drowsy and leaned against me as I snugged her in on my right.

I'd only had one beer, but the darkness and the wind whistling through the cracked-open window had an almost soporific effect, and I had to blink myself awake several times.

I turned up the radio and sang along. "Keep your motor runnin'. Head out on the highway!" I planned my own gifts to go with Nicole's new play table. I'd give her those little Hot Wheels models of cars. A Classic Cobra. A '55 Thunderbird with round side windows. Maybe make a mobile of them over the table. And a soft leather tool belt to sling across a three-year-old's overalls.

Whether it was my voice or the radio that caused it, when we were east of Houghton Road and heading into the open desert, Nicole woke with a start to find herself in an unfamiliar car without her parents. She began to cry. Her fists hammered at the car seat and she kicked and flailed in her fury.

The seat belt sprang open and the car seat slid sideways. I reached with one hand to recapture the loose belt but couldn't find the receiving end of the buckle.

I glanced down in my attempt to secure the seat, so I didn't see the car hurtling toward us in the wrong lane until it was too late.

It was nobody's fault. Just one of those cosmic coincidences where everything that could go wrong, does. And this was one I couldn't fix with penance at the Fault Tree.

CHAPTER 21

Dupree replaced the phone in the cradle and heaved a sigh.

"Bad news?" Nellis asked.

Dupree shook his head. He wasn't sure he wanted to get into all the ugly details with his new partner. "Just family stuff."

Nellis nodded and turned back to his computer screen.

Dupree's eldest daughter, Bitsy, was eighteen now, but it seemed like yesterday that he'd watched her take her first steps across the creaky front porch of his mother's house in Baton Rouge. To the new father, the world had seemed fraught with peril, but it was the peril of a sharp-edged coffee table or a gravelly spill from a trike. He hadn't known enough back then to worry about the kind of pain he was feeling now.

Bitsy had phoned to say she was leaving home and never wanted to hear from him again. He'd tried to be patient — even reasonable — when she first brought that boy home with her. But the kid had BAD written all over him. What kind of eighteen-year-old has a spider tattoo with the words "Widow Maker" etched into his chest? Dupree put his foot down. Bitsy couldn't see Spider again.

"I've got the background on the manager from the Guardian Motel," Nellis said, snapping Dupree from his thoughts. "He was picked up for check kiting twelve years ago, but he's been clean since then. We haven't found anything new on the motel guests since yesterday. John Samson in Unit One is a snowbird here from Detroit. Sixty-eight. No record. Lorraine Clark is visiting family in the neighborhood. We haven't been able to track down the other three names; they're probably fake." He flipped the small spiral notebook closed.

"Can the manager ID any of them?" Dupree asked.

"Maybe one. Says the guy has checked in a couple of times before and his face looked familiar. Early fifties, six foot, two-twenty or two-thirty, receding hairline. Hell, except for the age, that could be me."

"Have him look at mug shots and start with anybody with a home invasion or burglary charge."

"Will do. And I checked on the disinherited friend, Marjorie Lamar. Her husband left her with a pile of money. He was the descendant of the guy who started Prince Steamship Line. She's got a multimillion-dollar house in Skyline Estates and just does the museum thing as charity work."

"Then she doesn't need the money. Ask some of the others from the Desert Museum. See if they were having a fight about something. They're both widows; maybe they were going after the same guy." Nellis jotted a note.

"What about the pharmacist?"

Nellis flipped his notebook back two pages and read from the straight-line, squared-off printing — a love letter to an accountant. "John Stephanos," he said. "Born in 1971, graduated from Mesa High School in '89, got his bachelor's degree in health administration from Grand Canyon University in Phoenix in '93. No wants, no warrants. Married to Josie Dryer in '94. Divorced one year later. No kids."

"Did you ask Forensics to take a look at Mrs. Prentice's medical bills?" The forensic accounting team had gotten busier in the last few years, unearthing money-laundering schemes and frauds as well as motives for murder.

"It looks like she was significantly over-charged for the prescriptions she got at Best Aid. I guess she didn't realize it until she refilled this prescription last week. But we won't know whether that was a fluke or a systematic fraud until we get into the pharmacy books."

"Let's get a court order."

Dupree nodded and made another note.

"Did you find out anything else about Cadence Moran?" Dupree added. She had touched off a pang of unexpected sympathy in him, with her bruises and wide, sightless eyes.

"Yeah, I ran her name through the system too. No trouble with the law, but there was a record of a car accident eight years ago. The other car had a bunch of soccer players from Australia. I guess they were jet-lagged, maybe confused. They forgot which side of the road to drive on. Three people dead, two of the Australians and the three-year-old girl riding with Moran."

CHAPTER 22

I groaned when I woke on Sunday morning, my muscles as tight and bunched as a head of cauliflower. I needed physical activity, not only to ease the soreness but also to stretch my mind away from the ways people could hurt each other. Maybe housecleaning was the answer. Something to make me feel renewed but not make me think.

When I clean, I plan all my movements like the face of a clock. I moved the vacuum cleaner forward and back from twelve to six clockwise, then the same twelve to six counterclockwise.

When the scrubbing and dusting were done and I felt virtuously clean, I loaded a week's worth of underwear, T-shirts, and jeans into a gunnysack for the laundry. I made sure I had enough quarters, cinched the top closed, slung the sack over my left shoulder, and headed out.

Lucy's new and improved contours felt

familiar, but there was a different heft and weight to the cane. The steel shaft made it stronger but also made it heavier. I wound up stepping elegantly with it, instead of using the windshield wiper motion that the mobility instructors recommend.

"Have to give you a more formidable name now, I guess. How about Lucille? Lucinda?"

The coin-op laundry was two blocks to my left.

A circus of birds played at the feeder in front of the Arnolds' house until a dog with multiple tags on his collar scattered them with a bark. Thunder crashed in the distance, but there was no telltale odor of ozone to accompany it. No rain to cool us off today.

I stepped off the curb and into the street.

CHAPTER 23

He twitched involuntarily when the thunder cracked and pulled the baseball cap lower on his face. That woman probably lived or worked in the area, and he would need a good cover story if he were to keep circling the neighborhood. He had thought about loading the van with a rake, a hoe, and a bunch of garbage bags full of dead leaves. That way, if anyone asked, he would say he was going door-to-door looking for cleanup and gardening work.

No. He already had the perfect cover story. He rummaged around on the floor until he found the magnetic delivery sign under the backseat and slapped it onto the driver's door of the van. There. Legit. Now, if anybody asked, he could say he was lost and couldn't find the address he was looking for.

Another clap of thunder. He glanced at the towering clouds over the Tucson Mountains to the west. All bluster, just like his dad. There would be no rain in those clouds today. Just threats and noise.

He'd tried to talk to Lolly about the killing, about how it twisted his guts up, and how everything looked shadowed and darker to him now. "I did it for us," she'd said, as if that was reason enough. And it was. But he still felt the bricks of his carefully built identity crumbling and flaking away. He'd worked so hard to build the man they thought he'd never be, but the mortar wasn't holding.

Lolly had found her strength. Now he had to find his. And that rebuilding couldn't start until he was sure there was no witness against them.

He didn't know if the dark-haired lady would be here on a Sunday. If she worked around here she wouldn't be back until Monday, and he'd have to try again. But if she lived here, maybe he'd see her in a yard, or through a kitchen window, or coming back from church.

He started at the Guardian Motel and made slow, methodical circles of each block.

There. Ahead. One block down on the left and coming his way. She had a white canvas bag over her shoulder and used that wooden cane like a la-di-da prop. Putting on airs?

Or did she need it? Maybe she had a bad hip or knee. Maybe he'd banged up her leg the other day.

He checked the side mirrors and the empty street ahead. The only cars in sight were tucked nose first into their gravel driveways. No cops nearby, no Sunday strollers, no witnesses in the front yards.

He lined the car up on the yellow stripe and took aim.

CHAPTER 24

An engine roared.

I stood still in the middle of the road, sure that if I jumped in one direction, the panicked driver would pick the same one. I was safer standing still and hoping that he saw me in time.

My knees confirmed that fight or flight weren't the only two options in a crisis. They chose freeze.

I held my breath and waited for that telltale screech of brakes or the forced rubber sound of swerving tires. It never came.

CHAPTER 25

"How do you want to handle the Strouts, August?" Nellis said. "Separate rooms or together?" He shrugged off his jacket like a boxer getting ready for a championship fight.

Dupree looked up from his notes and glanced first at the Strouts, who sat on separate benches in the hallway, then back to his partner. "It looks like they're already fighting. That may work for us. Put 'em in separate rooms."

Nellis nodded, patting left and right for his pack of smokes. "I'll take a backseat with Priscilla Strout. Something about that woman makes my skin crawl."

Dupree raised his eyebrows twice in a Groucho Marx leer — "She does look a lot like Carole Martini" — invoking the name from Nellis's crash-and-burn romance.

"Don't start, August."

Dupree smiled. "Let's talk to the husband

first." He turned back toward the hallway and gestured for Arlen Strout to join them.

"Is this going to take long?" Strout asked, impatience and resignation swirling together in the words. Dupree took his time sitting down and straightening his papers. Nellis turned a side chair around and rested his hands and chin on the back.

Arlen Strout was little more than five and a half feet tall, with a farmer's tan across his biceps and a cowlick poking up like Indian feathers from the back of his head. Old acne scars dappled the hollows of his cheeks. "Tell me more about your wife's grandmother, Mr. Strout. Had you ever met her?"

"Yeah, a couple of times. She came over when Priscilla's mother died last year."

"So you've never been to her house?"

"No . . . yeah . . . I don't know. I don't remember."

If they could identify any of the prints inside the house as Strout's, they might be on to something.

"I dropped Priss off there once. That's all." He turned away from the detectives, sitting sideways in the chair to avert his gaze.

Nellis flipped back a couple of pages in his notebook. "You ever been arrested, Arlen?"

Strout's head jerked up and he met Nellis's gaze with a steely stare. "Six years ago. Possession."

"Possession of what?" Dupree asked. Just because Nellis hadn't found an arrest record didn't mean there wasn't one. Six years ago, Arlen Strout would have been a juvenile, and those records would be sealed.

"Cocaine."

"Here in Arizona?"

"Tacoma. Priss and her mom moved here three years ago. I followed them down, and we got married a couple of months later."

"Did you all three live together?"

"At first. But then we got our own place out in Catalina." Strout's face told the story of those three-to-a-house days: he hadn't liked the enforced supervision. Maybe jail time held the same threat for him.

"Where were you and your wife on Thursday night, Mr. Strout? Say, between eight and midnight?"

Strout stiffened, but his answer came easily. "I'm a night watchman at that taser company out by the airport. My shift starts at eight."

Dupree knew the place. They were the largest seller of tasers to police forces around the world. He wondered if they knew about their security guard's criminal history.

"That's quite a commute for you. All the way across town, it must be, what, thirty miles each way?"

"Priss likes to have the car, so I take the bus. It takes about an hour, hour and a quarter, with transfers."

"Can you prove you were out there all night long?"

Strout met his gaze without blinking. "I punched the time clock every hour on my rounds. And my partner was there the whole time too. Never even went for a dinner break, we ordered pizza in."

"Arlen, do you think your wife had anything to do with her grandmother's death?"

"Priss? Shit, don't be ridiculous." He waved away the notion with one hand, but that hand shook. "I mean, we're short on money and everything, but killing somebody? That's not Priss's style."

"What is her style? Stealing from her grandmother?"

Strout's eyes darted away.

Dupree and Nellis got up, leaving Arlen Strout in the interview room.

"Let's see what the grieving granddaughter has to say." Dupree led the way into the next room.

CHAPTER 26

Nellis leaned against the mirrored wall in the interview room, while Dupree sat at the end of the table, affording himself a view of only the woman's profile. Priscilla Strout was on her second Diet Coke. She wore a white halter top today, tied inches above the waistband of her shorts, revealing a narrow waist but pale and flabby belly. She clicked the nails on her thumb and ring finger together like a Morse coder with an urgent message to deliver.

"Are you sure I can't smoke in here?"

"I'm sure. We'll take a break in a few minutes." Dupree eased back in his chair and crossed his legs. All the time in the world.

"I really want a cigarette."

Dupree uncapped a bottle of water and placed it in front of her. "Did your grandmother keep valuables in the house?"

"I don't know. I'm not even sure she had

any. I only went there a few times. Mostly we talked on the phone."

"You know about her old TV show though, huh? Sounds like she was a real celebrity around here."

Sergeant Richardson had confronted Dupree this morning, waving a stack of e-mail printouts in his face to punctuate the urgency. "She was the fairy godmother to every damn kid in Tucson!" he'd said. "Now they're all over fifty and don't want their happy memories disturbed. I've been fielding calls all morning!"

"I guess I sort of knew it," Priscilla replied. "Dad had this scrapbook with a bunch of old pictures in it. We left it in Tacoma."

The celebration of a life — arrayed on the page, pasted down, titled, remembered — cast off in the interest of traveling light. Dupree remembered watching his wife cutting out news stories about his arrests, taking time out of her busy weekends to go to scrapbooking classes so she could showcase his achievements. Would his daughter Bitsy some day jettison Gloria's scrapbooked chronicle of his career?

He thumbed back to his notes from the last phone conversation with Juanita Greene, when she'd told him about returning to Wanda Prentice's house. Both Arlen and Priscilla Strout would have been too short to leave that nose print on the window, but Priscilla might have gotten someone else involved. Who knew what kind of friends she'd been making while Arlen worked?

He put a tick mark next to the note that said "coffee can." "There were coffee grounds all over your grandmother's kitchen, but we didn't find any kind of can or bag for them. What kind of container did she keep her coffee in?"

Priscilla's face showed alarm, as if she'd just been apprised of a pop quiz in a subject she hadn't studied for.

"Oh, *that* thing. Well, she did keep some money buried in the coffee can on the counter." She peeled the label from the bottled water in front of her.

"How much?"

"Never more than twenty or thirty dollars. It was for tips to the delivery people. The church basket. Stuff like that."

"What's that coffee can look like? Do you remember the brand?"

"It's not a real can, not like you get from the store. It's more like a decorative canister. Painted metal, with a red and green design."

It was the most detail Priss had provided for any part of her relationship to her grandmother. Dupree bet she had raided

136

the canister on her visits to the house. But the notion of delivery people was a good one. He'd follow up on any deliveries to the house: UPS, pharmacy, groceries, pizza.

"Did she have any good jewelry?"

Her hand jerked upward to rake her hair, successfully tipping the water bottle on its side.

"Oh, God. I'm sorry. Let me clean that up." She dug through her purse for Kleenex.

"Her jewelry," Dupree prompted.

"Nothing really good. A gold chain. Her wedding ring."

Dupree let her think that he hadn't noticed her slip off the yellow ring and drop it in her purse.

"Don't you get lonesome — bored — with Arlen working all night?" Dupree pictured *A Day in the Life of the Strout Household:* soaps on TV, Arlen snoring in the late afternoon, Priscilla looking for attention, conversation, any kind of stimulation by the time the sun went down.

She squirmed in her seat.

"What were you doing Thursday night while he was at work?"

"Nothing. I watched TV. Read a magazine."

"You had the car. You didn't go out?"

She shook her head.

"Who did you meet, Priscilla?"

Priscilla shredded the Kleenex into damp confetti. If anxiety were an indicator of guilt, he could have arrested her right then and there.

"No one."

It was a damn lie, and they both knew it.

CHAPTER 27

"Are you okay?" A woman's voice, high and fast with concern.

I groaned and rolled onto my back. "What happened?"

"I was looking out my kitchen window and saw this car come down the street and clip you. Are you sure you're all right?"

I was sure that I wasn't. I had landed on the bag of laundry, so my ribs and arms weren't as sore as the last time, but everything else throbbed as if I'd been thrown out a second-story window carrying a barrel cactus. There was new gravel rash on my face and one tooth wiggled when I tried to talk. My left hip was frozen with pain and I could feel a wet, bloody gash on my knee. I shook like a palsy victim, adrenaline masking the terror inside me.

I pawed the ground, in search of Lucy/ Lucinda. There. Thank God she was still in one piece.

"Did you see the car? Get the license?" A whirlwind roared between my ears and my teeth made grinding sounds. I wasn't sure I was making sense or even if I was saying it out loud. I tried to calm my heart with little sips of air.

"You're the blind lady from down the street, aren't you? Oh, my God, they hit a blind person." Her hands fluttered from my face to my hips like a wounded dove trying to take flight.

I didn't know why she thought running over a blind person deserved a different penalty from hitting anyone else, but then I remembered the game we used to play as teenage drivers. "Two points for the little old lady in the wheelchair!" Maybe I was the butt of the joke now and merited two points in somebody's Sunday joyride. But it was no joyride from this side. I had never felt so vulnerable, so unable to protect myself.

"Did you see the car?" I repeated.

"No, not really. Just a glimpse. It was big and boxy. Maybe an SUV or a minivan. Tan." Oh great, now kids were taking joyrides in minivans. "And it had a company name on the side. Like one of those magnetic signs."

I tried to stand, but my hip and knee

refused to hold my weight.

"You need someone to look at that knee. Let me give you a ride to the hospital. And we ought to call the police." She grabbed me around the waist and I leaned my weight against her.

"I don't think I can make it as far as your car. Do you mind calling an ambulance?" I think I managed both sentences before I blacked out.

A half hour later, I was lying on the examining table in an emergency room cubicle close to the hospital lobby. I could hear the tense conversations of patients and families waiting to be seen, the cessation of their pain forestalled by a six-page hospital entry form and the magic trick of a medical insurance card. The smell of ammonia filled the warm air, and paging announcements spurted from overhead speakers every few seconds. A gurney with a squeaky wheel was passing by when a swish of the curtains surrounding my bed announced an arrival.

"I'm Dr. Santos." A deep voice with too many emergency room nights behind it. "Let's see what we have here. Car accident, huh? It looks like the car got off easier than you did."

I grunted agreement as he swabbed my knee with something cold and stinging, then blew on it to cool or dry it, just like Aunt Caroline used to do with our scrapes and cuts when we were kids. I was hoping he'd plant a kiss on it the way she used to, to make it feel better.

Dr. Santos checked my limbs, my range of motion, and the inside of my mouth. "That tooth isn't going to fall out today, but you'll want to have your dentist check it soon."

He collared an orderly to push me up to X-ray and we passed the squeaky gurney again as it headed back to the lobby. There was something in that sound that made me pause. My head throbbed in the same rhythm as the squeak.

What had I heard when the car ran me down last Thursday night? An engine out of tune, certainly, but there's nothing unusual about that in Arizona, where the majority of cars on the road look like contestants in a demolition derby. What else? The rhythmic squeak of the gurney continued down the hall.

That was it! I'd heard a squeak in the left front suspension of the car on the night Mrs. Prentice was killed, and heard it again this afternoon as I spun away from the oncoming car. Metal on metal, a dry grating sound that echoed in a left-to-right pattern around the front wheelwell.

After the X-rays confirmed no broken bones, Dr. Santos stitched the gash in my knee, declared me "bloodied but unbowed," and pronounced me well enough to go home. My knee felt as big as a football and throbbed in announcement of its discontent.

But the most grievous damage was that done to my self-confidence. Would I ever be able to cross a street alone again? Raise my head and step confidently into the dark? I limped out to a waiting taxi, now clearly using Lucinda for support.

Dupree and Nellis arrived only thirty minutes after I phoned. Nellis, smelling of breath mints, wheezed onto the couch. Dupree paced from my kitchen to the front door and back again. The afternoon sun had warmed his earthy aftershave into something primal and passionate.

"I'm positive it was the same car that I heard Thursday night. Same engine, same suspension problem." The sun slanting through the front window warmed only half of my face. I scooted to the left to enjoy it.

"Did you smell antifreeze again?" A smile in Nellis's gravelly voice, but not the right kind. He didn't believe me.

"No, I didn't notice it this time."

Dupree was quiet. This was the first time

that either detective had been inside the house. I'll bet the room looked Spartan to them. Furnishings chosen the same way I pick my clothes: neutral colors so I never have to worry about an unintentional clash. No extraneous furniture for me to trip over. No family photos. No mirrors or pictures on the walls.

From where he was sitting on the couch, Nellis probably couldn't see the one piece of artwork I do have in the house, above my bed. It's a three-dimensional picture of the buttes and mesas at Red Rock, all carved by computer out of layers and layers of paper, to shape the scene. I use my hands to see that picture, including the feathered wings of the eagles in that placid sky. I bet that by now my fingers had left grimy paths, like smoke, where they had so often read that desert landscape.

"I know it was the same person, and now we have a description of the car."

"Tan? Could be a minivan or an SUV? And she doesn't remember what the sign on the side said? I guess it's a start, but it doesn't narrow it down much. Who was this witness who saw the car?" Nellis used a singsong voice, as if he were listening to a story made up by a child.

"I'm sure she gave her name to the cops

or the ambulance attendants. She lives right on that block where I was hit."

Nellis grunted. "You know, if you're not using a red and white cane, drivers can't be expected to know you're blind. You weren't even in a marked crosswalk. If they hadn't left the scene we might not even cite them for this accident."

I shook my head. I knew I couldn't help the police much, but I desperately wanted to. How else could I dare to take a sightless step across a street again? Breathe deeply and know that I was safe in my darkness? I had to make them believe me.

Detective Dupree was softer in his reply. "We'll talk to the neighbor who helped you. Maybe she can tell us more about that sign on the car door — whether it had a logo or a picture, maybe printed letters or italics. Anything she can give us will be a head start."

His comments were more open-minded than Detective Nellis's, but it still sounded like he was humoring me, and humor was the last thing I needed. If it was the same car in the neighborhood today, I was in a killer's sights and his aim was getting better.

CHAPTER 28

Nellis unwrapped a stick of cinnamon gum, wadded up the foil, and started the car. "That was a waste of time, huh? She wasn't much of a witness to start with. Antifreeze? And an engine that needs a tune-up? And now this big news: it also has a squeak in the suspension! What a crock of shit. Coming out here when we ought to be following real leads."

Dupree heard the frustration in his partner's voice. He still couldn't understand why Nellis had requested a transfer from Robbery. He'd been doing well there. Give him a good bank robbery or white-collar crime and Nellis could shine. But Dupree wasn't sure that his new partner had the heart for the kind of purposeful infliction of pain and misery you'd see every day in Homicide. It damaged you in ways that etched lines into a previously smooth face and made the heart go gray with grief.

They'd only worked two murders together so far. One of those was a jeweler's wife who'd been taken for ransom, and the suspect had been apprehended in Tucson's Garden of Gethsemane, a life-size biblical reconstruction done in concrete, where the money exchange was to have taken place. Of course, she was already dead by then. The second case was an abused woman who'd finally had enough and killed her husband. "She put him out of her misery," Dupree had quipped. Nellis didn't get it.

"That's what Homicide is all about," Dupree said, opening a stick of gum for himself. "Following a hundred bad leads in the hope of finding one good one. Hey, something I've been meaning to ask . . . why would anybody use antifreeze in the desert, anyway?" He'd never found it necessary growing up in saunalike Louisiana.

"Still feeling like a newcomer, August? Antifreeze works just as well to keep things from boiling over as it does to keep them from freezing."

Dupree nodded. That made sense. "And what other real leads did you have in mind?"

"Shit. I mean, maybe this blind lady was there and everything, but we don't even know if the car she heard belonged to the killers. How's that going to help us? God-damned snowbirds." Nellis blasted the horn at the slow-moving Cadillac in front of them, seemingly as much angered by the car's Michigan plates as he was by its speed.

Dupree shrugged and tested his seat belt. "You never know. There was a blind lady back home who could ID somebody by the shape of his fingers or the sound of his breathing."

Nellis continued as if he hadn't heard him. "Now this second hit-and-run. Probably nothing more than a blind lady not using a red-tipped cane and not walking in a crosswalk. Hell, she might even be one of those people who like to be in the middle of a crisis, so they make things up to stay involved. Attention junkie, know what I mean? And did you get a look at the tatas on that woman? Talk about an attention junkie." He whistled his admiration and continued, "I'll bet that's the kind of thing every woman knows, even if she can't see herself in a mirror."

Dupree looked back at the road. "Did you hear the sarge this morning? He's getting a lot of heat on this one. All those baby boomers who remember Wanda Prentice from the TV show have started a reward fund. It's already up to thirty thousand." Maybe Wanda Prentice wouldn't wind up in a tiny plot paid for by the county after all.

He used his cell phone rather than the police radio under the dash to call the Homicide Unit. "Linda? Check for me if anybody on our burglary or home invasion list drives a tan minivan or SUV."

"Nobody," she replied two minutes later.

"Yeah, that would have been too easy."

Nellis picked up the prescription receipt and waved it at him.

"Linda? One more try. How about a John Stephanos?" He read her the pharmacist's home address, thumbing the medical receipt while he waited.

"A blue BMW, huh? Thanks anyway."

CHAPTER 29

It was only sundown, but I'd had as much as I could take for the day. I limped into the bedroom, settled gingerly onto the bed, and braced my damaged knee between two pillows to create a tent that would keep the weight of the blanket off my stitches.

Wanda Prentice had been dead for three days now, and I hadn't been able to do a damn thing to help solve her murder. The only thing I'd succeeded in doing was drawing the attention of a madman who seemed intent on running me down.

A mourning dove, probably bedeviled by the neighbor's cat, gave an eerie late afternoon call just outside the window. Four monotone, plaintive notes.

It sounded like, "Who looks for you?"

CHAPTER 30

On Monday morning, the shrieking pain in my knee kept me in bed until an ice pack and a double dose of aspirin had taken effect and I could hobble to the living room. When I phoned the shop to ask for the day off, Walt didn't even ask for a reason, so I didn't have to admit being hit-and-run prone. I also didn't want to tell him that I had a serious case of the heebie-jeebies, second-guessing every move I made.

Juanita's call woke me from a deep sleep on the couch at eleven, and I told her about my latest visit with the cops.

"Detective Nellis treats me like I'm communicable."

"Don't let it bother you." She paused, then changed directions. "Say, do you want me to do a grocery run for you? I could do it over my lunch hour."

Kevin's shopping trip had only provided enough for our boiled dinner; I was running low again.

My loose tooth felt more solidly attached today. Maybe it would take care of itself and I could avoid a trip to the dentist. I winced and flexed my knee. "It's probably a good idea for me to keep moving. If you swing by here first, I'll go with you." I groaned and slid out from under the ice pack.

She arrived an hour later. I used Lucy as a crutch to the car.

We parked near the front door of Raley's and stopped to buy a dozen fresh green corn tamales from a Mexican family that was selling them out of the trunk of their car in the lot. Once inside the store, I turned to the right and headed to the only section where I was comfortable: produce.

My head swam with the mingled odors. Bright, acidy tomatoes; sharp, oniony leeks; fecund, almost too-sweet bananas. I reveled in the slick feel of the cucumbers and handled the Idaho potatoes as if they were chunks of mined ore.

I love the produce aisle, and if I could do all my shopping there I would be happy. But put me in the frozen food section or in front of the shelf of packaged rice and I am as lost as if I stepped onto an alien planet.

We filled the top of the shopping cart with the foods I could identify, then headed to the coldest part of the store. Juanita opened a freezer door and read off my choices. "Beef Stroganoff? Macaroni and cheese? Meatloaf?" We selected a week's worth of entrees that wouldn't put much strain on a loose tooth. When we got home, I would label each with a Braille tag to identify the dish, the cooking time, and the temperature required.

I paid at the register and limped behind Juanita as she pushed the cart to the car.

"Here's a good one, Cadence. There's a car over there with a sign in the window. 'For Sale by Owner.' Well, who the hell else is going to be selling a car? For Sale by Car Thief? For Sale by Mother-in-Law?"

As we stowed the bags in the trunk, a car passed down the aisle behind us and sat at an idle at the end of the row. The driver revved the out-of-tune engine to keep it from dying. I smelled antifreeze.

"Juanita. Don't be obvious, but check out that car at the end of the aisle."

"Yeah?"

"What kind is it?"

"Chevy Lumina, I think. You know, a minivan. Maybe five years old or so."

"What color?"

"Light brown."

"Does it have any kind of signs — like

company logos — on it?"

"Yeah, there's something painted on the door, but I can't read it, he's turning."

I gulped so loud that I thought that distant driver might hear me. The car wasn't moving fast enough to create that telltale suspension squeak, but I knew it was the right one. He was still here. And he was following me.

"Get the plate number. Now." I heard the minivan turning away from us to the left.

"It's not an Arizona plate. California, I think. It has seven digits. Let's see. Five . . . MSU . . . and the last three are either zero eight eight or zero three three. Something like that."

"Can you see the driver?" I heard the car coming back toward us in the next aisle.

"Sort of. He's got a baseball cap on. White guy. Maybe in his twenties. Dirty blond hair." Her voice tilted back up to me from a downturned chin. "He's looking this way."

I kept my back to the cruising car. The Chevy turned right and moved away from us. I tugged her toward her car. "Quick. Let's follow him."

"Why?"

"This is the guy who ran me over twice now."

Juanita pulled me to a stop. "Girl, you're jumping to conclusions. It's just a guy look-

154

ing for a parking space."

"His engine needs a tune-up," I said. "You can smell the antifreeze, and if he speeded up, I know we'd hear that squeak in his suspension. And the lady who helped me said it was a tan minivan with a sign on the door. How much more do you want? We can't let him get away this time!"

"Are you nuts?" Juanita asked. "Just call the cops. That's what they're for."

I realized how irrational I was being. Of course I wouldn't be of much help in a car chase. I pulled my cell phone from the bottom of my purse.

This time the detectives had to listen to me. I called their direct extension instead of going through 911.

"Detective Nellis? This is Cadence Moran —"

"Yes, Ms. Moran, what is it now?" Barely restrained patience there.

"I'm down at the Raley's on Grant, and I think the guy who ran me down is here in the parking lot." I put my hand over the mouthpiece and whispered for Juanita to keep an eye on the car.

"Why do you think it's the man who ran you down?" Like he was talking to a dangerous idiot.

"It could be the same kind of car that my

neighbor described — it's a tan Chevy Lumina — and it smells like antifreeze —"

"Ah, antifreeze again. Do you have the plate number?" Humor the poor woman is what it sounded like to me. I repeated the license information. "I'll make a note of it. Thanks for calling."

Oh yeah, it was loud and clear: *I'm just being polite but I have absolutely no intention of making this a priority.* It was just one more unlikely avenue of investigation for him and he already had too many "possibles" and not enough "sures." Or maybe it was just one more complaint from a silly blind lady whose judgment he didn't trust much in the first place.

"Is he still here in the parking lot?" I asked Juanita.

"No, he headed west on Grant."

"Let's follow him."

"The cops have got the number now, Cade. Let them find him."

I knew she was right, but I still felt a shiver move up my spine as if the killer had reached out a dark, horny hand and placed it on my shoulder.

CHAPTER 31

"Hand me that screwdriver, Lolly."

He'd waited until the movie theater parking lot was full of matineegoers, then knelt down to unscrew the plates from an old Nissan in the back row. They were the reddish-brown plates that were supposed to be reminiscent of Arizona copper mines but instead looked like peanut butter left too long in the sun.

Now that they were back at his house, he could swap them for the original plates on the van.

"They look right at home there," she said, handing over the screwdriver.

She was right. The stolen plates looked just as dusty and banged up as the car did. He screwed the plates in place and kicked up a little dirt to cover the fresh tool marks.

"We need to talk, Lolly." He sat down on the bare earth, leaned back against the rear tire, and patted the shady patch of dirt next to him. She scootched over.

"Nobody was supposed to get hurt," he said.

"What did you expect me to do? She was coming after you!"

"I guess, maybe, we should have just run away."

She glared at him. "Run away? Easy for you to say. You don't have to put up with all the shit at home like I do. And she was asking for it, the bitch."

"We'll find a way to be together —"

"Not without money, we won't. And that old woman was the best source of money I know. Didn't she go on and on about all her treasures? Egging me on all the time?"

Money. It was all he could think about. It shouldn't be up to Lolly to get the money so they could leave. That was his job. He was the man, and he should be providing for her. Protecting her.

"You know, what you did back there —"

"What *we* did," she corrected him.

"We. I'd never let you go to jail for that, Lolly. If we get caught, you tell 'em you had nothing to do with it. I planned it all. I killed her. Okay?"

She draped her arm across his shoulders. "We won't get caught. And we'll be smarter next time."

Next time? His stomach recoiled at the thought. But what other choice did they have? Leave Tucson in the dead of night with a half tank of gas and no plans? Beg for money in front of the McDonald's when they got hungry? And that's only if he could get her away from her old man. He wouldn't put Lolly through that. He had to find a way to get some money and get her out of that house.

"What time do you have to get back?" he asked.

"Pretty soon. He'll be getting up to go to work."

He rose and dusted off the seat of his pants, then helped her up and wrapped his arms around her. If they could only stay like this — just the two of them, with no one else in the world to interfere. And soon they'd have even more reason to be together. He breathed in the sweet scent at the nape of her neck.

"C'mon. I'll give you a ride back home," he said.

The old Econoline started without complaint and he turned right to join the interstate heading north into town. Maybe he could rob a bank. Hit a convenience store. Just one score like that would give them enough money to get out of town. And maybe it wouldn't involve killing.

He'd always thought that loving Lolly was a good step in his life. He'd never felt so whole. Together, they could do anything. But killing, and a life on the run, was not what he'd thought their life together would be.

He unrolled a pink wad of Bazooka and popped it in his mouth. He ought to be using sugar-free gum. He hadn't checked his blood sugar for days, and worrying about Lolly and the killing had thrown his levels out of whack. He pulled into the Walgreens parking lot, leaving Lolly in the car while he went in to get testing supplies.

"Can I see you again tonight?" he asked when he got back in the car.

"I don't know. He's started checking up on me. Calling from work."

He pulled to the curb at the corner, out of sight of her front door, and tugged her toward him. "I'll take you away. I will. Please believe that. It won't be long now."

CHAPTER 32

"August, wait till you get a load of this." Dupree looked up as Nellis bustled across the room, shoved a pile of papers to the side, and plugged in the portable tape deck. The tape spun lazily from one side of the cassette to the other. The woman's voice was scratchy but audible.

"Randy? It's Priss."

Dupree raised an eyebrow and leaned in closer. "What the hell is this?" He turned off the electric fan he'd plugged in next to his desk, in order to hear the tape more clearly.

"It looks like Ms. Grieving Granddaughter of the Murder Victim is dumber than we thought. She made this call from your desk phone yesterday afternoon after her interview. Mowray thought he overheard something weird when he walked over to escort her out, so he got Communications to make him a copy of the call," Nellis said.

"Hey, Good-Lookin'," the tape continued. A male voice. Deep but young.

"How about if we get together tomorrow night instead of Thursday? I've been so uptight, what with the police and all."

"The police?"

A whispered reply. *"I can't talk right now. I'm down at the police station."*

Dupree paused the tape. "Any idea who this guy is?"

"Randall Owner, according to the number she dialed."

The voice on the other end of the line erupted. *"Priss, are you fucking nuts? Calling me from the police station?"*

"Hey, I don't have a cell phone, and it's easier to call you from here than from home. Relax, they don't know anything about you. So, what do you say, tomorrow, same time as usual?"

There was a pause and then, *"Fine."*

A dial tone. No good-bye.

"Get a tail on that woman right now."

Dupree pulled to the curb behind the unmarked car. They were four houses away from Priscilla and Arlen Strout's house but with a clear view of the front door and driveway.

"What have you got?" Dupree asked the

young undercover cop, Heidi Rodriguez. Nellis pulled out a piece of nicotine gum.

"The husband left at six-thirty, on foot. A radio car said he got the bus out to the airport from the next block over."

"Yeah, he's on the night shift."

"The missus got back here at seven o'clock and carried three big Kmart bags into the house."

"Spending money like somebody who expects to come into an inheritance, huh?"

"Clothes shopping by the looks of it. She pulled a red blouse out of one bag on her way to the door."

They sat silently as the darkness settled around them. All the lights were on in the house. Dupree made himself a note to have the Strouts' old Chrysler checked for a radiator or hose leak. It didn't exactly fit the description of a tan minivan or station wagon, but eyewitness accounts were often wrong, and in the right light or in a stressful situation, that could be how you'd describe the big white beast.

It was a damn shame he couldn't make the same leap of faith and morph Stephanos's blue BMW into a tan minivan. Everything they were getting back said this lousy pharmacist got his bachelor's degree in criminal conspiracy and fraud instead of health administration.

Nellis trigger-flipped his Zippo.

"Not here. She'll see you," Dupree said.

Nellis groaned and shoved the lighter back in his pocket.

It was almost nine o'clock when Priscilla Strout finally made her move, wearing tight jeans and what Dupree guessed was that new red blouse. She left one light burning inside but extinguished the porch light as she slipped out the front door. She drove straight to the Bum Steer bar with the detectives' surveillance vehicle tucked into the same lane three cars back.

Dupree gave her a head start, then sent Rodriguez inside to handle surveillance. He could hear the band's bass amplifier from here; it shook the two-story wooden building like a series of well-timed earthquakes. He wiped a hand over the dome of his head and tugged at his earlobes. It had been a long day and looked like it was going to be a longer night.

He tried his daughter's number again. "Bitsy, honey, you know I just want what's best for you. Call me. We can talk about this." Was she going to keep screening her calls for the next decade just to spite him?

A few minutes later, Heidi Rodriguez slipped into the seat behind him. She was in her late twenties and wore her dark hair in a loose ponytail. The white jeans and spaghetti-strap top made her look more like a college student than a cop. Dupree hung up the cell phone and half turned to the backseat.

"Whew, that's one noisy bar," she said. "I had to wait to get the stool right next to Strout before I could hear anything."

"Who's she meeting with?"

"A young guy. Light brown hair, six one, two hundred pounds. His name is Randy, so it's gotta be the right guy. And based on the amount of tar on his boots and under his nails, I'd say he works as a roofer or on a paving crew."

Nellis groaned under his breath.

"Does it look like business or pleasure between them?" Dupree asked.

"Can't tell. I heard him ask her if she was alone tonight. She said, 'Yeah, for the first time in a long time.' "

"We'll stop them on the way out and take him downtown. Find out what he and Strout have going."

Rodriguez unfolded herself from the backseat and retraced her path to the front door of the bar.

Nellis let out a long sigh.

"What's all the whining about?" Dupree

asked when Rodriguez was out of earshot.

"Shit. It sounds just like Carole. Remember when I told you that she said I was never home and never talked to her? Then she declared Wednesday night girls' night out, only I find out that Carole is the only girl involved." He paused. "And that the paving crew she was hanging with at the bar was laying more than asphalt."

Dupree shook his head in commiseration, then turned his attention back to the front of the bar. He'd been hoping for proof that Priscilla Strout was involved with her grandmother's murder and that she would lead them to her accomplice. Was it Arlen, who was already pushing for information on the will? Or maybe this Randy Owner? Owner was tall enough to have left that nose print.

Had Owner been convinced by love or by money? Was he a hired thug Priscilla Strout had found to do the dirty work, or was there something going on between them? He imagined Owner's car coasting to the curb in front of Wanda Prentice's house. Mrs. Prentice would have recognized her granddaughter, but did she put up a fight because she didn't know the man? Did she threaten to tell Arlen about his wife's nighttime activities?

A splash of music brightened the air when

the door to the bar opened. Priscilla Strout and Randy Owner came out together, walking hand in hand toward a black truck in the back corner of the lot. Rodriguez was on them like a beagle on a rabbit.

"Gotcha'," Dupree said under his breath.

CHAPTER 33

A tan Chevy Lumina with California plates. At least my bogeyman was gaining definition. I wondered if the detectives had been successful in tracking it down. Or if they'd even tried.

I'd have to tell Kevin and the guys at the shop about it. Have them keep an eye out for the car. And I ought to alert my neighbors too.

I shivered, even though the evening temperature was almost ninety.

I didn't want to be alone with my thoughts tonight, and I had the perfect solution. At my request, Juanita had asked for one of the tapes of *Wanda's Story Hour* that had been delivered to the police station.

I tapped it into the slot on the VCR and pushed Play. Jewelry box–ballerina music came through the speakers, then a soft, sweet voice asked all the children to gather around to hear a story.

I pictured a dozen pajama-clad children plopped on cushions at her feet. She would have been dressed like a princess.

Wanda Prentice's tone had changed over the years, but that decades-old tape held the essence of my friendly neighbor's voice. Lilting. Honeyed. Smile-curved around the edges.

I spent the night with Wanda Prentice and *The Little Engine That Could.* They made me feel better, even though, more often than not, I was The Engine That Was Too Scared to Even Try.

CHAPTER 34

Nellis waited until Officer Rodriguez had put Randy Owner in her car, then tucked Priscilla Strout in the back of his Crown Vic. He and Dupree remained silent during the trip from the bar to police headquarters, letting the specter of jail and culpability take shape in her mind.

"Does Arlen have to know about this?" she whined as Nellis escorted her to an interview room.

He didn't answer.

Dupree shoved Randy Owner into a separate room. While he fidgeted, Nellis did a computer check for wants and warrants. The records indicated a conviction for grand theft auto when he was twenty-one. Nothing since then.

"Looks like he specialized in Corvettes," Nellis said "Maybe Randy's been a good boy for the last five years, but it's more likely that he's learned not to get caught."

"Ah, the things you learn in prison," Dupree agreed. "You take the lead with Priscilla Strout. Maybe she'll be a little more forthcoming tonight."

"Tell me about Randall Owner," Nellis said to Priscilla as they entered the room.

"Is that his name? He told me to call him Randy, but I didn't know if that was his real name."

She twirled a lock of hair around her index finger and pleaded with Nellis from under downcast eyes. "You don't have to tell Arlen, do you?"

"You mean the same way you didn't tell him about stealing your grandmother's ring?" Dupree asked from the back of the room.

"Steal it! She gave it to me!" Priscilla Strout twisted the ring again and ricocheted between their unresponsive faces. "Well, she would have given it to me if I'd asked."

Nellis herded her back to the original topic. "How long have you been meeting Randy Owner?"

"A couple of months. It's not really an affair, not like that. I was just looking for a little excitement." Her crossed legs twined together like a man-eating vine. "Sometimes we'd get a room or go back to his place. Sometimes we used the back of his truck or some other car."

Nellis kept his eyes on the notepad in front of him, waiting for her to fill the silence.

"Randy always gave me a present, and I made sure no one ever saw me."

"A present?" Nellis looked up, but Priscilla avoided his eyes.

"Usually about forty bucks. Please don't tell Arlen. You don't know what he's like." Dupree couldn't tell if she was more afraid of Arlen's fists or of losing her extracurricular income.

"You have any other boyfriends, Mrs. Strout?"

"Not really. Well, nothing regular. Sometimes if I meet somebody nice I'll maybe make out with him. But that's not really —"

Nellis leaned back in his chair and linked his hands behind his head. "I see. You're hooking."

"Well, I don't have enough money to go out on my own. Do you have any idea how long it's been since I even got to buy a new pair of shoes? And it was perfectly safe . . ."

"Yeah, up until the point where you and one of these boyfriends decided to rip off your grandmother. What was it? Did you just get tired of waiting for her to die? Did she wake up while you were ransacking the kitchen?"

"I swear. I was with Randy last Thursday. I never went to my grandmother's house."

"Prove it." Nellis shoved the legal pad toward her. "Write down every place you went on Thursday night and every person who can verify you were there."

Nellis joined Dupree at the wall. He flipped to the page in his notebook where he had written the tag number that Cadence Moran had called in, underlined it twice, and pointed it out to Dupree.

If that plate number had anything to do with Randall Owner or any of Priscilla Strout's other boyfriends, Dupree knew they were going to have to do a full-on Catholic-style-bended-knee mea culpa to the blind woman.

CHAPTER 35

I jerked awake, but having my eyes wide open didn't help. I could still imagine the demon-racing engine and spinning tires that had pursued me in my dream. The phantom face in the car was in silhouette, but bright lights had cut like knifepoints through the darkness.

I'd fallen asleep after the ten o'clock news and it was barely midnight now, but I felt like the nightmare had lasted for days.

Someone wanted me dead. And in the still-air silence of the night, I heard his approach with every breath. Did that short, sharp sound come from a neighbor's house, or was it the squeal of my rusty screen door? Was that muffled clunk a stray dog in the garbage can, or the footfall of a predator in the next room?

I'd done what I could to identify that car for the police, but what could I do to protect myself in the meantime? Should I move in with Juanita until I knew he'd been caught? Or, heaven forbid, move back in with my mother?

I didn't think the licensing folks would take kindly to a blind person with a gun, but I could carry a knife. And Lucy, now that she had been reinforced, would make a good weapon.

I pulled the sheets up to my neck, then snuck one hand out to rest on the bedside telephone. I'd stay on guard until I heard the early morning sounds of traffic and conversation and coffeemakers. Then I'd do my best to fortify the house. String a bell across the windows and doors so that I would hear a surreptitious entry. Hide weapons in each room where I could find them if I needed them.

There would be no more sleep tonight.

Chapter 36

Dupree shoved away from the wall in the interrogation room and preceded Nellis out the door. It had been a long night, first with surveillance and now with questioning. He glanced at the clock; a new day was about to begin.

"What do you think?" he asked once the door to Priscilla Strout's interview room had closed behind them.

"Guilty as sin."

"Not if she's got alibi witnesses that can place her in a bar with Randy Owner last Thursday night."

"They'll have to be some pretty damned good witnesses to convince me," Nellis said.

They entered the small interview room where Randy Owner waited. Dupree shoved an empty chair away from the table with his foot, spun it around, and sat down with his arms folded across the back. He compared the mug shot to the man sitting across from him. Nothing had changed. Owner still had long sideburns and the tattoo of an empty-eyed skull on the left side of his neck.

The Miranda warning was on the table in front of him. Owner had willingly signed it, saying he didn't know why the police had picked him up, but he had nothing to hide.

"Okay, Randy, let's start with how you know Priscilla Strout."

Randy shook his head. "I never saw her before tonight. I just met her there in the bar."

"We've got a recording of her phone call to you, Randy."

"I swear to you, I never saw her before in my life." Sweat beaded his forehead.

"Priscilla Strout says you were with her, murdering her grandmother, last Thursday night."

"What? The bitch is nuts! I haven't killed anybody!"

"But you were with her last Thursday?" Dupree challenged him.

"No! I told you, I just met her." Owner gulped and his eyes skittered left-right, on the hunt for a get-out-of-jail-free card.

"You're not helping yourself here, Randy." Dupree consulted the file again. "It says here you've got a black Toyota pickup. You have any other cars?"

"No, sir."

No tan SUV or minivan, Dupree thought. That made Owner a less likely suspect. But the phone call from Priscilla Strout in the police station proved that they were in cahoots on something.

Dupree wasn't going to release Owner until they'd had a chance to check his car. There might be bloodstains or fibers that could link Owner to the murder. Hell, there might even be a radiator leak. Rodriguez was off getting the warrant right now.

"Sit tight. We'll let you know if we have any other questions." And one of those questions was why Randy Owner wouldn't admit to knowing Priscilla Strout. What did he have to hide?

Owner was chewing his cuticles down to blood as Dupree and Nellis left the room.

CHAPTER 37

"If you loved me, you'd do it," Lolly said, catching her breath. She'd taken the bus out, but the walk from where it let her off had winded her. He hoped the bus driver wouldn't remember her if the cops came asking.

"We can just leave. Today. You'll never have to see him again." He wrung the baseball cap between his hands, transmitting the urgency and anxiety to the cloth rather than to his voice.

Sunlight sat heavy and hot on his shoulders, and beads of sweat snailed down the back of his neck. He never thought he'd be talking about killing in the bright light of an Arizona noon. Hell, he never thought he'd be talking about killing at all.

"He'll find us." She hung her head, blond hair cascading across her cheeks, her eyes wet with tears. "He'll never let me go. This is the only way."

He knew she was right. He'd never stop hunting for her. He'd bring her back, no matter what it took. Especially when he found out why they'd run.

He had to die.

"Where is he now?"

"Asleep. That's how I got out of the house." Her lips weren't quivering anymore. She stood straight and wide-eyed.

He knew he had to match her courage. Prove that his love was as strong and deep as what she'd shown.

He stuffed two pillowcases with underwear, T-shirts, and jeans and threw a denim jacket over his shoulder. They wouldn't be coming back here.

An hour later, Lolly was tapping her foot to an unheard song on the drive across town. The house was still and quiet when they arrived, the curtains pulled shut across the front window. There was a low hum nearby from a neighbor's window air conditioner. It was early afternoon; the guy should be sound asleep.

"It's for us," Lolly said, handing him her keys. Her voice was low, more breath than volume. She wrapped her arms around his neck and opened her mouth to a deep kiss.

"You wait here." He put a finger to his lips and then to hers, and got out of the car. He didn't need the house key; the door was unlocked. He pushed it open and stepped inside. The living room was dark as a theater. A faucet dripped in the kitchen.

He crept down the hall to the closed door at the end and turned the knob.

Strong, steady snores from the bed. He took three steps forward, willing the man to wake up, to face him, to understand why he was going to die. It was time to make all those "bad seed" predictions come true.

He took a deep breath, unsnapped the buck knife from its sheath at his waist, and pulled the blade sharp and hard across the man's throat. At the last moment, the old man had opened his eyes, wide with fright but no recognition of the avenging angel in front of him.

He jumped back to avoid the spray of blood, then waited until the gurgling was over before he turned back toward the door.

He had to do something to make sure the cops didn't immediately think of Lolly as the killer. What would throw them off?

He went into the bathroom and wiped the knife on the towel that hung, still wet, from the shower door. He could smash the man's bones, upend heavy furniture, and make sure the murder looked like the work of a man. Would that be enough?

No, wait. He found his way into the kitchen and tore off a paper towel to mask his prints. Then, with a fury he thought he'd already expended, he yanked ice cubes, cookies, cornmeal, and flour from the cupboards and refrigerator and dashed them across the floor.

There was no reason for the cops to tie Lolly to Mrs. Prentice's death, so they wouldn't automatically think this one had anything to do with her either. It would be the work of the same crazed burglar who attacked Mrs. Prentice.

He jammed the paper towel into his pocket. Dry mouthed, he grabbed a handful of chewing gum packages from a bowl on the coffee table on his way out. He spit out the gum in his mouth, opened the new pack, and tried to still his shaking hands as he approached Lolly in the van.

"Is it over?" Her eyes were bright with excitement.

"Yes." He held out a handful of the Bible Gum packages he'd taken from the house.

"Thanks." She ignored the Bible card inside the pack and dropped the cellophane onto the sidewalk beside the car.

He wasn't sure if she meant thanks for the gum or for the murder.

"We've still got one more person to take care of," Lolly reminded him.

CHAPTER 38

Dupree pushed his spine against the desk chair and leaned back into the cool rush of air from the fan. He'd been at it for only a few hours, but the words were blurring in front of him; he had to restore his concentration. He thumbed through the stack of interview sheets on the desk.

What was he missing? They'd canvassed the area for four days, checked all traffic stops or parking tickets in the neighborhood that night, tracked down known burglars and home invasion specialists and followed up on their alibis.

The phone tips hadn't been any help at all, but they all had to be verified too. Hundreds of them. The killer is hiding out in a cave, one caller said. As if there weren't a thousand caves in southern Arizona, including the massive Kartchner Caverns that could have hidden a hundred fugitives.

Crime scene techs had been all over

Randy Owner's truck but hadn't found any link to Wanda Prentice or Cadence Moran's hit-and-run. They'd had to release Owner, but Dupree cautioned him not to leave town. They still had to check out Priscilla Strout's other alibi witnesses to prove that Randy Owner was with her that night.

So far they'd tracked down three stores that made regular deliveries to Wanda Prentice's house: the pharmacy where she'd had a fight, a grocery store, and a sandwich shop. They weren't done with the list, but right now none of the delivery guys looked promising. Unless maybe that pharmacist had used a delivery as cover to get into her house and kill her.

Nellis said his money was still on Priscilla Strout. Maybe she got tired of waiting around for her inheritance. Maybe she got one of the guys she was sleeping with to kill Wanda Prentice.

Dupree rose and walked to the window overlooking the St. Augustine Cathedral to the north. The sun on the chalk-white domes and towers threw blinding glints of light back at him. The only new information was that Wanda Prentice had kept money in a coffee canister, and that canister was missing. It was looking more like a burglary gone bad.

Sergeant Richardson had left another stack of baby boomers' outraged e-mails on his desk to spur him on.

Nellis had put in a request yesterday for information about the license plate that Cadence Moran had phoned in, and now Dupree spread out the faxes that had arrived from California. Nellis had tried four possible combinations. Juanita Greene had been pretty sure about the beginning of the plate, 5MSU, so he'd started with that and tried adding 088, 033, 038, and 083. That last one wasn't an assigned number, so the California DMV had faxed them the details on only three cars.

"Any luck?" Nellis asked, setting a greasy bag of churros and *pan de huevo* on the desk. Sweet breakfast treats for instant energy.

"Nothing from the phone tips." Dupree uncrumpled the top of the paper bag and gestured to the faxes in invitation. "But take a look at the responses we got to your license inquiry. I got the local cops to pay a visit to these three. This one" — he picked up the top fax with sugar-crusted fingers — "zero three three, belongs to a '66 Mustang owned by an employee of the Department of Justice in Fresno. Zero three eight is on a dark green Subaru up north in Smith River,

California, and the car's still there. But this one could be interesting."

He licked two fingers and handed Nellis the last fax. "Zero eight eight. A 2000 tan Chevy Lumina, owned by a Darren H. Toller, twenty-seven, of San Diego," Nellis read.

"And Juanita says the plate is on a Lumina. It matches."

"Does he have a record?"

Dupree shook his head. "He's either clean or he's smart."

"Let's check in with Ramona," Nellis said, crumpling the bag to preserve the last two churros. "She left a message that she's found something interesting on the pharmacist."

The Forensic Accounting squad was on the same floor as the Homicide detail but all the way across the building. Dupree spotted Ramona Fuentes in the corner, her fingers flying across the keypad on an old adding machine.

"You still use that old thing?"

"My fingers know it best. And it prints out whatever I'm adding so I can double-check myself." She wore rimless glasses that magnified her eyes. Dupree would have sketched her as a goldfish.

"Here. Let me show you what I've got. Overcharging is the least of this guy's crimes." She fanned a deck of prescription receipts across the desk. "First, he's not telling any of these patients that there are generic equivalents for the drugs they've been prescribed. Then, he doesn't include any coverage by a patient's secondary insurance carrier. So when the patient shows up, she finds out her prescription's going to cost a hundred and thirty bucks, and that Medicare will only cover thirty of that. That's what your murder victim discovered."

She tapped a stack of insurance forms. "Then he goes ahead and rebills both Medicare and the secondary carrier."

"So he's made money off the patient for the higher-priced drug and then been repaid — sometimes twice — by the insurance companies," Dupree said.

"Could this just be ignorance?" Nellis asked. "Maybe the guy doesn't know how to do the paperwork."

She shook her head. "It doesn't look like it. They get it wrong about a third of the time. And Stephanos has approved every one of the transactions."

"Is there any pattern to it?" Nellis asked.

"The victims all seem to be seniors, but I don't know what else they have in common. It includes all kinds of medication: painkillers, sleeping aids, cancer drugs, cholesterol drugs. Maybe they only pulled the scam on customers who looked like they were well enough off that they wouldn't notice if their medical bills went up from twenty to a hundred and twenty bucks."

"How much so far?" Dupree said.

"About thirty thousand for the one month I've looked at. But that's not the worst of it. I checked with the lab. The blood pressure pills Wanda Prentice was charged a hundred and thirty bucks for were generics."

"So what's he doing with all those branded drugs he kept?" Dupree asked.

CHAPTER 39

Lolly had wanted to go back inside.

"I need to pack some things."

"It's too dangerous. We'll buy whatever you need."

"With what? Our good looks?" she sneered.

She was right. His last paycheck and the nineteen dollars from the Prentice house hadn't gone far.

He drove to the Tucson Mall on Broadway. The stolen plates weren't enough protection. He couldn't take the chance someone had seen the van. They needed a new car.

Massive parking lots were tucked at odd angles around the mall. A thousand vehicles shimmered in the July heat. There were enough stores and movie theaters here to guarantee that the car wouldn't be missed for a while.

The van threatened to stall as they idled down the rows looking for a likely target.

The engine had overheated when he'd swapped license plates earlier, and he'd had to walk back to a gas station for a gallon of antifreeze for the radiator. He'd be happy to get rid of the old van and move on to something more reliable.

"How about this one?" Lolly pointed to a tiny Mini Cooper with all the windows left open.

"Too flashy. Too small."

They kept prowling. At the end of a long row on the south side of the shopping center they found the perfect vehicle: a small pickup truck with a hard plastic cover over the bed. The windows had been cracked open — a good sign that the owner expected to be at the mall until the temperatures made the truck too hot to get into. Maybe a store employee. Perfect.

He put the van in park, opened the driver's door, and told Lolly to slide over. She had driven the van before and would do fine as long as she was just following the other car through light city traffic.

"We'll head north toward Mount Lemmon," he told her, easing into the front seat of the Mitsubishi. It was a little smaller than he would have liked, but it was an anonymous car, and if it was just the two of them traveling, it would do. He unbraided two plastic-coated wires under the dash, just like his brother had taught him to do, and sparked the engine to life.

"Follow me. And Lolly? Don't do anything to make the cops curious."

"Kill the engine," he said after Lolly had angled the car into position.

She switched the motor off and got out of the van to join him. Less than forty miles north of Tucson, the air was cooler at this elevation and he breathed in the sweet mountain air.

He used his shirttail to wipe every hard surface inside and outside the van — steering wheel, mirrors, seat adjustment, glove box, visors, dashboard, and door handles.

Together they moved all their belongings into the back of the new pickup truck. They'd stopped once on the Mount Lemmon highway to get a gallon container of gas. He splashed the liquid over the front and rear seats, then wiped down the gas can before he threw it down the hillside.

Reaching into the van, he moved the gearshift to neutral with a gloved hand and let the car roll forward till its front tires touched the sandy edge of the cliff. He ignited a matchbook that was three-quarters full and tossed it into the driver's seat. The gasoline-soaked fabric ignited with a whoosh.

Stepping back as the flames grew higher, he leaned all his weight against the back bumper. The van inched forward, hesitating at the sandy lip for a moment before it plummeted down the mountainside. It seemed like a lifetime before it came to rest among the burned, skeletal branches of what had once been a grove of old evergreens. The car's tan contours began to blacken in the crackling flames until it looked at home in the already burned wasteland.

"Just one more thing to take care of, then we're out of here."

CHAPTER 40

I couldn't afford many more days without making some money, so Tuesday morning I limped down the street to the shop. After two too-close calls with that car, and a sleepless night full of unknown sounds, I made sure not to step into the street if I heard an engine anywhere nearby. Probably paranoia on my part, but I wasn't taking any chances. When the street held only the riotous sound of cicadas, I swung my leg around in a stiff arc in hopes of keeping the stitches in place and stepped out into the street. There was a gooey dampness in the gauze over my knee by the time I reached Walt's front door.

There was no noise of search dogs or police walkie-talkies on the block now, but it had already been five days since Wanda Prentice's murder. I hoped the information on that California license plate would help them. I didn't want to think about more sleepless nights, wondering if I would be the next victim.

Nellis had sounded so dismissive about the license plate. Had he ever checked into it? Maybe I should call Dupree when I got home. Maybe he'd be open-minded to following up on it.

"Whoa. What happened to you?" Turbo greeted me.

"Another run-in with a car. The police think it has something to do with that murder down the block. Think maybe the guy's after me too."

"Yeah, right. Because you'd make such a good witness."

I ignored him and headed for Walt's office but got the same treatment there.

"What do you want me to work on today, Walt?"

"The way you look, you ought to be working on yourself! I've junked cars with less damage on them."

That sounded so much like the day he'd hired me that I had to laugh. Although it was years ago, I could still remember the desperation in my voice. Walt had heard it too. I was practically begging. "Give me a try. Any car you have in here. I'll do a full tune-up and have her singing 'Back Home Again in Indiana' in thirty minutes flat."

Walt had guided me to the carcass of an original VW Bug and I traced its rounded contours with shaky hands. There was more rust and Bondo than there was paint. I touched and tapped and breathed in the scent of every part of that car, from the pitted chrome around the headlights to the rough ovenlike surface of the tailpipes. When Walt started it up, I heard the wheezing and rales of an engine on its deathbed. This was a landscape I recognized, a territory I could explore even without my eyes.

A half hour later, when I turned the key and the engine gave that unmistakable VW growl of a healthy sewing machine on megavitamins, I knew I had a job.

"I've got some stitches in my knee," I told Walt, coming out of my nostalgia, "so I can't do much kneeling down but —"

"How about you just pack wheel bearings for Turbo? You can do that without moving around much."

"Thanks." I hadn't realized how weak I really was. Even the walk to the shop had taken a lot out of me. By the time Turbo and I had repacked the bearings on an old Pontiac and mounted new tires for the car, I was about done in.

I told Walt I'd try to make it back in the next day, but he brushed aside my good intentions. "Don't come back until you can do the work, Stick. I'll pay you for the next couple of days, anyway. You were kind of on the job when you got hit Thursday, you know? Just consider it my civic duty."

I smiled my thanks, wormed out of my overalls, and baby-stepped back home. It was only midafternoon, but I felt like I'd been on my feet for a week.

I tapped up to the gravel driveway at the house and breathed in the honeysuckle smell at the edge of the property. Yeah, I was tired, but maybe I'd take just a moment to spray the plants and savor that special Arizona blend of airborne water and dust.

Juanita had always insisted that she would only plant things that the Arizona Highway Department grew in the medians of the state's freeways. "If the Highway Department can't kill 'em, then I can't either." But I loved to garden, to get my hands deep into good soil, and I mostly chose plants for their texture and fragrance. This year I had planted pots of lavender, soft velvety lamb's ears, sweet-smelling pineapple sage, and Mexican feather grass, as delicate and brushlike as its name. Almost two dozen pots were clustered into fragrant families across the gravel in my front yard. Most of them wouldn't last more than one season in this heat, but if I was religious about watering them, they might have a chance.

I breathed in the scent of my next-door neighbor's struggling imported roses and once again laughed at the incongruity of an unsighted person wanting to garden in a land of thorny bushes and cacti.

A car idled just down the street. Going nowhere fast. I didn't hear the *ca-chunk* of a misfiring engine like the car that had run me down, but I still didn't like the notion that somebody — somebody silent and unmoving — was watching me from that car.

"Cadence!" My neighbor, Mr. Lotz, called from behind the roses.

I jumped, then cleared my throat to mask the nervousness.

"Mrs. Arnold down the block said you'd been hit by a car. What are you doing out of bed? Can I help you with anything?"

"I'm okay. Just banged up my knee."

"Can I bring you some chicken soup?"

His wife made a mean chicken soup. "Absolutely. I'll trade you for some fresh green corn tamales. Come on in."

He followed me to the front door and took the house keys from me when my trembling fingers missed the lock.

As tired as I felt, it was still nice to have

someone around to keep the bogeyman
away.

CHAPTER 41

"Why's she staring at us?" Lolly whispered.

"Shhh."

They hadn't waited on the Mount Lemmon highway to watch the van burn. Better to be far away if anyone noticed the flames. But he couldn't leave town with that one thing dangling. He'd promised Lolly. The woman who had talked to the cops was the only thing standing between them and a safe new life.

He'd seen her twice in this neighborhood now. Once on Thursday night when they went into Mrs. Prentice's house, and then again on Sunday when he'd almost been able to get rid of her. He knew his chances of finding her again were good, and there she was, right there in the front yard watering plants. Just like she was waiting for him.

"Cadence!" A balding head peered around the rosebush next to the driveway. He couldn't hear every word, but he got the gist of it. "Mrs. Arnold down the block . . . hit by a . . . out of bed? Can I . . . ?" The neighbor came around the hedge and toward the woman with the hose. The woman replied and pointed to her knee. Then the bald head followed her to the front door.

He wasn't worried. He knew where she lived; he could take all the time in the world.

Chapter 42

After Mr. Lotz left, I took a quick shower, not so much to get the grime off as to cool down. The doorbell rang as I stepped out of the tub. I pulled on a T-shirt and sweatpants, gave my wet head a rub with the towel, and approached the front door, my nose close to the jamb. That earthy scent of aftershave again.

"Hello, Detective. Are you alone?"

He gave a grunt of surprise. "How did you know it was me?"

"Your aftershave."

"No, I mean, before you opened the door."

"Your aftershave." I smiled, but he didn't laugh in response. "That's a joke. I heard your police radio. Come on in."

I ushered him in and offered a cold drink. Using my forefinger to gauge how full the glasses were, I added ice and returned to the living room.

"I have a favor to ask of you, Ms. Moran.

Something that may help us with this investigation."

I didn't encourage him, knowing how flawed my help had been so far.

"I want you to meet with Mrs. Prentice's granddaughter."

"What good is that going to do?" She was probably already blaming me for not calling the cops when I heard that muted scream.

"We think she knows more than she's telling us. If she was there, just having her see you at the station may make her think you're there as a witness against her — that you can identify her. Or maybe you'll catch her in something that you know was a lie from that night."

"You think being blind gives me special powers of ESP, Detective?"

"Please. She might have been one of the people you heard running from the house. You owe it to Mrs. Prentice."

I wished he hadn't said that. I hugged my elbows and ducked my head.

"Please, Ms. Moran. You're all I've got."

"I'll do it." And heaven help us all if I'm your only hope.

Dupree took me down to the station. In the car, he filled me in on Priscilla Strout's story about going barhopping on Thursday night.

I recognized the route through the lobby to the elevator but lost my sense of direction on the way to the interview room.

Priscilla Strout was already seated when we got there, drumming her fingernails on the table. It must have been a different room from the one they had taken me to the night after the murder. This table sounded like metal rather than Formica.

"There's a small table three feet in front of you, Ms. Moran," Dupree said. "And an empty chair on its left. Mrs. Strout is seated on the right side of the table." I took two steps into the room and Dupree shut the door behind us.

"Mrs. Strout? This is Cadence Moran, the witness who came forward the night your grandmother was killed," he said.

"Call me Priss." Her voice came from waist level, almost in front of me. She wore an overwhelming fragrance of gardenia with undertones of vanilla, much too liberally applied. I moved forward until my fingers brushed the edge of the metal table.

Priscilla Strout was silent, maybe uncomfortable around people with disabilities, or maybe wondering whether I knew she had a part in the murder. Finally she said, "I know who you are. I saw your picture in the paper."

I waited, wondering where to start. I knew so little about that night — the car, the killer. How did Dupree think I could trip her up?

"What kind of shoes are you wearing?"

There was a pause while both Strout and Dupree wondered where I was going with this.

"High-heeled sandals. Red," Strout said, as if the color could possibly make a difference to me. "I always wear high heels. I have trouble with my Achilles tendon and they're the only shoes I'm comfortable in."

"Do you always wear the same perfume you have on today?"

Priscilla was happy with the change in topic. "Isn't it wonderful? It's called Camellia Nights and I've worn it for years. I think it's just about the sexiest thing I've ever smelled."

At last, we'd found a topic she could get excited about, although I bet that the name was really Gardenia Nights.

I thanked her and tapped my way to the door. Dupree joined me, then made sure the door was closed behind us. He led me over to his desk and I sank into the guest chair, my hands resting on the dog's-head cane.

"It's not Priscilla. She wasn't there."

"How do you know?"

"Two things. First the shoes I heard were not high heels. The footsteps were different from the sound high heels make. These sounded thinner, like a flat leather sole. But you'd have to confirm that she only has high-heeled shoes at home. Otherwise, who knows what she was wearing that night?"

"What's the second thing?"

"The perfume. I didn't smell it the night I heard Mrs. Prentice scream. And as heavily as she wears it, it would have been obvious if she was anywhere nearby."

"Well, that fits her story of being out on the town that night."

I was feeling a grim satisfaction in at least clearing one suspect, until Dupree added, "Now we just need to prove she didn't get somebody else to do her dirty work."

CHAPTER 43

When Nellis returned to the squad room, Dupree told him about Cadence Moran's scent memory and the confirmation of flat-soled shoes running from the murder scene.

"I wish you'd stop believing every damn word that comes out of that woman's mouth, August. She hasn't been right about anything yet." His ruddy cheeks ballooned with his sigh.

"Oh, I take some of it with a grain of salt. But she might be worth listening to every now and again."

Nellis didn't seem willing to give her that much credit. "Just because she didn't smell that woman's perfume doesn't mean Priscilla Strout wasn't involved in this. We've only found Randy Owner so far. Who knows how many other guys she's fucking? And get this . . . I checked car thefts for the night Mrs. Prentice was killed. A '67 Corvette was stolen from a bar on Wilmot about eight o'clock that night."

"Maybe that's why Randy Owner doesn't want to fess up to being with Priss. I wonder what he was driving when he met her that night? Let's swing by her house and ask her. And make sure she doesn't have any flat-soled shoes."

It took almost two hours to get a search warrant and retrace the route to Catalina.

They stopped at the wheeled plastic garbage can at the curb in front of the Strouts' home before they approached the house. Taco Bell wrappers and a pizza carton. "If she threw those shoes away, she didn't do it here," Nellis said.

Arlen Strout answered the door, bare-chested and with a can of Coke in his hand. A Cardinals game was blaring from the TV in the living room.

"We have a warrant to search the premises, Mr. Strout," Dupree said, handing him the paperwork.

"Help yourself." Strout opened the door wider. "But where's Priss? Isn't she with you?"

"What do you mean? An officer brought her home more than an hour ago."

Strout shook his head. "I've been here all day."

Dupree turned to his partner. "Check with Ogilvy. He was supposed to bring her home. Maybe they had car trouble."

Nellis moved off to the kitchen, his cell phone at his ear. Dupree and Strout remained standing, glaring at each other like hesitant duelists, each unwilling to take the first shot.

"Tell me, Mr. Strout, did your wife ever get a prescription filled for her grandmother? Ever do any shopping for her at the Best Aid?" Randy Owner wasn't the only candidate to be Priss's accomplice. Maybe she and John Stephanos had already talked about how hard it was to wait for her grandmother to die. Maybe that's why Stephanos blew up at Mrs. Prentice at the pharmacy.

"I don't know. You'd have to ask her." His arms were locked and loaded across his chest.

"Where's my wife?" Strout snarled when Nellis returned to the living room.

"Officer Ogilvy dropped her off here a little after three o'clock. He didn't stay to watch her go in, but she was walking up the driveway when he pulled away."

"Your Chrysler is still here," Dupree said. "Do you have any other vehicles?"

Strout shook his head.

"Maybe she just walked up to the corner store?"

"An hour and a half to go to the corner store?"

"It's too early to file a missing person report," Dupree said. "But we'll tell all mobile units to be on the lookout for her. In the meantime, let's check around here and see if there's any clue where she's gone."

Strout followed Nellis as he searched the kitchen and living room. Dupree headed straight for the bedroom closet.

Turquoise sandals with a strap between the toes. Cowboy boot mules with high stacked heels. Black stilettos that he would have loved to see his wife in.

"Doesn't your wife have any flats, Mr. Strout? Any sneakers?"

"She's got problems with her feet. Said it was gonna have to be either high heels or orthopedic shoes."

"Are there any suitcases missing? Any toiletries?"

Strout checked under the bed, where two canvas suitcases collected dust, then the bathroom. He came out carrying a toothbrush in one hand and a bottle of perfume in the other.

"Everything's still here."

They checked the trunk of the Chrysler in

the driveway before they left. No Priscilla Strout and no flat shoes.

"Think she ran?" Nellis asked.

"Either that or that jealous husband in there just wants us to think so. We might be looking for another body."

CHAPTER 44

Dupree returned from the taco wagon on the corner with a greasy paper bag in his hand. Five-fifteen and they still hadn't had lunch yet.

The phone rang, interrupting his first bite. He answered and listened. "We'll be right there."

"What's that about?" Nellis asked.

"We've got another body. A man this time — a James McDougall — but it might be the same MO. Killed with a knife and nothing but the kitchen was touched."

"Let's go." They rewrapped their almost-lunches and dropped them in the trash.

It was six o'clock by the time they got across town to the tan-colored brick house on the quiet cul-de-sac on the north side of the city. Crime scene tape was strung from the prickly pear cactus on one side of the yard to the six-foot saguaro on the other. They ducked under the tape and Dupree greeted the officer at the front door.

"Who found him?" Dupree asked.

"A guy from his job." He chin-gestured to a man in a denim shirt just outside the crime scene tape. "McDougall was supposed to help him do some work on his house today."

"Keep him there. We'll want to talk to him later."

Dupree preceded Nellis into the house. The curtains were still drawn and it was cool and dark in the living room.

"Do people really live here?" Dupree muttered. Everything was a pristine, icy white. Clear plastic casings covered the white sofa and two side chairs, ivory lamp shades retained the clear acetate ribbons that were wound around them at the store, and a two-foot-wide strip of heavy-duty plastic covered the pale shag rug in a trail that led from the front door to the kitchen.

A large wooden crucifix, complete with the thin, tortured body of Christ, hung over the sofa. There was a well-thumbed Bible on the coffee table, along with a bowl of wrapped chewing gum and candy, but Dupree didn't see any other books. He also didn't see a television. Had the thief taken it? Or was this a household that distained that kind of blasphemy? It would have been difficult to see the picture if the television had been plastic-wrapped anyway.

"The body's in here," a second officer said, waving them into the bedroom.

Dupree knelt beside the bloody bed, waiting until the medical examiner finished taking the liver temperature. Probably in his late forties, McDougall had been a bear of a man, jowly and big fisted, with a day's worth of stubble gracing his cheeks and chin. He lay on his back, one arm and leg hanging off the bed, a gaping gash across his throat. The spilled blood was a dark red Rorschach against the white bed linens, pajamas, and rug.

"Looks like they didn't wait for the homeowner to wake up this time," Nellis said.

"And it doesn't look like the front door was forced either. How long ago?" Dupree directed his question to the medical examiner.

"Three to six hours."

Dupree rose from the squat and followed Nellis to the kitchen. Cupboards had been flung open and emptied: pinto beans, rice, and coffee grounds speckled the floor. The refrigerator had an automatic icemaker, and its plastic bin had been yanked from the machine and hurled to the ground. A broken jar of spaghetti sauce mimicked the bloodstain in the bedroom.

Dupree knelt to retrieve the blood-smeared bath towel on the floor and placed it into an evidence bag.

"The killer wiped the bloody knife on the towel, then came in here. McDougall didn't interrupt a burglary in progress."

"And nothing but the kitchen touched. Ransacking a house is not unusual, but when it's only the kitchen . . . think we've got a copycat?" Nellis asked.

"Maybe. Some of the details of Wanda Prentice's murder were in the paper and on the news. Or maybe it's one killer who just likes doing things a certain way. There was a knife used in both attacks. See if the coroner can match the wounds."

They rejoined the first officer in the front yard.

"Mr. Hutchins," Dupree said after introductions were made, "you were to meet Mr. McDougall this afternoon?"

Tim Hutchins had a bulbous nose dappled with sun-damage cankers. He cleaned an ear with his little finger while he answered. "Yeah, our shift starts at seven, and Jim said he'd help me hang an overhead light before we had to go to work."

"He was supposed to come over to your place?"

"I was supposed to pick him up. His car's in the shop. There was no answer when I got here, but the door was unlocked so I went in. I found him there in the bedroom. Haven't seen anything like that since I last went hunting." He shook his head.

"Did you notice anything missing in there? Was anything taken?"

"I wouldn't know. Never spent much time in the house. But check with his daughter; she should be able to tell you."

"His daughter?" Dupree looked to Nellis for confirmation. Nellis shrugged.

"Beatrice. She's seventeen." He stopped, then searched the detectives' faces. "Oh, please don't tell me she's in there too."

Seventeen. Almost his daughter's age. "We need to find her," Dupree said. "Do you know what school she goes to?"

"She's not in school anymore; he's been homeschooling her."

"Any idea where she'd go?"

Hutchins shook his head, and Dupree drew a question mark after Beatrice's name in his notebook, then added another after Priscilla Strout's name. Two women missing.

He didn't want to think of the possible reasons that a seventeen-year-old, who should have been home on a Tuesday afternoon, was gone when her father was found murdered.

"Find out what kind of car McDougall drives and whether it's still in the shop. And let's get a picture of Beatrice out on the wires. I don't know what we're looking at here, but when kidnapping is the best of the options, you know the rest are downright pitiful."

CHAPTER 45

The six o'clock news was just ending. They didn't have any details but said there had been a possible kidnapping and another murder in Tucson. I guess we really had graduated to big-city status.

"Cade!" Juanita called from the front porch.

I turned down the TV and went to unstring my warning bell and unlatch the screen door. "Didn't expect to see you today."

"I just wanted to check in after our adventure in the parking lot yesterday. And I brought dinner. Any word from Dupree on that license plate?" She brushed past me cradling a big paper bag with both arms.

"Nothing yet. Want something to drink?"

"Thanks. We look like twins today," Juanita called from the kitchen where she was unloading her groceries. "White T-shirts and jeans. Great minds think alike, huh?"

"It's almost a uniform for me." I wore only black and white shirts, and I'd stitched an X into the neck of the black shirts so that I could tell them apart. As if thirty seconds in the Arizona sun wouldn't have told me anyway.

"But today's too damn hot for the jeans. What are you cooking?" She already had at least one container open and it smelled great.

"My mom's *carne adobo.* She was cooking all day and made us up a to-go bag with the beans and salsa. All we've got to do is grill the steaks."

"I'll let you light the grill." Open flames didn't sit well with my finger-friendly style of cooking.

"You mind going over the bills while you're here?" I asked.

"Sure. Let me get the fire started first."

She dumped charcoal into my hubcap-size Weber grill while I poured a glass of red wine for her and iced tea for me. We took our drinks to the kitchen table to go through the bills.

My electricity bill was as low as ever, but the cost of water in the desert was skyrocketing. After Juanita filled in the payee line and the amount, she positioned the check in front of me and placed my left forefinger on the signature line. I know there are computers that could help me, but I loved Juanita's running commentary as she read through each letter.

When the bills were done we gave the steaks a scant five minutes on each side and served big plates, towering with the meat, tortillas, beans, and salsa. I poured a second glass of iced tea.

"Hey, I've got a new sign for you," Juanita said. "I was driving along in a construction area today, and the sign says 'Double Fine Zone.' Great, huh? Double fine, even better than fine. But they ought to put it up someplace like the Grand Canyon. Someplace *really* double fine."

I folded a chunk of beef and a fingerful of beans into a tortilla and thought about Double Fine Zones. Double the happiness; life would be good. But I couldn't picture anybody else there with me. There was nobody at the shop I was interested in. Turbo and Danny were years younger than I was and treated me like a sister. The two detectives were the only new men I'd met in more than a year. Dupree already had a wedding ring on, and I could understand perfectly well why Nellis didn't.

"Say, what do you want to do for your birthday?" Juanita asked between bites.

My birthday. Tomorrow. These hit-and-runs must have shaken me up more than I realized. I'd been so focused on planting ice picks, knives, and screwdrivers in every room that I'd completely forgotten the date. I usually looked forward to my birthday for weeks, because it meant my annual plane ride with Kevin. I hadn't heard from him yet about scheduling one this year.

I tapped the side of the plate. "This is my birthday celebration. Thanks for a great dinner."

When we were done, I walked her to the front door and rehung the tinkling bell trip wire across the threshold. Mindful of the electric bill I'd just paid, I turned off all the lights. Nobody here needed them anyway.

CHAPTER 46

"Okay, every squad car and news outlet in the city has her picture," Nellis said. "It'll be on again on the late news and then in tomorrow's papers."

Dupree sat at the foot of the narrow bed in Beatrice McDougall's room, holding a wallet-size snapshot of the girl with both hands. The date on the back said she was fifteen years old in the picture, but there didn't seem to be any more recent photos around. Long, straight blond hair past her shoulders. She was young enough to still have baby fat, and her smile had a vague air of sadness, as if she had only enough energy to raise one side of her lips.

Like the rest of the house, everything in the girl's room was done in shades of white. Glossy white furniture. Nubbly ivory bedspread. Off-white rag rug covering most of the floor. There were strips of sticky tape on the wall, the adhesive scars marking locations where pictures or posters had previously hung. Dupree wondered if they were taken down because of content, because the girl's tastes had changed, or because they added too much life and color to the otherwise icy white room.

"We're just about done out here, sir," the Crime Lab technician said from the doorway. They'd spent the last four hours dusting, photographing, and taking samples from the house and the body.

"Thanks. Did you find anything?"

"Just this." He held out two small evidence bags. "We found this piece of chewed gum out by the sidewalk. It smells like Bazooka, but we'll check to be sure. And right beside it we found this." He handed over the second bag.

Dupree turned the bag over in his hands. "A gum wrapper, Bible Gum brand. And the Bible card that goes with it. There's a bowl of them in the living room. So maybe our thief helped himself to one?"

"Could be. There are some great prints on that wrapper." The Crime Lab technician grinned like he had the inside scoop on the lottery numbers and hadn't told his ex-wife.

Nellis and Dupree set out on opposite sides

223

of the street to interview McDougall's neighbors. The first officers on the scene had done a preliminary canvass and had noted the addresses where neighbors had something to offer. Unfortunately, none of them had been around earlier in the day when McDougall had been killed.

"What can you tell me about your neighbor, Mrs. Carlyle?" Dupree asked the harried mother of twin eleven-year-old boys in the house across the street.

"They've only been there a year or so. I think they used to live on the east side of town. Beatrice — that's the daughter — said something about going to Palo Verde High School for a while." She swatted absently at the Star Wars combatants behind her.

"I thought she was homeschooled."

"She is now. Her father was very possessive, you know, and he didn't like what she was learning in public schools."

"Homeschooling must have put quite a burden on him, raising a daughter by himself like that. Where's Mrs. McDougall?" Dupree sketched two Jedi light sabers to remind him of the interview.

"He said she died when Beatrice was little. Didn't go into details. It was hard to get him into conversation at all."

Dupree flipped back to his notes from the

interview earlier in the day with Hutchins. Both men were on-call plumbers working the night shift. If McDougall was home-schooling Beatrice in the daytime, he wouldn't have much time left to chat up the neighbors.

"He loved that little girl," Mrs. Carlyle continued. "But I don't think she liked being kept on such a short leash."

"Why do you say that?"

"I heard them arguing last week, out in the front yard. He said, 'I mean it this time. I'll move us out of state.' And she said, 'You'd better hurry, then, 'cause the minute I turn eighteen I'm leaving anyway and you can't stop me.'"

Dupree thanked the woman and left, wondering whether every teenage girl was hardwired to make that threat. And whether the standoffs ever ended happily.

CHAPTER 47

As unexpected as an icicle in the desert, the sharp crack of a twig outside my bedroom window sent alarms ringing up and down my spine. I held my breath, waiting for a second sound that would tell me what kind of predator waited there and what direction he was going.

Something rustled in the thick lantana that carpeted the narrow flowerbed under my window. Was that the swish of fabric? An inhaled breath? Why the hell hadn't I planted a cholla cactus?

I reached out to grab the butcher knife I'd positioned within easy reach on the bedside table, then gulped. It wasn't there.

I groped from one corner of the night-stand to the other, my terror rising — Kleenex, alarm clock, telephone — but no knife. I knew I had left it there when I'd armed the house before going to bed.

Was he already inside, standing an arm's

length away and grinning at my vulner-
ability?

Thirty seconds. A minute. Nothing but
silence from the backyard.

I wanted to move but couldn't make
myself do it. My heart raced with panic. I
didn't want to be the hysterical woman the
cops refused to respond to after a while.
Neither did I want to be the dead one they
would read about in the morning paper.

Slowly, slowly, I reached out to take the
cordless phone from its cradle and pull it
under the covers with me. I punched in 911
but didn't push Send yet.

I eased one leg from under the sheet, moving in one-inch increments as I stretched
toward the floor.

My toe connected with the sharp point of
a blade and I jerked back in surprise. When
my heart slowed, I reached down and
retrieved the knife from where it had fallen.

This killer wouldn't have to terrify me. I
was doing a damned good job of that myself.

I spent the rest of the night with my hand
cradling the phone, the predialed number
all ready to go.

CHAPTER 48

Wednesday morning, Dupree checked the messages as soon as he got to his desk. Priscilla Strout had not come home during the night and Beatrice McDougall had still not been found.

"Any news?" he asked Nellis.

"Nothing on McDougall. Priscilla Strout doesn't have a cell phone, and the bus driver on that route doesn't remember her, so I was thinking, how does she get out of there? I pulled the LUDs from a pay phone at the Circle K a couple of blocks away. There was a call to Randy Owner's cell phone just ten or fifteen minutes after Ogilvy dropped her off."

"Good work. Have you tracked down Owner?"

"That's the best part. I just heard back from his boss. Owner left the job site yesterday after getting a call and didn't show up this morning. And get this, the boss checked back through their records for me. Three months ago, their crew paved the cul-de-sac where the McDougalls live, and they had a job just a couple of blocks from Wanda Prentice's house the week before she was murdered."

"That's good enough for me." Dupree holstered his Glock and grabbed his jacket from the back of the chair. Officer Rodriguez had executed the first search of Randy Owner's house after they'd picked him up at the Bum Steer. Dupree was looking forward to seeing the place for himself.

They took I-10 south to the Kino Parkway exit and headed toward Owner's house, a scant half mile from the western edge of the airport property.

"I could have sworn that Priscilla Strout was in the clear after what Cadence Moran told us," Dupree said, wincing as they raced through a yellow light at the intersection.

"Yeah, I thought your witchy woman might finally have been right about something."

"Hell, she was probably right about the high heels and the perfume. But I guess that doesn't prove Randy Owner wasn't there. Any word on that missing Corvette?"

Nellis shook his head.

Dupree had phoned for more units to join

them, and two cruisers were already parked around the corner from Randy Owner's house when Dupree and Nellis arrived fifteen minutes later. It was a worn-down neighborhood: dead grass and weeds where there should have been lawns. Tinfoil lining the west-facing windows to keep the sun at bay. Shallow front porches that hadn't seen a welcome mat in twenty years.

"You guys made good time." His words were almost lost to the shriek of a massive departing jetliner overhead.

"We haven't seen any activity," a black officer said. He was the older of the two in the first patrol car, and the buttons on his uniform were pulling apart from what looked like an extra ten pounds since he'd bought the shirt. Dark sweat rings blossomed under his arms.

Dupree nodded and looked at the tiny house that sat apart from its neighbors. Pink stucco with small windows; the house couldn't be more than two rooms wide. The front yard was bisected by a cracked concrete walkway, and the wooden ramada was only big enough for a single car. Randy Owner's black truck was nowhere to be seen.

Nellis organized their approach. "Hanks?" he said to the black officer, "you and your partner go around back." Dupree could see straight across from one yard to the next, with only a junked car and an empty aboveground pool to block the line of sight.

Nellis indicated the other officers with this chin. "We'll take these two with us."

They gave the officers a chance to get in place around the side of the house, then approached with their weapons held to their thighs. The murders had involved knives and not guns, but they couldn't take the chance that Owner didn't have a gun as well.

Nellis and Dupree braced the door, with the uniformed officers pressed close to the wall behind them.

"Randy Owner!" Nellis called. "Tucson Police Department. Open up!"

Silence from the house.

"You've got five seconds, Owner! Come out with your hands up!"

Nellis got a nod from Dupree and holstered his gun, took a deep breath, and moved one step back for better leverage. The policeman beside him craned his neck to the side to see through the grime-encrusted window.

"Ah!" Nellis jumped at the tap on his shoulder. He spun around, fist cocked to protect himself and get enough room to get to his gun. He didn't need to.

Behind him stood a woman no taller than a child, hands on hips and elbows held wide. Her thin hair was cotton candy white and she wore two sweaters — one pullover and one cardigan — on her small frame. She'd cut holes in her sneakers so her bunions wouldn't rub.

"I've been trying to get your attention," she said. "I live across the way and I've been yoo-hooing since I saw you pull up."

Nellis released some of the tension with a long exhalation. He caught Dupree's grin and returned a headshake.

"You'll have to step back, ma'am." He ushered her back toward the curb.

"I said I was trying to get your attention," she repeated.

"Well, you got it. Now go back to your house and I'll send an officer over as soon as we're done here."

Dupree stifled a grin and watched the woman purse her lips and shuffle back toward the street. Nellis confirmed their timing with fingers one-two-three, raised his knee to his chest, and kicked hard next to the doorknob. The door splintered in a foot-size pattern and he kicked once more to clear the frame completely.

Officer Hanks and his partner had come in through the back and met Nellis and Dupree in the kitchen. "All clear." They holstered their weapons.

A black Naugahyde weight bench, complete with a set of weights and two chrome dumbbells, filled the left half of the living room. A big-screen TV and matching black Naugahyde reclining chair took up the rest. Priscilla Strout would have been happy with the upgraded TV but otherwise wouldn't have thought this house much better than her own.

Dupree moved toward the bedroom. A month's worth of dirty clothes on the floor. No Randy Owner.

"Excuse me, Officer!" A voice as thin and reedy as straw. Dupree turned to the parenthesis shape of the old woman silhouetted in the front doorway: the ghost of desert summers past and present.

"That's what I was trying to tell you. Mr. Owner got home about three-thirty yesterday afternoon. Then he came out with a suitcase and raced out of here in that black truck like his tail was on fire."

"Put out an APB on Owner's Toyota," Dupree directed. "They've either run off together, or Arlen Strout got to them first and made sure they weren't going anywhere."

CHAPTER 49

I woke to the sound of birds. Little birds, not the big piñon jays or starlings. Maybe a warbler. One sounded like a pugnacious loading dock boss giving orders: *witchety-witchety-pit-chek!* He was answered with a high-pitched plaintive song: *sweet-sweet-sweet-sitta-see.* Happy birthday to me. I knew that by late in the day, my mother would remember and place a call. Until then I was probably on my own.

I made coffee and double-checked the security precautions I'd added to each window and doorway. The tilted chair was still in place by the back door, the bells across the front door hadn't rung during the night, and the tin cans I'd lined up on the windowsills were undisturbed. Despite my night terror, I was fine.

I decided to treat myself to a mechanic's version of a spa.

I put my favorite Lalo Guerrero CD in

and turned the sound down low. *"Vamos a bailar — otra vez,"* he crooned from the living room. I filled the tub with the hottest water I could stand and squirted in dishwashing liquid for a sudsy treat. Then I grabbed the foot-long file from my tool kit, the chamois that I used to wash special cars at the shop, and the plastic tub of grainy ProSoap.

I eased myself into the tub, taking care to keep my knee and its itchy stitches out of the water. I was going to have to rise crane-like on one leg to get out. No way my stitches would let the knee bend enough to use both legs. Using the ProSoap as an abrasive, I filed away as much of the callus on my heels as I could, then rubbed the rest of myself with the heavy leather chamois. Not quite Elizabeth Arden but the best I could do under the circumstances.

I draped the chamois over my face and sank lower. I was feeling vaguely guilty about taking pleasure in celebrating a birthday knowing that Mrs. Prentice would never have another of her own.

Was there anything else in her house or on the street that I should have suggested Juanita check? It sounded like they'd already covered the house and neighborhood thoroughly.

And what about the Chevy Lumina from the grocery store parking lot? At least the police now had definite information there — a real license plate to track down — but I didn't know if they were doing anything with it. Something was nagging me about that car. The antifreeze smell was right. The engine noise was right. And it matched the description my Good Samaritan neighbor had offered. I guess I hadn't expected the car to be as new as Juanita said it was — only five years old. It had sounded older than that. I couldn't even trust my ears anymore.

The phone rang just as I started to add more hot water. Balanced on one foot until I could get my damaged knee clear of the tub, I wrapped myself in a big towel and grabbed the phone.

"Did you think I'd forgotten our annual flight?" Kevin asked. "Happy birthday, by the way."

"Thanks, Kev. Are you at work already?"

"Yep. I came in early so we could still get in an airplane ride this afternoon. Are you up for that?"

"Absolutely. I'd love it." I'd been afraid that his work and family obligations would have meant missing my birthday treat this year.

"Can you meet me at the Avra Valley Airport at four? I've got my boss's plane lined up for us."

I grinned and agreed.

I poured a second cup of coffee and called Dupree again. This time he was in. "Did Detective Nellis tell you about getting the license plate on the car that ran me down?"

"Good morning to you too, Ms. Moran." We shared the moment with separate sips. "Yes, he told me, and we've received information from the California authorities already."

"You haven't found him yet." It wasn't a question.

"No. But we'll get him. We've got the information in every cruiser in the county." He paused. "Does the name Darren Toller mean anything to you?"

"No. Is he the guy in the Lumina?"

"Yeah. But he's just one of the people we're looking at. There is something else, though. There was another killing yesterday, very much like Mrs. Prentice's, although we're not telling the media about any similarities between the two. And a seventeen-year-old girl may be in danger. I want you to be especially careful."

I remembered hearing about the murder and kidnapping on TV. "Is there anything I can do?" Aside from arming myself with tin cans and ice picks, that is.

"You've been a big help already. Just take care of yourself."

I put on jeans and a white T-shirt, and then added my best silver concho belt and soft Kaibab moccasins in celebration. All dressed up and someplace to go.

CHAPTER 50

"We may have a break on that Chevy Lumina," Nellis said, putting down the phone. "The San Diego cops went back to reinterview Darren Toller's neighbors. Nobody knows where his ex-wife is, but one neighbor has a number for his mother. She's in Florida now." He set the phone to speaker and dialed the Florida number.

"Mrs. Toller?" he asked when the woman answered.

"It's Bolivar now. But my first husband's name was Toller."

"I'm with the Tucson Police Department and I'd like to ask you a few questions about your son."

"Darren? What's wrong? Has he been hurt?" Her voice was fragile and thin across the wires.

"We think he might have been a witness to a crime, but we're having trouble finding him."

"Oh, my. I don't know how I can help. Darren calls about once a week, but he's just moved to Arizona and I don't think he's settled down yet. Where did you say you were calling from?"

"We're with the Tucson police, Mrs. Bolivar."

"Oh, dear. I don't know what to tell you. When he called last week he said he'd found an apartment, or maybe he said a house — something that he was renting by the week."

Dupree jotted a note. They would canvass all the motels and rental units in the area.

"Did he leave you a phone number or does he have a cell phone?"

"No cell phone. And he didn't leave a number. He said he might be moving again, but he'd stay in touch."

Nellis frowned. "Did he say anything else? What street it was on? Or what neighborhood?"

"No, I'm sorry, I just don't remember anything else." She paused. "But where's Steven?"

"Who's Steven?"

"His son. He's ten. Darren told me that Steven was traveling with him for a little while, and then he was going to drive him back to Fresno where he lives with his mother."

Of the two sets of footprints at Wanda Prentice's murder scene, the Crime Lab had said one was from a size-nine Nike, and the other was from a flat-soled woman's shoe in size seven. The Nikes could have belonged to a ten-year-old boy with big feet. But who was the woman? And what link could there be between Wanda Prentice and a newcomer to Tucson like Darren Toller? Maybe they met at the Desert Museum — every Tucson visitor went out there. But if that was the case, how did Toller and James McDougall fit together?

"Does your son belong to a church, Mrs. Bolivar? Is he very religious?"

"Oh, my goodness, no. Neither one of us. Although we'll probably pay for that in the next life."

Nellis nudged Dupree and pointed to a line in his notes. Juanita Greene had said the car in the grocery store parking lot had some kind of sign on the door. Dupree nodded, and Nellis asked the question. "What kind of work does your son do, Mrs. Bolivar?"

"Carpentry, home repair. That kind of thing."

"Does he have a sign for that business on his car?"

"I think he has something small painted

241

on the driver's door. Something like 'I Can Fix It,' with his phone number. But, of course, that was his California phone number."

Dupree made sure the woman knew how to contact them in case Toller called her again.

"Get her phone records," he told Nellis after they hung up. "If we can identify the phone he called from — even if it's a pay phone — at least that will narrow it down to a neighborhood. From there, well, you know the drill.

"And we'd better start praying that he didn't see a sign for a rental apartment when he was driving past. If that's the only way it was advertised, we'll never find him."

That covered everything they could do to find Toller, but there was one more suspect that Dupree wasn't willing to walk away from yet. "Rich, see if MacDougall or his daughter were on any prescription drugs and if they ever shopped at that Best Aid on Swan."

Of course, if the McDougalls got drugs from John Stephanos, it didn't mean they'd met him at the pharmacy. Especially the teenager. Maybe that was what Stephanos was doing with the drugs he was squirreling away.

CHAPTER 51

At three-thirty I called a cab to go meet Kevin. We drove northwest on the freeway toward the Avra Valley Airport in Marana where Kevin's boss kept his private plane, a little two-seat Cessna 150. In the years that Kevin had been taking me flying, I'd come to treat the Cessna like a favorite pony at a children's ride. Sure, there were faster and newer planes around, but I knew this old Cessna like a familiar song.

"Happy birthday!" Kevin said when I walked into the office thirty minutes later. He pushed a heavy plastic tub into my arms. The heady scent was unmistakable.

"Jasmine! It smells great."

"For your front porch. It should climb right up that post in no time."

"You're wonderful." I reached up and pulled his cheek to my lips.

I left the potted jasmine in the airport office and we walked around the plane together on a preflight check. The Cessna was a high-wing single engine, no bigger than some of the cars I worked on. I ran my fingers along the edge of the propeller, checking for gouges or dings that would change the vibration and balance as we climbed, then did the same for the leading edge of the wing. I traced the smooth, hot metal dimpled by rivets that held the thin sheets in place.

We circled the plane and Kevin checked the trim tabs, elevator, and pitot tube. I tugged the chock from under the front wheel and climbed into the passenger seat. When he started the engine, the little plane bounced around like a tractor in a rutted field.

He pulled the microphone from its hook on the instrument panel and told the tower who we were, where we were, and what we wanted to do.

"Wind's not too bad today," Kevin said to me, then keyed the mike and acknowledged the tower's response.

"Here we go." He revved the engine to fifteen hundred RPM to check the magnetos, left and right. The rudder pedals on the floor tap-danced as Kevin tried to keep us centered on the taxiway.

A crosswind hit the plane on the right side

and jostled it like a friend sharing a joke. Kevin called tower control with our plane number and readiness to depart. When we heard the confirmation over the head-phones, he slued the plane into a sharp turn and came to a stop at the end of the runway.

"Okay. Ready?"

"For this? Always."

"You can read the yoke if you want," he said, placing my hands on the steering device in front of me.

"Thanks." I kept my touch as light as a breeze so Kevin could move the yoke as he needed to.

He kept talking through the takeoff. "Sixty . . . seventy. We're almost at takeoff speed. And up." The yoke pulled back toward my chest as Kevin drew the nose of the plane toward the sky. "And left on the crosswind leg." The plane canted to the left with his words and we continued to climb.

Kevin read out the altitude, airspeed, and heading information as we climbed, guiding my hands to the relevant gauges as he spoke. "Want to go do some turns around Picacho Peak?"

I grinned at him, knowing that he would be watching for my reaction. Truthfully, I didn't care where we did the turns, I just liked turning.

Ten minutes later we had leveled off at three thousand feet and Kevin gave me the controls. "How about a perfect two-minute turn?" he asked.

From an aerodynamic point of view, the perfect 360-degree turn should take two full minutes. At that rate, you wouldn't even be aware of turning. I could swear that I'd seen a couple of little old ladies do that same thing in Cadillac convertibles before I lost my sight, and I didn't think there was anything perfect about it at all.

"Here goes nothing."

I turned the yoke to the right and the wing dipped. Then I depressed the rudder pedal and the plane banked into the turn.

"Too much right rudder," Kevin said. I nodded and let up a little on the pedal but held a steady backpressure on the yoke.

"I thought this might help get your mind off that murder and your hit-and-runs," Kevin said as we tucked deeper into the turn. He nudged my knee with his own to remind me about the proper pressure on the pedal. I suppressed a groan. It had taken all my willpower to get my bandage-wrapped leg into the cockpit and in position. It was already throbbing where the stitches had pulled tight.

"Flying blind is one of those things that

focuses the mind wonderfully." It wasn't just the murder I wanted to forget. It was the teeth-grinding terror of hearing an unrecognizable sound in the night. I wasn't sleeping much.

I pictured the terrain that Kevin could see but I could not: the dark, volcanic boulders of Picacho Peak above the brown desert floor. Gray-green scrub brush dotting the landscape everywhere except the arroyos and washes. No water there, just the sandy traces of last year's monsoon runoff.

"Is there any more news from the cops?" Kevin asked, belying his desire to keep me from thinking about the murder.

"I talked to Dupree this morning. He said there's been a second murder, this time with a kidnapping. They're looking for somebody named Darren Toller, driving that Chevy Lumina I told them about. Maybe it means they're getting close."

We turned and dipped and climbed for another half hour before Kevin said we had to head back to the airfield. The plane seemed to go faster — surer — with Kevin at the helm. Like a horse rented to tourists at a dude ranch, the Cessna made the return trip to home base a great deal faster than the trip out.

Leaving the plane, I felt weighted, heavier

than I had in the air. But that was just physical. Mentally I felt light as helium, uplifted and buoyed by my birthday flight.

I kissed Kevin good-bye, shifted the new jasmine plant to my hip, and tapped my way outside to wait for one of Tucson's few taxis for the ride home.

"I'd offer you a lift, but I've got to go pick up the girls on the other side of town," Kevin said.

"No worries. You've already made my day." I didn't know then how wrong I was.

Chapter 52

The sun had just dipped below the horizon as he pulled to the curb down the block from the woman's house. He couldn't leave town until he knew she was no longer a threat. Not with what it meant for him and Lolly.

He would have waited on the far side of the house, but that was where the nosy, bald-headed neighbor lived, and he didn't want to give the man another look at him. The guy hadn't noticed them when they'd been here in the new truck yesterday, watching her water the plants, but he didn't want to chance it. He unfurled a new piece of bubblegum and began chewing.

He still had a good view of the woman's house from here. Red brick, with potted plants on the gravel yard and the concrete porch. The screen door was warped and torn at the corner and the paint was faded on the wooden posts that held up the porch overhang.

A horn honked in the distance and jerked him back to his surveillance. If this lady worked a regular job, she should be coming home soon. The sky deepened in color around him, rivers of coral and purple across the horizon.

And there she was, in a light-colored sedan pulling into the driveway. She was alone in the car.

He'd thought he might have to wait until full dark to avoid being seen, but that honeysuckle hedge did a good job of hiding the little four-door from the neighbors. Dusk would do just fine. He wouldn't have to take the chance of waiting on the street any longer.

He took a deep breath, pulled the buck knife from the pocket of his denim jacket, and tested the edge against his thumb. "Stand up!" the dream voice ordered. "And finish what you start," he reminded himself out loud. He owed it to Lolly to have the same courage she had shown.

He snicked the truck door shut behind him.

Now. Do it now. Before your hands start shaking and your knees give out.

He was at the back bumper when she opened the car door. He reached in, grabbed a handful of dark hair as she turned to face him, and pulled her head back as far as the headrest would allow. He raked the knife across her pale, exposed throat.

Blood spurted over his hands and across her shirt, deep brown-red in the dying light. She didn't make a sound.

CHAPTER 53

I had to wait almost an hour for the cab, so it was close to eight o'clock by the time I arrived home, and then it took me a few minutes to find the right bills. I keep the singles flat in my wallet, fold the fives in half, the tens in thirds, and give the twenties one fold the long way. When I'd sorted out the right amount, I jammed the wallet back into my jeans, juggled the jasmine plant and my cane, and got out of the car. The taxi pulled away and I tapped up the gravel driveway.

Lucy hit metal where I didn't expect any to be. A car. An ice-edged breath, Dupree's words of caution ringing in my ears. I patted the shape of the taillights and trailed my fingers across the length of the bumper, relaxing when I traced the raised dots on the Braille bumper sticker Juanita had put on her car in my honor: IF YOU CAN READ THIS, YOU'RE TOO CLOSE.

"Juanita?" Maybe she was already inside.

Then I smelled it. Coppery, metallic. I tapped around to the driver's side and pulled the already unlatched door wide open. Something soft and wet rolled onto me and I jumped back with a scream, dropping the potted plant.

Backpedaling across the gravel, I lost my balance and landed on my butt, my palms crushed into the sharp-edged stones. My legs were pinned by the weight that had fallen from the car. I made small mewling sounds and scooted as far away as I could.

When I had regained my breath, I moved forward cautiously and felt the ground around me. A double-sided metal button in the gravel, like the kind you have on a jeans jacket. A denim-clad leg. The softness of a pliable, downy arm, covered by something wet and sticky. I moved my hands up the torso and read Juanita's face with my fingers, the same way I had when I asked her what she looked like now. The wisps of hair near her ears. The almost snub nose. The generous lips.

Then I found those other wet, leering lips on her throat, where no smile belonged.

And tumbling from her lap, three small boxes wrapped in crinkly paper and set off by curled ribbon. Birthday presents.

I screamed again. But this time the scream was met by an answering groan from the woman I held in my arms.

I sat stiff and upright on the couch. Detective Dupree leaned over me and sighed.

It hadn't taken long to get help for Juanita. Mr. Lotz from next door heard my cries and came tearing around the side of the rosebushes so fast that I bet he was still picking the thorns out. He called 911 right away, and while it seemed like a decade before the ambulance arrived, the first cops got there in only three or four minutes.

Police radios now echoed from a circle-the-wagons formation in front of the house. The front door stayed open with the movement of police in and out. Dupree had been talking about me rather than to me for the last few minutes. I felt like an eavesdropper. Interested but not participating. Numb.

"Get the forensic techs in here," Dupree said. "And get some samples from this woman so she can get cleaned up."

I was still covered with Juanita's blood and held my hands, palms up on my knees, like unwelcome visitors. Someone knelt beside me, held my hand at the wrist, and scraped under my nails.

"Ms. Moran, can you hear me?" Dupree's

voice now came at me straight on. Hunkered down in front of me. "What time did you expect Ms. Greene to get here tonight?"

"I knew she'd probably come by — it's my birthday — but we didn't set a time."

"And when you found her, did you hear anything outside? Footsteps? Voices? Maybe a car starting up?"

I shook my head, my cheeks wet with tears. I had nothing to tell him and I wasn't going to play detective anymore. No more antifreeze. No more out-of-tune engines. No more California license plates. Look what happened when I tried to interfere.

"Does she have any enemies?"

"Just me."

"What do you mean?"

"This is my fault. He attacked her because he thought it was me."

Dupree's silence told me more than any "there there" pat on the shoulder could have. It told me how close my own death had been.

"Why don't you go get cleaned up? We'll need your clothes bagged for evidence. And don't worry, we'll have a police vehicle outside the house tonight."

I rose like a sleepwalker, followed the female officer Dupree had assigned to me, and shut the bedroom door behind us.

I started to unbutton my shirt, but my fingers froze into icy sticks. My imagination had always been much sharper than my eyesight and now I relived Juanita's attack as if I had witnessed it. Strong hands bared a throat. Eyes opened wide. A burning, tearing, severing across the neck. Not even enough time to scream. The loop played without ceasing behind my open eyes.

I knew that if I hadn't told the police I'd heard that scream, this wouldn't have happened. If I hadn't insisted I could identify the car, everything would still be okay. If I hadn't made Juanita call in the license plate number, my friend wouldn't be in a hospital bed now, fighting for her life.

I asked my patrolwoman-babysitter to check on Juanita. She came back into the room a moment later, saying that she was still in emergency care, but, barring any complications, she was expected to live.

I wished I could say the same about myself. Even Dupree's promise of a police guard didn't seem like enough. The madman had found me three times now. And all three times it had ended in near death.

What was to stop him from coming back to finish the job? I wrapped my arms around myself but kept shuddering.

CHAPTER 54

Dupree ran a hand through his thinning hair and glanced out Cadence Moran's living room window. The swirling police lights gave it a carnival atmosphere outside. Squawks and bleats from the police communications channel echoed from the radio he had clipped to his belt, the volume lowered to such a level that it sounded like a faraway storm.

He shook his head and went to join Nellis in the front yard.

"Think it's the same guy?" Nellis asked.

"Unless we can turn up some crazed ex-boyfriend or someone with a grudge against Juanita Greene. You find anything out here?" Juanita Greene had been loaded on a gurney and hustled to the hospital within moments of the ambulance's arrival. All that was left in the driveway was her Toyota and a dark stain that had already seeped into the gravel.

"She lost a lot of blood, but it looks like she might have been turning her head, so she avoided the worst of it. EMT says she'll probably make it."

"Just one across the throat?" Dupree thought of her bright smile. The cockeyed way she'd look at you when she really disagreed with your train of thought but wanted to be polite.

"Yeah, looks like he was aiming for the carotid but was in a hurry. Maybe a hunting knife — the lab might be able to tell us more," Nellis said.

"Anything from the canvass?"

"The neighbor who called 911 remembers a car waiting at the curb a couple of days ago, but nothing today." Nellis gestured to a uniformed policeman unfurling yellow crime scene tape across the front of the yard. "He talked to the lady across the way. She says there was a light-colored vehicle parked down the street for a while. Doesn't remember much about it but says it wasn't familiar to her. Whoever it was, it's gone now."

"I suppose asking for a plate number is a waste of time?"

"Maybe we've already got it," Nellis said.

Dupree turned away from the pulsing police lights and back toward the house.

"Keep the press away. We don't want him to know she's still alive."

CHAPTER 55

I had given the policewoman my blood-stained clothes but couldn't make myself lie still in bed. I grabbed fresh clothes from the closet and rejoined Dupree at the front door.

"Detective?" I stood in the open doorway and tugged the T-shirt down over my sweatpants.

"What is it, Ms. Moran?" Dupree's soft voice.

My God. I just wanted out of this. But if there was even the slimmest wisp of hope that it would help them find the man who did this . . .

"Over by the driver's door. In the gravel. I just remembered. There's a metal button — from a denim jacket, I think. It doesn't feel like the same kind of button I have on my jacket, and Juanita wasn't wearing one."

Dupree told his partner to look for the button. Nellis's cigarette-laden voice called back to him a moment later. "Got it."

A gust of desert night air swept across the back of my neck like bat wings.

I could feel his presence as cold and hard as that metal button in the detective's hand.

CHAPTER 56

Juanita's brother Books came by to pick me up the next morning. I made sure I recognized his voice before I opened the door. Juanita had been moved from intensive care. It looked like the worst was over.

Like Juanita, Books had his father to thank for his height, but some long-recessive gene had given him a soft voice to go with it. I strained to hear him over the traffic noise.

"Can she talk yet?"

"Just a little bit. She asked to see you."

"What do the doctors think?"

"That she was damn lucky. He hit her just as she was opening the car door, and she must have turned her head or she would have died right there. But she'll make it. She's a real fighter."

I turned to the window so Books couldn't see my face. I agreed with his assessment of Juanita's strength, but "a real fighter" had been one of his sister's "phrases most in need of eradication." "Did you ever hear somebody say, 'He won't make it, he's always been a wimp — never could stand pain'?" she would ask. "Nope, it's always, 'He's a real fighter, he won't give up that easy.' Where are all the Caspar Milquetoasts of the world? Where are the guys who say, 'Hoo-boy, I didn't bargain for this — I'm checking out'?"

"What do the police think?" I asked.

"They're not coming right out with it, but I think they believe the guy was after you. That he made a mistake."

I knew he was right. "We look like twins," Juanita had said, not recognizing it for the dark prophecy it was. We rode another few minutes in silence.

He waited until he'd turned into the hospital parking lot and shut off the engine.

"Juanita told us to take care of you."

Rooster, Books, Cahill, and Chance, like all the John Wayne movie posters rolled into one. Juanita's brothers would be a formidable defense if I needed one. All but Chance had been football players in college, and two of them had gone on to pro ball for a while. Part of me wanted to nestle in their protective arms, have them surround me, keep me from harm.

"I appreciate that, but Detective Dupree

263

said they'd put a police watch on the house. And this guy would have to be really stupid to come back and try it again. He'd have to know I'd be on alert for him."

"Begging your pardon, Cadence, but it's not easy to be prepared for an attack when you're blind." A soft-voiced rebuff.

I knew he was right. Early on in my darkness, I'd almost walked into an open elevator shaft in an office building downtown. It was only the change of air — a subtle, cool drift against my face at the last minute — that kept me from taking that next step. With this killer, I wouldn't even know what direction danger was coming from. He could be waiting inside my house, or leaning against a telephone pole on the corner. He could be the pizza delivery guy or someone bringing a car to Walt's for repair.

Books offered his arm to escort me into the hospital.

We crossed a lobby awash in foreign sounds. A rondo of words in what sounded like Tagalog off to my side. In front of me, a soft conversation in Spanish between two young voices. More of Juanita's family?

"We're heading upstairs for a minute," Books told them, then directed me to an elevator on the right.

A swish of soft cloth and the scent of floral

perfume when we entered the hospital room. Juanita's mother. I held out my hand. "I'm so sorry, Mrs. Greene."

She took my hand with one arm and hugged me with the other. "*Gracias a Dios.* She's going to be okay."

Another smell among the strident hospital odors: nicotine and spearmint gum. "Detective Nellis?"

"Yes. Detective Dupree and I are both here. Can you join us for a few minutes, Ms. Moran? We have some questions for both you and Ms. Greene."

"We'll be outside," Books said, moving his mother toward the door.

"Juanita?" I approached the bed and felt the blanketed shape in front of me, then skated delicately over the IV attached to the back of her hand. "Don't try to talk."

"Ummmm."

I traced the heavy gauze packing under her chin and the puffiness over her temple.

"Water."

Nellis put a plastic mug in my hand and I guided its straw to her lips.

"Do you think you're up to a few questions, Juanita?" Dupree asked.

The straw dipped with her nod.

"What time did you get to Ms. Moran's house last night?"

Juanita cleared her throat but it still came out as a croak. "Sunset."

That meant that she'd lain maimed and alone for almost half an hour before I found her. She must have been gasping for breath as I ploddingly unfolded and recounted my bills in the taxi. I winced with the pain of that knowledge.

"Do you know who attacked you?"

She didn't respond, but I felt her cushions move and interpreted that as a small negative shake of her head.

"Did you see anything? Can you tell us his race? Height? Did he say anything?" Nellis asked.

"She wants the writing pad," Dupree said. A moment later he read Juanita's words. "Came from behind. Tall. White. Bone-handled knife." More scratching sounds. "Stinky?" he asked. "Stinky like what?"

It took her longer to come up with the words this time. "Rotten fruit?" Dupree read.

"Maybe a homeless guy," Nellis mused. "Maybe this doesn't have anything to do with the Prentice killing at all."

"I don't know," Dupree said. "Seems to me that if we add this attack to Ms. Moran's two hit-and-runs, and now a second similar murder, it's unlikely that it's just random violence." He paused. "Juanita? Do you know anything about James McDougall, the second victim? He's a plumber — works for Garcia Plumbing — out by Silverbell."

A gurgled "no" from Juanita.

"How about you, Ms. Moran? Anything about him or his daughter, Beatrice? She's seventeen. Here's her picture."

I hoped he was showing the picture to Juanita because it wasn't going to do me any good. "They don't sound familiar," I said. "And I don't think I've used Garcia Plumbing."

Dupree scratched something into his notebook. "I was thinking, maybe there's a way to draw this guy out. Make sure he knows that he's got to try again . . ."

CHAPTER 57

Dupree, lost in planning how to attract the killer's attention, jumped when his cell phone rang.

"August? It's Paul Wheeler."

Dupree remembered the Santa Cruz County sheriff's deputy. They had worked a hijacking case together last year that left three people dead and almost a million dollars in stolen computer chips still on the loose. It was Paul's insight that had tracked and then stopped the thieves, but that was almost four months later.

"I haven't been out there yet, but I've got a report from Arivaca that may be of interest to you. They found the body of a female down there. Maybe eighteen or so. It looks like knife wounds, but maybe that's damage from the animals that got to her."

Dupree cussed under his breath. When there were multiple murders like this in Tucson, the killings were most likely gang or drug related. But these three victims — Wanda Prentice and the two McDougalls — didn't seem to fit that category. Did he have a serial killer on his hands?

"Where'd they find her?"

"You know the ghost town, Ruby? About ten, twelve miles from Arivaca? They found her in the abandoned schoolhouse there."

"You think it's my girl?" Beatrice Mc-Donald may have been a kidnap victim or part of the crime. Either way, she could have wound up dead.

"Can't say for sure. But I saw your APB on the missing seventeen-year-old and thought you ought to know."

Dupree had heard about the old mining town an hour south of Tucson near the Mexican border but had never been there. The town used to have as many as two thousand residents and had a short, colorful history as one of the biggest copper and silver mines in the area. But the ore ran out in the '40s and the town didn't last long after that. "I thought Ruby was private property now, you had to get a permit to go in."

"It's easy to get through the fence. And they're starting restoration on the buildings still standing — you know, make it a real tourist attraction — so people have been in and out of there."

"I can be there in an hour. Can you meet me at Arivaca Junction?"

Interstate Highway 19 met Arivaca Road about forty miles south of Tucson. From there it would be another twenty-five miles to the ghost town, and Dupree thought the trip would be faster with someone who knew where he was going.

"I'll be there." There was a moment's silence on the line, then Wheeler said, "I hope I'm wrong about this."

"Me too."

Nellis agreed to return to the phones at headquarters, continue the search for Darren Toller's Chevy Lumina, and follow up on any other tips for finding Beatrice.

"Let me know as soon as you're sure," he cautioned Dupree.

Forty-five minutes later, Dupree took Exit 48 and pulled his car off the road at the end of the exit ramp. Paul Wheeler was already there, the seven-point blue star on his county sheriff's vehicle disguised by a thin layer of dust.

"Let's take the Explorer," Wheeler said, thumping the door of his SUV. "It's already dirty, and this road's just going to add to it." Dupree locked his car and joined the deputy.

"What are the circumstances?" he asked as they angled southwest on Arivaca Road.

"The Santa Cruz County coroner's out there now. It looks like the woman has been there a couple of days. There's not much left of her. Animals got to her. Buzzards. Insects. But the age is about right."

So was the timing. Beatrice McDougall had been missing for two days now. Dupree grimaced in the sunlight and pulled down the visor to cover his eyes.

"This sounds like a banner year for you down here," Dupree said.

"Only if you consider two hundred or more dead border crossers to be something to brag about. But yeah, the numbers are up this year. The illegals head out into the desert — no water, no food — the only thing that's important to them is getting across. But murders? That's not so common."

It was clear that the illegals had more to fear than just the desert. Human coyotes to prey on them. Armed vigilantes who wanted to stop them. Robbers, thieves, border patrols, killers, and other devils.

Twenty miles later they reached the outskirts of Arivaca, not much more than a ghost town itself, with only a hundred and fifty full-time residents, not including

271

the cattle.

At the junction of Pima and Santa Cruz counties, only spitting distance from the Mexican border, Wheeler turned back to the southeast as Ruby Road went from paved surface to gravel. There was no conversation. Each man traveled his own road of assumptions, hypotheses, and hopes as they approached the remains of the old mining town.

Ruby, and the adjacent Pajarita Wilderness, were a scant four miles from the border. The route through the water-carved and wind-etched Sycamore Canyon had become the new highway for illegal aliens entering the United States. Maybe this young woman was one of those sad travelers who tried to brave the desert with too much hope and too little water. If so, that meant that Dupree still had a chance to find Beatrice McDougall alive.

They pulled through the gate and onto the dirt road that was the main entrance into what remained of Ruby, Arizona.

Dupree huffed a laugh. In his mind, he'd painted Ruby as a complete Western town, with wood-planked sidewalks and hitching rails for long-gone horses. Something like Old Tucson on the west side of town but without the gunfight reenactments and ice cream shops. Instead, Ruby was rubble.

Fifteen or twenty tin-roofed, stucco-walled shacks dotted the land. The jailhouse was about the same size and shape as a four-horse trailer but with fewer windows, and the former infirmary was infirm in its own right: dry slatted-wood walls caving in on themselves. They passed an old outhouse, the wood so warped that the door no longer shut for privacy.

The desert had all but reclaimed the land from the old miners. Tumbleweeds and cholla cactus graced the side streets like lazy pedestrians who no longer bothered to look in both directions before crossing.

Wheeler turned left at the first fork past the main gate where the hard-packed dirt path was still clear.

"They said she was found in the school-house." He pointed to an L-shaped build-ing ahead of them.

A Santa Cruz County sheriff's vehicle and two green and white Border Patrol cars lined the narrow lane; the coroner's station wagon was parked up against a creosote bush like a tethered horse. Wheeler pulled off the road and tucked the nose of the SUV against a scrub oak that looked as down on its luck as the town did.

"Who found her?"

"The guy who owns the land now. He wants to fix this place up, the next Disneyland."

Dupree rolled his eyes and turned full circle around him. A tourist attraction? What kind of tourist would think this was something he ought to pay to see? He shrugged and opened the car door, trading air-conditioned luxury for a hot-gust glimpse of hell. The coroner came through the empty schoolhouse doorway, pushing a gurney laden with a thin, lightweight body draped in black polyurethane.

"What can you tell us, Doc?" Wheeler asked.

"I can't tell you for sure how long she's been out here. Depends on how fast the coyotes got to her. I'll have a better idea when I do the autopsy."

Dupree pulled the wallet-size photo of Beatrice McDougall from his shirt pocket and handed it to the coroner. "Can you tell if it's my missing seventeen-year-old?"

"Not now, I can't. I'll let you know."

"I've got a set of the prints we gathered at the girl's house."

"Don't know how much good that's going to do." He ducked his head at the small, sad package on the gurney. "Like I said. The animals . . ." He tucked the photo under the black bag and started to move off.

Dupree held up his hand and the coroner stopped. He took the zipper in both hands and slowly pulled it down the front of the bag. She had a thin facial structure, but the features that would have made her face come alive were gone. Long, light brown hair. She wore a T-shirt, stained red in more places than it was white, and a flared light blue skirt with silver rickrack on it.

Both the hair and skin looked a little darker than the photo of Beatrice, but it had been two years since that picture was taken. Age could have made a difference, or maybe it was a trick of light when the photo was taken. There was nothing here that would give him permission to say, "Don't worry, it isn't her." And who would he tell, anyway? She had no family anymore. No father to wonder where she'd gone on that last, inauspicious Tuesday afternoon.

"You find any kind of ID?"

The coroner flipped a clear plastic bag with a yellow-stained note on top of the gurney. "We found this in a corner of the room. 'Maria Consuelo Ibarra' with an address in Bogotá, Colombia. But we don't know if it was hers. It might not have anything to do with her at all."

"I'll take that." Wheeler tucked the evidence bag into his shirt pocket. "We'll send an inquiry down to Colombia, but don't hold your breath about getting anything back real soon."

They waited until the coroner's van had negotiated a tight U-turn and passed through the main gate. Wheeler waved his thanks to the Santa Cruz County deputy who waited by the car and escorted Dupree to the Explorer.

"I've never wanted a coroner to tell me he couldn't confirm it was my victim before," Dupree said as they got back in the car.

"Oh, hell, I want him to confirm it," Wheeler replied. " 'Cause if she's not yours, she's mine."

CHAPTER 58

I listened to enough of the news to know that they hadn't found Darren Toller and the Chevy Lumina that was chasing me. Frustrated, I shut off the TV and made myself an iced coffee. What I really wanted was to go sit in the backyard and let the late afternoon breezes play over me. Pretend that I could see the full moon rising. Listen to the rustle of my neighbor's cottonwood tree. Now that's a Double Fine Zone.

But the backyard held too many quiet corners. Too much private access from the narrow alley. Too much footstep-cushioning dry grass in the yard.

I took my drink to the kitchen table and called Dupree.

"Detective Dupree's desk." I could almost smell Nellis's cigarettes.

"It's Cadence Moran."

"Dupree isn't here right now. Can I help you?" It was the first time that he hadn't immediately dismissed me in a conversation.

"You haven't found Darren Toller's car yet, have you?" I didn't mean to sound accusatory; I just wanted an update.

"No, not yet."

"If it's leaking fluids as badly as I think it is, he's either going to be buying lots of antifreeze or he's going to have to take it in for repair. Have you had your officers check repair shops?"

There was a momentary silence. "They've been on the lookout for him everywhere."

Would it kill the guy to say, "Thanks, Cadence, we hadn't thought of that"? Or even, "That's a great idea but we're already on it"?

"The car's old enough that he probably wouldn't take it to a dealership," I said. "More likely just a local repair shop."

"I'll make sure they check them. Good night."

I was mentally congratulating myself for giving such good advice until I realized that the killer could just as easily bring the car into Walt's for repair. And then what would I do? Hope he didn't see me?

I double-checked the placement of bells and cans and ice picks around the house before I made dinner.

CHAPTER 59

Dupree couldn't leave it alone. After Paul Wheeler dropped him off at his car at Arivaca Junction, he followed I-19 south to Nogales instead of returning north to his desk in Tucson. He had to know if the girl in the ghost town was Beatrice McDougall.

The Santa Cruz County coroner wanted to wait until the next morning to begin the autopsy. "I've got these two gentlemen to do first," he said, combing his thinning black hair across his crown from ear to ear and patting it in place. "A knife fight over a woman they apparently both thought they were married to."

"They can wait." Dupree nodded at the almost flattened polyurethane bag on the table.

Paul Wheeler came in, accompanied by a gust of air from the pneumatic doors. "August, didn't expect to see you again so soon."

"I have to know now," Dupree said.

Wheeler took in the tense situation, crossed the room to stand next to the coroner, and turned him around for a private conversation. Although his voice was soft, it carried clearly to Dupree by the door.

"Can we do this favor for our friend from Pima County? If it isn't his missing girl, he still has a chance to save her. And if it is her, he's got to find the guy who did this." The coroner, still not happy about anyone else setting his schedule, sighed, then nodded.

"Gowns and gloves are over there" — Wheeler pointed at a cupboard on the far wall — "if you want to stay."

Dupree nodded his thanks, pulled a crinkly paper gown from the stack, and leaned against the wall, out of the way of the coroner and his work. He hated this part of the job. The stench of decaying human flesh clung to the back of his throat for days after an autopsy. And the matter-of-fact dissection of organs and tissues — the crack of the chest as it was opened, the buzz of saw blade against skull — made him question the life force inside us. Where was the soul in all this jumble of silvery red flesh and sinew? What exactly, among all these bones, muscles, and wet tissue, set us apart from other creatures?

The coroner turned on the overhead microphone to add his verbal sound track to the drama. Time, weight, condition, coloration, gender, age, length — the easy part of forensics because it dealt only with facts, not with speculation about how or why. It didn't answer who she was or why she was huddled against a cold iron stove in an abandoned schoolhouse in the middle of a desert ghost town.

"Hand me one of those Ten Cards," the coroner said, nodding toward a short stack of white fingerprint cards on a desk against the wall. Dupree did as he was told.

"It looks like we've got enough tissue left on this one finger to get a print." He turned the girl's hand palm up and showed Dupree the intact ring finger on her left hand. The other fingertips had been lost to the desert. He inked a small roller and gently pressed it to her hand, then took the ring finger, as tenderly as a piano teacher showing a new student the right key, and placed the pad against the ninth box on the card. He handed the card to Dupree.

"I'll send it to our forensic team for analysis, but if you want to take a quick look, see if there's some similarity to the prints of the girl you're looking for . . ."

Dupree retreated to the desk against the far wall and lined up the new print card and the one he'd brought from Tucson. Saws whirred across the room.

"Does the person you're looking for come from a poor family?" the coroner asked as he worked farther into the body.

"I don't think so. Maybe not rich, but paying the bills okay. Why?"

"This one didn't live well. The leg bones and rib cage show evidence of rickets."

Rickets. Poor nutrition. The photo of Beatrice McDougall did not look like a child with rickets. He breathed an unworthy sigh of relief. Maybe this was a girl from a poor neighborhood in Mexico or South America. Was she the Colombian Maria listed on the scrap of paper found at the school? Colombians could be this blond and light skinned.

Beatrice McDougall's prints were on the card on the left. They'd lifted the prints from her bedroom — the headboard, the hairbrush, her homework notebook — and had a complete set of all ten fingers. Using a magnifying glass, he peered at the ninth box of both cards. This wasn't his specialty, but he knew what to look for. The coroner waited at the autopsy table behind him.

"The relative size of the prints is the same," Dupree said, moving the magnifying glass from the card on the left to the card on the right. "Both have a radial loop . . ."

He stopped and looked up at the coroner. "But the similarity ends there. The bifurcations and ridges don't look at all similar to me."

"Let me take a look at that," the coroner said, stripping off his gloves. He bent low over the cards. After a few moments of comparison he confirmed it. "Congratulations. We have a dead girl here, but you still have a shot at saving a live one out there somewhere."

CHAPTER 60

The phone blasted me from sleep at midnight. I grappled with the Kleenex box and narrowly missed slicing my wrist with the bedside knife before I answered it.

"Hello?"

No response.

I fumbled the receiver back into the cradle, turned over, and pulled the sheet up to my chin. I had almost settled my breathing when it rang again.

"Hello? Who's there?"

Nothing but silence on the line. Or was there someone there? I tried to distinguish between empty air and living, breathing air, and my panic rose.

Was he checking to make sure I was home? That I was alone? Or was this a misdialed number from some still-daylight time zone? Someone who didn't trust his English enough to say, "So sorry to bother you, I must have a wrong number"?

I hung up. "You're being stupid," I told myself aloud. "Making something out of nothing." I got up to go to the bathroom.

Splashing cold water on my face, I took deep breaths to slow my heart rate. I had this house wired with noisemakers and weapons in every room. No way someone was going to get inside without my hearing him. And no way that a wrong number should spook me like this.

I hefted the ice pick I'd left in the bathroom as a handy weapon and crossed the hall, heading back to bed.

I stopped, frozen by the rhythmic squeak of the rocking chair in my bedroom. Had I brushed by it as I went into the bathroom and set it rocking? Or was the killer now only five feet away from me, relishing my horror?

Seconds stretched into lifetimes as I waited — breath frozen in my throat, ice pick held ready — for the chair to stop moving. How long does it take for a rocking chair's motion to cease? Not as long as the feeling of icy terror that gripped me.

I lunged toward the chair and stabbed down with the ice pick. The attack was met with empty air and a soft *pfft* as the cushion exploded in a feather storm.

CHAPTER 61

Dupree slammed the phone back in its cradle. Nothing. It was Friday already, almost two full days since they put out the APB on Darren Toller and the California plate number they got from Cadence Moran, but the car was nowhere to be found. And now he was looking at the driver for both kidnapping and murder. Attempted murder too, if you added the attacks on Juanita Greene and Cadence Moran to the list of crimes.

He scratched his scalp through wiry hair. Damn.

Nellis was across the room with a telephone held to each ear, coordinating a search of the rental units and car repair shops in the area. Every police car in the city had Toller's mug shot clipped to the dashboard. Officers stopped at real estate offices, grocery stores, pharmacies, and repair shops in every neighborhood from

Catalina to the Benson Highway. Pima County sheriff's officers searched the neighborhoods and highways outside the city for the Chevy Lumina with the California plate. No one had seen Darren Toller.

The phone tips for both Toller and Beatrice McDougall continued to flood in. Sightings were claimed from the Four Corners area to Mexico. Dupree and the task force members had roped in as many volunteers and police officers from the administrative and traffic divisions as they could to handle the calls. It would take months to sort out whether any of them were solid leads.

Nellis kept insisting that the pharmacist, John Stephanos, was just as viable a suspect as Toller, but they hadn't found a way to tie him to McDougall yet. McDougall didn't take any prescription drugs, and, unless he'd paid cash, he had never shopped at that Best Aid store.

The only good news, if you could call it good news, was confirmation that the girl in Ruby was not Beatrice McDougall. A microscopic comparison of a cross section of that girl's hair to the hair in Beatrice's brush at home showed an entirely different appearance. Both hair samples were straight and the same thickness, but they differed widely in the pattern of pigment in the cortex. Paul Wheeler said the Santa Cruz County forensic team would do a DNA comparison, but he thought it was safe to say that the body was not that of the missing seventeen-year-old.

Dupree turned his attention back to the stack of papers on the desk. They'd had no luck with the neighborhood canvass at the McDougall murder scene. One neighbor thought he had seen Beatrice in a tan minivan down the block from her father's house the day before the murder, but no one remembered seeing a car on the day McDougall was killed.

The phone on his desk bleated again. He barked a greeting.

"It's Gary Cheney at the front desk. There's a man here to see you. Says it's important."

Just what he needed. Another well-intentioned citizen who thought he had all the answers. Or another one of those psychics who knew they did. The last one that called said Beatrice could be found in the shadow of a thirty-foot saguaro with a cactus wren's nest in it. As if that didn't describe most of the area around Tucson.

"What does he want?"

"He says his name is Darren Toller."

Dupree sprang to attention. This could be a joke, or maybe Cheney hadn't heard the man right. Maybe he was saying this was *about* Toller.

"Blond hair? Round face?" He held up the copy of Toller's California driver's license.

"Yes."

"Does he have a young boy and a seventeen-year-old girl with him?"

"No."

Cheney was being careful with his words; Toller must be standing right in front of him.

"Tell him I'm in a meeting, but I'll be right there. Whatever you do, don't let him out of your sight."

Dupree hung up and grabbed his sport coat off the back of the chair. He reached over and depressed the button on his partner's phone, disconnecting the call. He spotted the two newest recruits on the unit, John Garnet and Aaron Phipps, at the coffeemaker.

"Get Garnet and Phipps. Darren Toller just walked in the front door. He's waiting for us in the lobby."

They agreed that Nellis would position himself in the lobby first, and the other two officers would go down the back stairs and come in through the lobby door. Dupree gave them a one-minute head start.

He paused behind the glass railing on the mezzanine level. Cheney was sequestered in a small bulletproof cubicle on the far north side of the lobby, where he could check IDs before admitting anyone to the building. There was a plate-size vented area at mouth height to speak through and a sliding tray he could push out like a teller at a bank's drive-through window. Cheney spotted Dupree at the top of the stairs and gestured with his head toward a blond man seated in one of the lobby's dozen well-padded armchairs.

The man was heavyset, but it looked like fat rather than muscle. He wore an untucked pale yellow shirt over loose khaki pants. His legs were spread and he leaned forward so that his elbows almost reached his knees. His head hung down and his hands were clasped as if in prayer.

Dupree made a quick scan of the room. He recognized a public defender he'd worked with standing near Cheney's cubicle. A Latino family huddled uncertainly in the middle of the room. Nellis was on the far side of the family in front of the large glass display case, in a position where they would not block his view of Toller. Phipps and Garnet were entering the lobby from the Stone Street side.

Dupree unsnapped the guard over his Glock and descended the stairs. His right hand gripped the gun in the leather holster. "Darren Toller?" he said as he neared the man.

"Yes, I wanted to . . ."

The man rose in a rush and reached for Dupree's right hand. Dupree jumped back, grabbed the man's shoulder, and spun him around, then grabbed the back of Toller's collar in an attempt to regain control.

Toller kept spinning, his arms wild and loose, and knocked the gun from Dupree's hand. It clattered on the tile floor and slid between Toller's feet. He bent at the waist and reached for it.

Gunfire blossomed from the street side of the lobby. To Dupree, it was all in slow motion. Nellis made a dive for the Latino family in the center of the room, brushing them into a heap of arms and legs against a row of chairs. The public defender held his briefcase up against his face like a hockey mask. Garnet and Phipps were frozen in target shooter stances by the lobby entrance, their bodies silhouetted by the sun coming through the glass doors behind them.

Toller lay like a broken marionette, his

blood pooling on the tile floor.

"Toller! Where is the girl?"

Toller's eyes grew wide, then dimmed into unconsciousness.

The desk sergeant called for an ambulance while Dupree knelt in the rivulets of blood seeping from Toller's head. He didn't care about preserving the scene. He had to find Beatrice. He felt for a pulse on Toller's wet, red neck and lifted one closed eyelid.

"He's still alive. Get him to the hospital. And I want someone with him the whole time, in case he regains consciousness."

He turned to Phipps and Garnet. They had reholstered their weapons and looked pale and shaken.

"What the hell did you think you were doing? This is the only man who can lead us to Beatrice McDougall! And you go for a fucking head shot?" Their pallor increased.

"It looked like he was going for your gun . . ." Phipps ventured.

"Get his wallet, anything in his pockets," Dupree told Garnet. "Maybe he's got something on him that can lead us to the girl."

Garnet retrieved a butt-shaped brown leather wallet from the back pocket of Toller's pants. There were two keys — maybe ignition and trunk — on a beaded key chain in the front pocket.

The paramedics arrived in a flurry of activity, took readings, started IVs, and hoisted Toller's body onto a gurney.

Dupree opened the wallet, thumbed past the California driver's license and the Costco card, then took out a Wells Fargo ATM card. "Start with this." He handed it to Nellis. "Find out where there's been recent activity. It doesn't look like he uses many credit cards, but if he's withdrawing cash, he's probably doing it close to home."

Folded into the wallet's bill compartment, Dupree found a receipt for a weekly apartment rental of a hundred and forty dollars. It showed that Toller had rented "Unit A" five days ago, but no address was given. The signature on the receipt was illegible, but it was flowery and flowing — probably a woman's handwriting.

"You two start with this." He passed the receipt to Garnet. "We need to find someplace with a Unit A that rents for a hundred forty a week. Go! She may still be alive."

He collared a uniformed police officer who had rushed to the lobby at the sound of gunfire. "Come with me. We're looking for a tan or brown Chevy Lumina parked nearby. It may still have California plates."

And please, God, let it also have a ten-year-old boy and a healthy seventeen-year-old girl inside.

CHAPTER 62

I perched at the foot of the bed and felt it shift when Juanita turned over.

"You must be feeling better."

"I am." Her voice was still soft. "Why?"

"Because you're already on the second chocolate milk shake, and that one was supposed to be my lunch."

"You should know better than to leave anything chocolate unattended around me." She cleared her throat.

"Feel up to talking a little bit?"

"Sure. Just keep the chocolate coming."

I filled her in on the forensic team's work in my driveway and the discovery of the metal button. "Gene Howard was part of the team. I didn't know the guy they had dusting for prints, but Gene said there were hairs wrapped around the bottom of the button and they'd probably be able to get DNA from them."

"The latent print guy, really low voice,

sounds like he ought to have four balls? Probably Brodie, the guy who printed Wanda Prentice's house. He's new — just moved here from Colorado — but he's good." She took another long draw on the straw. "If I don't move around too much, I should be able to get back to work pretty soon."

"Are you kidding? He almost killed you!" I had spent much of last night selfishly thinking about what my life would be like without my confidante/friend/taxi driver/bill payer. I grimaced, remembering the assassinated rocking chair cushion and my night terrors.

"Not for lack of trying," Juanita said. She sucked on the chocolate again. "I forgot to tell you about the sign I saw at the Baptist church on my way over to your house. It's one of those where you slip in the letters, you know, so you can announce the topic of this week's sermon. Know what it said? 'Smoking section or nonsmoking. Where will you spend eternity?' "

"That's not funny today."

"Of course it is. Hey, Cadence, I'm going to be fine. He missed me. Well, almost. And the police are going to catch him."

I was still trying to figure out how to keep Juanita in the hospital when Dupree entered the room. His soft-soled shoes made delicate sucking noises across the linoleum.

"Hey, August," Juanita said. "How you doing?"

"Better than you. Although you're looking pretty good there." He placed his hand on my wrist and greeted me as well. The fatigue was clear in his voice.

"Where's your partner?" Juanita asked.

"He's trying to track something down. Actually, that's the reason I came by. We've found Darren Toller, the man who owns that car you saw in the parking lot."

"Yes!" Mine was a subdued celebration, a whispering announcer at a golf match. I felt a weight lift from my shoulders. "You've got him!" No more listening for clunky engines or rocking chairs. No more worrying that he'd come after Juanita or me again.

"He's been shot, but he's just come out of surgery and he's upstairs here. I know it's not exactly a regulation line-up, but if the nurses say it's okay, I'd like you to come see him. See if you can identify him."

Juanita was all business. "I didn't get a good look at the man who attacked me, so I couldn't give you an ID that would stand up in court, anyway. Cade, I'll need some help with my robe. It's on the chair to your left."

Dupree left the room but was back in a moment with a wheelchair. Once Juanita was settled in, I put one hand on the back handle and walked beside the chair while Dupree pushed. He was thoughtful enough to keep the pace slow for my aching knee.

We took the elevator to the third floor. Dupree greeted a policeman who was posted just inside the door to a private room.

"He still hasn't regained consciousness," the officer said.

I hung back after we entered the room. There was nothing I could help with here. The wheelchair rolled closer.

"I only saw him from the side," Juanita said. "And these bandages are covering part of his hair, but yes, this is the man who was driving the Chevy Lumina with the California plates we gave you."

Dupree pulled the wheelchair back toward me. "Thank you, Juanita."

"Wait a minute," she said. "Move me back up there a minute." The rubber tires moved forward and I heard her sniff.

"I know he's been in surgery and they would have cleaned him up, but this doesn't smell like the guy who attacked me. It was really strong. Like something that came straight out of his pores. Not like something you could wash off."

"What are you saying?"

"I mean, this may not be the guy who attacked me."

CHAPTER 63

"We've got it!" Garnet's voice over the phone was loud with adrenaline. "It's an apartment complex just off Swan and Grant Road, less than half a mile from the ATM where Toller's been getting cash. The manager says she recognizes his picture. He rented the unit earlier in the week."

"Get that property surrounded," Dupree said, "but do not approach. Do you hear me? We don't know if he's working alone." It had been three hours since Juanita Greene had identified Darren Toller as the man in the Chevy Lumina.

They'd found Toller's minivan in the pay lot next to the police station. Toller's mother had remembered the "I Can Fix It" sign on the door accurately. But there were no kids inside the car and no clues to where he'd left them. Dupree had the car secured for the forensic team.

If Toller died, they would have no way of

finding Beatrice McDougall. Juanita wasn't convinced that Darren Toller had attacked her. But if he was driving the car that Cadence Moran heard leaving Wanda Prentice's house, he was most likely the same person who'd killed James McDougall and taken his daughter. The rental apartment was their only lead.

He checked that he had a full clip in the gun and one in the chamber, and donned a bulletproof vest. Nellis arranged for the additional units they'd need and they raced to their unmarked vehicle.

"Why the hell didn't the apartment manager call it in?" Dupree clipped the curb with the rear tire as they careened around the corner. "We've had his damn picture up on every newscast since Wednesday."

"Says she's been out of town visiting her sister and just got back and saw it in the paper."

The Agave Arms was a small complex: six stucco apartments shaped like shoe boxes and painted a dirty turquoise, arranged in a U-shape around a central parking area. There was a palm tree struggling to survive in the middle of the court, and a small, rusted hibachi had taken root beside it. Nellis evacuated the other apartments. The complex was calm and quiet in the morning air. A piñon jay broke the silence with a squawk as it dive-bombed a slinking cat along the western edge of the last apartment.

Unit A faced the street at the bottom of the left leg of the semicircle. The curtains were drawn.

Dupree signaled the SWAT team into position, their metal battering ram held by the first two officers in line. He nodded to the team leader and at the same moment yelled, "Police!" They smashed once near the latch and the hollow wooden door gave way.

Dupree was the first one through the opening. He saw a younger-than-teenage boy in the room, dark and thin, with a Frito halfway to his mouth. The boy dropped both the chip and his can of 7-Up when the door burst open. Dupree moved through the rest of the small apartment, checking the bathroom, under the bed, and in the closet. There was no sign of Beatrice McDougall.

He reholstered the gun. "Where is she? Where's the girl?" The boy sat silent, his mouth agape.

A representative from Child Protective Services was already in the interview room, but Dupree didn't want her to tell the boy about his father. Dupree had to do that himself. He took a deep breath and pushed open the door.

Even three people in such a tiny room made a crowd. Steven Toller sat at the small metal table with his hands clasped in front of him. The tears had dried into dusty lines on his face.

Mrs. Govern from CPS had placed her chair against the wall but in a position where Steven could easily see her. She reached over, gave him a sad smile, and patted his back.

"Your father has been hurt," Dupree said. "The doctors are doing all they can and we'll take you to see him just as soon as possible."

Ten-year-old Steven was steely in his posture but panic rose in his eyes, like a crash test dummy that had come to life the moment before impact.

"We're looking for a girl named Beatrice. She's seventeen years old with blondish hair. Have you seen her? Did your father bring her home in the last few days?"

Steven looked at him with confusion. "I haven't seen a girl like that. We've been up at the Grand Canyon. We got back real late last night. My dad said he was going to straighten everything out."

"Your dad was going to straighten what out, Steven?"

"We saw his picture on TV last night and the reporter said the police were looking for him. Dad said he was going to go down to the police station to explain everything. Tell them they were looking for the wrong man."

Was Toller giving himself up? Or were they looking for the wrong man and Toller was really coming to tell them that?

Had Toller reached for Dupree's gun? Or had he stuck out his hand for a shake?

"Let's go over exactly what you've done since you got here." Maybe there was evidence that could still place Toller at the scene, and this kid was lying for him. Or maybe Toller snuck away from the rental apartment while Steven slept and killed Prentice and McDougall. But what was his connection to the two victims?

Juanita Greene might be right: maybe Toller was at the grocery store, but he wasn't the one who attacked her and therefore not the killer. Dupree wasn't willing to give up yet, but there was a place in his heart — like a deep bruise too painful to touch — that said Toller was the wrong man and had been shot for no reason at all.

CHAPTER 64

The doctor told me that he was willing to release Juanita from the hospital, as long as she didn't expect to be home by herself. "She's got a lot of stitches and she's going to be sore for a while." A lot sorer than my banged-up knee, that was for sure. I knew how close we'd come to losing her.

Juanita's mother put on a full-court press to get her to move back home with the family, but Juanita refused. "She'd have priests in every room, going all extreme unction on me. *Caldo de queso* and pork adobo from here to the front door. There's no way."

Although I wouldn't have minded the adobo or the cheese-and-potato soup, I convinced both the Greenes and the hospital that I could take care of her at my place. "I'm a good cook and hell on wheels with a cell phone if there's trouble." I didn't want to tell them that I wanted the company to keep the spooks away at night too.

Books Greene gave us a ride home from the hospital.

Juanita stretched out on the couch, with each limb buttressed by soft pillows. I supplied the iced tea and started a big pot of posole, but the soup wouldn't be ready for hours. By noon, her restlessness was apparent. She had channel surfed past a sexy thriller and two good cooking shows, her nails tapping on the end table. When she threw the newspaper across the room, I knew I'd have to accommodate her wishes or tie her down.

"I've got to get to work," she announced. "Just to check in. We're losing too much time."

"He almost killed you, Juanita. You're going to need some time to get your strength back."

"Who do you think you are, my Guardian Anglo?"

I smiled. "That's 'angel.' "

"Not in your case."

I knew when I was beat. I turned off the burner under the soup, called a cab, and followed her down the driveway to the street. A perfect example of the halt leading the blind.

"I don't think this is what the hospital had in mind when they released you," I said

306

when we arrived at police headquarters and shuffled toward her office. She ignored my comment and we headed to the DNA section rather than her Latent Print area.

"Gene? Are you here?" Juanita called.

He answered from a far corner on the left. "Jeez, Juanita. I thought I was seeing a ghost. Aren't you supposed to be in the hospital?"

"They said it was okay for me to get some exercise, so I thought I'd start with my mind."

"In that case, you're going to love this," he said. "We've got some new evidence on the McDougall case. They sent in gum and a wrapper from the crime scene. Your guys collected prints from the wrapper but haven't run them yet. When I get a chance, I'll check the gum for DNA."

"How far into it are you?"

"We got the brand of gum — it's Bazooka Bubblegum. That's as far as I got. There are about fifty other pieces of evidence that came in first."

"Bazooka, that sounds like a kid's brand. What have the cops said about that?" I asked.

"They're thinking we might have a kid, a teenager anyway, involved in this. But the gum could have belonged to the kidnap victim too. Or anybody just walking down the street. It was found near the sidewalk."

"Have you heard anything about that metal button from Juanita's attack?" I asked. In my mind we were talking about the same crime and the same criminal for all three attacks.

"Not my case," Gene replied. "Mark's working on the hair that was wrapped around the button, but just like all this other stuff, we won't have DNA answers for another few days."

"Doesn't stop me from checking it for prints," Juanita suggested.

"You think that's appropriate? Investigating your own attack?" Gene asked.

"Very." Juanita turned back toward me and we retraced our steps to her office. It was a large room but too full to echo much. She shared the space with the new latent print specialist, the supposedly four-balled Brodie.

I bumped into a stack of loose papers and string-tied envelopes when I tried to sit in the guest chair.

"Sorry, let me get that." Ah, that low-slung, shift-through-the-curves voice again, the one I'd heard out in my driveway with the police.

"Hey, Brodie," Juanita said.

"Hey, yourself. You look like you should still be flat on your back."

"You always say the nicest things. I don't think you've met my friend Cadence Moran."

"I was at your house the night Juanita was attacked. Uh, I don't mean that was a great way to meet you . . ."

We shared a four-handed shake. His were square hands, with short, strong fingers. A scattering of hair at the wrist. No callus on his third finger. Maybe he worked more with microscopes and computers than with pens and pencils. And no wedding ring.

"Is Brodie a first name or last?" I asked, as if Juanita were no longer in the room.

"The only name, really. My first initials are W.B., but I just go by Brodie."

"W.B. as in Warner Brothers?"

"Won't Bite."

I finally released his hands.

"Hope you didn't mind my retesting a few spots at Mrs. Prentice's house, Brodie," Juanita said.

"Go for it."

"Good. Looks like work has been piling up in my absence." Juanita flipped through the stack of papers. "Oh, here's one I'd love to catch."

"Which one's that?" Brodie asked.

"The ignition finger."

"What's that mean?" I said.

Brodie replied for her. "They found a human finger in a stolen Mercedes. Belonged to the owner of the car. He had one of those new high-tech security systems installed, you know? Car won't start without the owner's fingerprint? So they cut off his finger to use on the ignition."

Yuck. "How's the owner?"

"Don't know. Haven't found the rest of him yet."

Juanita moved over to Brodie's desk. "Here's the button you found in the driveway."

"Get your paws off that. There's no way I'm letting you handle your own evidence." Brodie moved back to his chair. A drawer opened and he unscrewed the lid of a jar. I pictured the rapid, silent twirl of carbon black powder across the raised design on the top of the button. Clear adhesive to lift the print. Then onto a card for microscopic comparison. "Shit. It's a partial but not big enough or clear enough to go on. Maybe they'll have better luck with the hair."

"Damn." Juanita groaned as she shifted position in her chair.

"C'mon, ladies," Brodie said, "I'm taking you out to lunch. Juanita, you don't look well enough to be here, and Cadence, you look like you could use a few pounds."

"I'm game, as long as lunch is a chocolate milk shake," Juanita said.

I stood up too quickly and listed to the right, coming chest to chest with Brodie.

"Sorry." I balanced myself with a hand on his shoulder. My fingers brushed past his cheek, then explored the rest of his face. His hair was loose and long, curling over his collar. Full beard and mustache trimmed close to the skin. A prominent but well-shaped nose. My hands traveled south to his collarbone. He would have looked good in suits, but I doubted that he wore them very often.

"Sorry," I repeated. "I should have asked first. . . ."

"Anytime." Brodie placed himself between us and escorted us to his car. I had to move two heavy, fist-sized cameras with long lenses before I could sit down in the backseat.

"Are you into photography?" I asked.

"Yeah, black and white. I still do it the old-fashioned way. Never went digital."

Great. Fingerprints and photography. Leave it to me to get interested in a guy whose hobby and work I could never appreciate. We drove to Sonic and placed an order for two cheeseburgers and three shakes. Over the last bite of burger I asked if they'd had any luck with the nose and handprints from Mrs. Prentice's front window.

"No word back from DNA yet," Brodie said. "But if we get a suspect, I can sure compare the handprints. The nose print is something else, but who knows? I got a conviction once, back in Colorado, with a lip print. Bank robber ran smack-dab into a glass door on his way out."

A metal button. A strand of hair. A nose print. That sounded like the ghost of a chance to me.

CHAPTER 65

"I told you we shouldn't have counted on her," Nellis said. "A fucking blind woman as a witness! Good God, what next? Rodeo clowns as security patrols?"

He broke a pencil in half and threw it across the room. There were only two other detectives in the office midday on Saturday. No one said anything about the missile.

"Maybe she didn't get it all wrong," Dupree said. "Maybe the antifreeze and the engine noise are right, but her imagination ran wild by the time she got to the grocery store parking lot. Thought he was following her everywhere."

"Well, she sure got the wrong car that time." He flung a tissue-thin printout across the desk to Dupree. "Two things. We just got confirmation from a motel at the Grand Canyon. Toller and his son were there until yesterday at four p.m. They'd been there for three days. Paid cash, but the manager has the license number written down and Toller used his California driver's license as ID when he checked in. No way he could have driven back by the time Juanita was hit or McDougall was killed."

"Could he have flown back?"

"There's no record of it."

Dupree scanned the information from the motel.

"And Toller died ten minutes ago."

Dupree looked up. "Aw, shit." The horror and injustice of killing an innocent man was going to stay with those two rookies for a long time. And having to tell Steven Toller was going to stay with Dupree. Should he have arranged things differently in the lobby? Not trusted two rookies with the sun at their backs? He should certainly have cleared the lobby of innocent bystanders before they surrounded Toller. Should he have taken a shooter's stance himself and not approached the man? He probably wouldn't be blamed for the man's death, but he knew it was his fault.

"Call Protective Services. I'll go over and tell the boy." He sighed. "What other leads do we still have open?"

"I told you at the beginning of this that my money was on Priscilla Strout. Now that she's gone missing and we can link Randy

Owner's work sites to both murder scenes, they're still at the top of my list. And Stephanos is dirty too. He'd be looking at a twenty-year sentence if Wanda Prentice blew the whistle on him."

"I'll check out the pharmacist's alibi. You keep looking for Strout and Owner," Dupree said, shrugging into his coat. Beatrice McDougall, Randy Owner, and Priscilla Strout. All three now loose in the wind.

And the only way to tell if they were victims or villains was to find them.

John Stephanos lived with his girlfriend and her twelve-year old daughter in a second-story red brick apartment off Broadway. The concrete staircase and walkway that led to the apartment shook with each of Dupree's steps.

The woman at the door had a thin rodent face, dun-colored hair, and skin pulled tight across her cheekbones.

"Ellen Dray?" Dupree explained his mission. "John Stephanos says you can prove where he was two Thursdays ago. During the evening hours."

She'd been expecting his visit, and it showed. She answered without hesitation. "He was with Amanda — that's my daughter — and me. It was Amanda's birthday and we took her to the movies and then out to dinner."

"Do you have any proof of that? Ticket stubs? Receipt from the restaurant?"

"Even better." She crossed the room to the Formica counter that separated the kitchen from the dining nook and picked up a small camera. "It takes videos. I filmed us outside the movie theater and when she was blowing out the candles at the restaurant."

Dupree screened the footage on the tiny display. Stephanos leaned in close to kiss Amanda's cheek in the first clip. In the second, you could read "Happy 12th Amanda" across the cake in blue icing.

And there was a time and date stamp in the bottom corner of the screen. Damn.

"What's that other shot at the end?"

"What? Oh, that's Amanda in front of the house. I wanted to get her new birthday outfit."

Dupree looked back at the screen. Amanda's new birthday clothes included jeans riding so low on her hips that she looked ready to step out of them.

"Whose car is that behind her?" He could just make out a light-colored, boxy shape.

"That's mine. It's a Honda."

And that would have given John Stephanos access to a tan or light-colored SUV or minivan like the one that twice ran down Cadence Moran. If only that time/date stamp didn't prove he was somewhere else at the time.

He wrote out a receipt and told her he'd need to take the camera with him. The crime scene techs could tell him if there was a way to alter the date or time code on the screen.

He called Nellis from the car. "Get a judge. We need to pick up a 2001 tan Honda Odyssey from Ellen Dray." He read off her address. "Get it tested for front-end damage from a hit-and-run. And Rich? Check for an antifreeze leak too."

He hung up then tried his daughter's number one more time, wishing there was some way he could change the time/date stamp on his own life.

CHAPTER 66

In my sighted days, my friendships were like the roots of a saguaro: widespread and superficial. For the cactus, it meant a wide anchor in sandy soil and the best chance at finding rainwater. For me, staying close to the surface meant that I didn't have to expose myself to the shame of my mother's alcoholism and my father's departure on the day I was born.

Now my friendships were fewer but deeper. Juanita and Kevin formed the nucleus of my social world. I rarely let in newcomers. W. B. Brodie might become an exception.

He'd escorted us into the house and, after asking my permission, answered the phone in the kitchen when it rang. It was Nellis.

"I'm sorry, but we've determined that Darren Toller, the man in the Chevy Lumina, was not the man we're looking for."

I'd been afraid of hearing that ever since

Juanita said he didn't smell like the man who attacked her. "Are you sure? I mean, odors can get washed off, or they're not even noticed in all the smells of a hospital."

"We're sure. He and his son were in Nogales when Mrs. Prentice was killed, and they were at the Grand Canyon the afternoon Ms. Greene was attacked."

"But . . . if he wasn't the man you were looking for, how did he get shot?"

Nellis cleared his throat. "It . . . ah . . . was a mistake. The officers thought he was going for a gun . . . resisting arrest."

Of course he was resisting arrest; he hadn't done anything! "Will you let him go as soon as he's better?"

"Mr. Toller died this morning."

I wrapped my arms around the Fault Tree.

CHAPTER 67

"Hikers found it early this morning." Dupree stood at the side of the twisting two-lane road that led to Mount Lemmon and peered down through the blackened trees to the shell of an Econoline van at the bottom of the ravine.

Mount Lemmon had always been a haven for Tucsonans: both a cool respite from the summer heat and an Arizona child's first chance to see snow. But the road wasn't traveled as much now, since wildfires had raced through the canyons claiming the homes, the vacation chalets, and thousands of acres of pristine wilderness a couple of years back. There was rebuilding going on, but Mount Lemmon had lost much of the natural beauty that had attracted the day travelers.

"Need a refill?" Nellis handed him a tall Styrofoam cup of coffee. "What makes you think this car has anything to do with the

Prentice and McDougall murders?"

"For the moment, it's just a guess. But the van hasn't been down there long, and based on the burn pattern, it looks like it was torched on purpose. And under the seat it's got one of those magnetic signs that says it's a Home Depot delivery service car. Didn't that witness at the second hit-and-run say that she thought there was a sign on the door? Lucky thing the guy didn't know how to set a good fire. Not much of it burned."

"Have the crime scene guys found anything yet?" Three highway patrolmen were taping off a wide area of the hillside around the vehicle and four members of the forensic team were already collecting evidence from the van.

Dupree shook his head. "Looks like they wiped it clean. But there's a metal can in the back that looks like the coffee canister Priscilla Strout described. I'll tell you what, when we get the van to the garage, I'm for damn sure going to check the suspension for a squeak and see if it's leaking antifreeze."

Unlike Nellis, he still believed that Cadence Moran had given them good information about the car that roared away from the Prentice house on the night of the murder.

"The plates don't match an Econoline van," Nellis said, ending a phone call to the MVD. "But the VIN comes back to a guy named Pickett. Gerald Pickett."

"What do we know about him?" Maybe they were finally on to something concrete that would lead to the killer. Something other than a sound or a smell.

"Not much. Nineteen years old. A Tucson address, no tickets, no wants and warrants." He paused. "Well, maybe we know one thing."

"What's that?"

"If he's our guy and he finds out the witness is still alive, he'll come after her again. He's that pigheaded."

"He wouldn't worry so much if he knew she was blind," Dupree said.

"I'm not going to tell him if you don't."

CHAPTER 68

Gerald Pickett's driver's license listed an address on one of those stop-and-start-again residential side streets on the east side of town.

"We know this place," Nellis said, shifting into park.

"The same block, anyway. Wanda Prentice's rental property, right? What were the renters' names?"

"Two units. Harmon and Garafulo," Nellis said after consulting his notes. He nodded at a freshly painted white house down the block.

"So maybe this is the link to Wanda Prentice. But where does McDougall fit in?"

The Pickett house was two doors down from the address shown as Wanda Prentice's rental duplex. A rusted sedan, shrouded by a car cover as dry and brittle as a tamale husk, was up on blocks in the driveway. Weeds grew through the cracked sidewalk and a summer's worth of blown debris decorated the chain-link fence to the west of the property.

Nellis thumped three times on the screen door.

"I'm coming! Hold your horses." A voice rough with cigarettes and Whataburgers, and a face to match. She had a beer in one hand and a remote control in the other. Gray haired, gray skinned, with T-shirt-clad breasts swinging freely near her waist. "Whatta ya want?"

"Tucson Police Department. We're looking for Gerald Pickett."

"Ha-ha." An exaggerated cartoon bray. "That's the funniest thing I've ever heard." Beer sloshed down her T-shirt. "Mr. Goody Two-shoes himself."

"What do you mean?"

"Gerry hasn't lived here since he was sixteen. Got himself 'emancipated,' you know. Went to court and everything. He said we were a bad influence on him — his own family, can you imagine that?" She took another swig of beer, but the laughter continued through the foam.

"Where does your son live now?"

"Hell, I don't know and I don't care. But if you see him, you tell him I was asking about him, right? Tell him I said, 'Look who

324

the cops are asking for now!' "

Nellis and Dupree moved down the block to Wanda Prentice's rental duplex. A pot of bright red geraniums graced the porch at one entrance, balanced by a healthy fern at the second door. The tenants looked like good enough friends to share the porch swing that sat midway between the doors.

A tall, thin man answered Dupree's knock. He was in his thirties, with a mountain bike over his shoulder.

"Oh! You surprised me! I was just going out." He dropped the bike and rested it against his hip. He wore a helmet with purple flames on it, a skin-tight Lycra shirt, and black bicycle shorts.

"Mr. Harmon?"

"I'm Ted Harmon."

Dupree explained why they were there. "Have you been a tenant here long?" Maybe he remembered Gerald Pickett from down the block.

"Almost five years. I'm an assistant in the Psychology Department at the U of A, and Mrs. Prentice has been a great landlady. I was so sorry to hear about her murder. Do you know what's going to happen to the property?"

"No, but you might want to check with her granddaughter, Priscilla Strout, or maybe Rocky Trillo at Wells Fargo. They should be able to tell you. Has the other tenant been here as long?"

"Sandy? No she's only been here a year. But she's a welcome relief from the last one."

"Why do you say that?"

"There were a father and daughter over there. Really weird. The whole place done in white. Never said anything to you if you saw him coming in or out."

"McDougall? Was that the name?" Dupree had his connection now.

"Yeah, pretty spooky with both him and Mrs. Prentice getting killed, huh? But there was something strange about that guy, I'll tell you that."

"What about the daughter? Was she friendly?"

"Maybe overfriendly. She'd come on like a real flirt when her father wasn't around. Then like a nun when he was. And always wearing white."

"How about Beatrice McDougall and Mrs. Prentice? Did they ever spend any time together?" Right now, Beatrice McDougall was the most solid connection they had between the killings.

"Not much. But I remember overhearing one conversation — I was waiting out on the porch to give Mrs. Prentice my rent check — and she said something to Beatrice about 'all the treasures' she'd gathered in her life. Something like, 'Wishing won't get you what you want. If you want something badly enough, you just have to take it. Make it happen. Nobody can stop you and nobody else can do it for you.' "

Dupree thought that the storybook-reading, museum-volunteering Wanda Prentice he'd come to know had probably meant the "treasures" of a life well lived and a family that loved you. He wondered how Beatrice McDougall had taken it.

Harmon shifted the bike back to his shoulder. "Is that it? I need to get to class."

"Do you remember a Gerald Pickett, used to live a couple of houses down that way?" Dupree pointed to the west.

"Oh, yeah. Those were some real fireworks. It was probably just a puppy love thing, but McDougall reacted like the boy was trying to lead his daughter into prostitution. Kept calling him 'a bad seed.' Even threatened to call the cops on the kid."

Dupree thanked him and watched Harmon pedal away. Adjusting the seat belt, he turned to Nellis in the car. "So these kids knew both murder victims and may have had a grudge of some kind against both of them. Unless Randy Owner's connection to both murder scenes pans out, or we get some concrete evidence against the pharmacist, I'd say these two are in it up to their eyeballs."

"And Beatrice is hardly a kidnap victim."

CHAPTER 69

Unable to convince the florist that I really wanted a bouquet of sweet-smelling herbs and foliage, I wound up sending a wreath of mums and gladioli to the mortuary handling arrangements for Darren Toller's funeral. Traditional flowers for the dead. But his death wasn't traditional or typical or even acceptable. I railed against a God who thought this was part of his overall plan. There was nothing planned or accepted here. Nothing except my hubris and misplaced ego in thinking that I could help solve a crime.

Juanita was napping on the couch when the doorbell rang.

"I'll get it. You stay still."

"We have a proposition for you," Dupree said by way of greeting.

Juanita made space for the two detectives on the couch and I got four cold drinks from the refrigerator. "Here's another good one," Juanita said, reading the inscription under the cap of a berry-flavored Snapple. " 'Screeched is the longest one-syllable word in the English language.' "

The detectives were silent, as if her comment had the weight of an omen.

"We know now that Darren Toller had nothing to do with Mrs. Prentice's murder," Dupree began.

The words were lead in my chest. "Screeched" may be the longest word, but "fault" is the heaviest.

"And that means that the real killer is still out there. He probably killed James Mc-Dougall, he's tried to run you down twice, and he's tried to kill Juanita, mistaking her for you," Dupree continued.

Nellis started to add something, but Dupree silenced him with, "We don't know enough about him yet."

I waited.

"We'd like him to try again." Nellis this time. No pussyfooting around with this guy.

I froze, like a small desert creature that scents a predator in the wind. "What do you mean?"

"We've kept Juanita's name out of the paper, so while the press knows there was an attack at this address, they don't know her identity and they don't know she's still alive," Nellis continued. "We want to tell them the attack was on you, but you're doing well and you're back home now."

"What good will that do?"

"It's going to alert this guy that he's not out of the woods yet."

"How the hell does he think a blind woman can hurt him!" I knew how pitifully unable I was to have stopped the killings or to have identified him.

"Maybe he doesn't know you're blind, Cadence," Dupree said. "I mean, why else would he have kept coming back?"

Had I so successfully hidden my handicap that I'd now put myself in jeopardy as well? Over the years of my sightlessness, I had forgotten that people expect the blind to be hesitant and risk averse in their movements. In the last eight years I had become so used to my home and work environments that I moved with the ease and confidence of a sighted person — a person with places to go and people to see. People to see. Huh. And he thought I'd seen him.

"What do you want me to do?"

Nellis again. "First of all, you and Juanita can't be seen together. We don't want him to realize there are two of you. Other than that, you just go about your normal life. Go to work if your injuries will let you. Walk the neighborhood if that's what you usually do. We'll have undercover cars posted outside and an officer here inside with you."

"You'd better give her some gauze bandages around the neck too," Juanita said. "He knows he cut me."

They waited for my answer. "I'll do it." The fraternal twin of Fault is Responsibility.

"What did you have planned for the week?" Nellis asked, like a secretary ready to clear my schedule.

"I want to go to Mr. Toller's funeral tomorrow. And if my leg feels good enough, I'll go back to work on Tuesday."

"Okay. August, think we can get a mention of how well she's doing in tomorrow's morning paper?" Nellis asked.

"That shouldn't be a problem. And they can reference her as someone who was there the night Mrs. Prentice was killed, but I don't want them going on about how important she is to the case. Don't want him getting the idea that we're protecting her. We want him thinking this will be as cool and comfortable as taking a dip on a hot July day."

I gulped.

When I escorted them to the door, Dupree turned back to me at the last moment.

"You're doing the right thing, Cadence. This is the only way to make it stop."

I nodded. Now if only I could make my mental recriminations stop as well. But that would be like trying to call back an echo.

CHAPTER 70

He and Lolly had taken the farthest cabin away from the lobby at the tiny motel in Madera Canyon. Forty miles south of Tucson, the manager boasted that the bedroom was in the United States but the bathroom was in Mexico. Here they could be out of the hot white spotlight of the police search in Tucson and wait for things to die down before they hit the road.

They'd been lucky to get a room. Madera Canyon was prime bird-watching territory and July was the best month to do it. He knew they'd have to leave soon; the credit card he'd stolen from a coworker's wallet at Home Depot would be discovered any day now.

Lolly was still asleep, stretched across three-quarters of the bed and snoring like a happy kitten. He kissed her on the forehead and snuck out of the room in search of coffee. In the lobby, he thumbed through a bird-watching pamphlet while he waited for the manager's daughter to pour two to-go cups. Then he spotted the morning newspaper on the table by the checkout desk.

It was the lead story in the local section. The same picture they'd used before, when she was leaving the police station. Head tucked down, holding on to the arm of the cop beside her.

He hadn't managed to kill her at all.

He tucked the paper under his arm and took the coffee with shaking hands.

He'd breathed easy last night for the first time in two weeks, comfortable in the knowledge that nothing could lead the police to them. And he'd dared to imagine a life with Lolly, safe and happy forever. Maybe a sweet little cabin like here at the motel, with pine trees and gurgling streams. They would learn to identify all the birds that showed up at the feeder: the elegant trogon, sulphur-bellied flycatchers, and painted redstarts.

He kissed Lolly awake and showed her the paper. "It's time to get out of town."

"Finish what you start," she reminded him, taking the cup of coffee. "That's what you always say. We can't leave until we finish it."

CHAPTER 71

Dupree had worn a dark charcoal suit today, knowing that he'd be attending Darren Toller's funeral. But he hadn't counted on the heat rearing its fiery head so early. Maybe he could leave the suit jacket in the car. Or, more likely, wear it when he arrived at the funeral, then take it off after the service began.

In the meantime, he had to get a handle on this Gerald Pickett. They'd been by the address shown on his driver's license, but it was now rented to a Susan Smith, who said she'd been there for six months and had never heard of him. Calls to TEP and the Water Department showed no electrical or water hookups under his name, and Qwest had no phone service for him.

Nellis was running a credit check and had a call into the personnel department at Home Depot, but so far nothing had turned up.

If Pickett was still in town, he was invisible. And if he was gone, who was driving his van? Dupree wasn't going to pin all his hopes on this guy, but the results were in from testing the pharmacist's girlfriend's minivan and that lead wasn't going anywhere. No hit-and-run damage and no fluid leaks.

Dupree shrugged into his suit jacket, picked up the copy of Pickett's driver's license photo, and stopped at Nellis's desk.

"Get this out to every cruiser in the city."

CHAPTER 72

Books Greene had come by my house before dawn to get his sister, and he swore he'd stay with Juanita at their mother's house. I wished she could stay with me, but I was also glad that at least one person would be out of harm's way.

Brodie picked me up at ten-thirty for Darren Toller's funeral. The coroner had released Toller's body to his family after the autopsy, and Dupree said Toller's mother was flying in from Florida. She'd decided to bury him in Tucson because they didn't have any kind of family plot of their own and because Toller had chosen Tucson as the place he wanted to live.

I knew his son would be there too, but didn't know about anybody else. Toller hadn't exactly had time to settle down and make friends in this town.

"Can you see any cops following us?" I asked Brodie.

"There's a small truck back there with two people in it. That's probably them. I didn't notice anybody else."

"That doesn't sound like any kind of unmarked cop car I've ever heard of."

"Probably what makes it such a good idea for surveillance."

We found a space right in front of the Saguaro Shadows Mortuary and entered the sparsely filled funeral home. Only a few hushed conversations to one side and a crying baby in the front of the room.

Brodie found two seats for us in the back, too close to a man who used beer mouthwash and a woman wearing a flagon's worth of lavender-scented perfume. Maybe people from Toller's apartment house. More likely just professional funeralgoers who had found a cool, reflective place to sit during a hot summer day.

The room gradually quieted, and a panting, heavyset man strode to the podium, shuffled his papers, and tapped twice on the microphone.

"Darren H. Toller was a good family man who will be missed by many," he intoned, then continued with the kind of Christian platitudes that made you wish you were a Buddhist.

The speaker — a local pastor or maybe

someone from the funeral home — noted that Toller's young son was in the room and wished him the strength to grow and mature the way his father would have wanted him to. A woman at the front of the room continued to sob. Toller's mother? His ex-wife? I adjusted the gauze and tape over my nonexistent neck wound.

There was no accusation in the speaker's voice, but my ears were ringing with self-condemnation.

Brodie and I followed a slow procession of cars to the old Evergreen Cemetery on Oracle. I hung at the back of the small crowd of mourners, but after a few minutes I patted Brodie on the arm and moved back into the forest of headstones and mausoleums on the other side of the drive. I heard the high-pitched whine of machinery start up nearby and pictured the cemetery maintenance crew, wielding weed whackers like gasoline-powered dental floss between the headstones.

Most of the markers were plaques set into the grass, creating shallow indentations that caught my feet. I tapped around me — nine o'clock, twelve o'clock, three o'clock — and stepped carefully so as not to tread across someone's grave. When I found a row of upright, waist-high headstones, I trailed my fingers across the gritty marble to read the names and dates. *Beloved husband and father. With the angels now. Gone but not forgotten.*

Darren Toller's should have said *Killed Because Some Pig-Headed Blind Woman Thought She Knew What She Was Doing.*

I heard a rustle of plastic and the rasp of a rake over dirt and gravel. "Sorry," I said. In my reverie I had almost walked right into the maintenance man.

"Huh." I must have interrupted his daydream as well. I heard the swish of his corduroy pants and smelled something sweet and rotten on his breath. I moved back toward the crowd of mourners. The raking sound followed me.

When I found the cherub on the headstone that had been my starting point, I moved three feet ahead and rejoined Brodie.

Brodie handed me a wadded tissue. "I hate to go to funerals on beautiful days," he whispered. I nodded, but my thoughts were still with the maintenance man whose foul air I could smell behind me. Why had he joined Toller's family and small group of mourners at graveside?

CHAPTER 73

He and Lolly had followed the car, first from the woman's house, then from the mortuary. Once he saw them park at the cemetery, he got out of the car, told Lolly to stay low in the seat, and grabbed a black plastic garbage bag and a rake that someone had left leaning against a marble headstone. He thought he would blend in better as a groundskeeper than as a mourner who'd risk having someone in that small crowd ask how he knew the deceased. His khaki shirt and corduroy pants looked enough like a uniform that he thought he could pull it off. He just wished those real maintenance men, with the cemetery logo over the breast pocket of their dark green shirts, weren't so close by. When they started looking at him with suspicion, he dropped the rake and bag behind a stone bench and joined the gathering at the open grave.

It was so funny it almost made him laugh.

He'd read all about Darren Toller in the newspaper. How the cops thought he had something to do with Mrs. Prentice and Mr. McDougall's deaths. He was getting blamed for everything. And then they shot him by mistake. That was a good lesson too. That's exactly what the cops would do to him and Lolly if they ever found them. Shoot first and ask questions later.

But that wasn't the best part. Getting this close to the witness, Cadence Moran, made the whole trip worthwhile. She was using that cane for a reason: she was blind. How could that be? A blind woman couldn't drive. Maybe he'd blinded her during the attack. No, she'd been using the cane earlier.

Hell, it didn't matter. Either way, she couldn't tell the cops a thing. He had nothing to worry about after all. And he'd gone to all this trouble to stop her.

They could walk away. Never think of this so-called witness again. They'd have to leave Tucson, sure, but that had been the plan anyway. A life together, just the two of them, without deceit and hiding and lying all the time.

A bubble of laughter rose in his throat and he covered it with a burp. The woman turned her head and sniffed the air like a bloodhound.

Could he really rest easy? The police had called her a witness. Blind or not, maybe she did know something.

The only way to know for sure was to ask her.

CHAPTER 74

Dupree waited well behind the Toller family with Officers Garnet and Phipps, who were on administrative leave until the shooting had been investigated. Dupree had not pointed them out to Toller's mother, Mrs. Bolivar. Better she didn't know. Although if she filed the expected lawsuit against the city, she'd know their names and faces soon enough.

The sky was a clear blue and the forecast was for more of the same. Mourners shuffled in the rising heat, already a hundred and not even noon yet. The men shucked off ties and dark jackets as the service droned on, and the women fanned themselves with remembrance cards from the mortuary.

Dupree saw Cadence Moran on the edge of the crowd. Her surveillance team had backed off once Dupree radioed that he would cover her at the cemetery.

Her new liaison with Brodie was interesting. Was it just the common bond of two people reacting to the attack on a friend? Or was it more than that? They seemed like a good match. But right now Cadence looked like as much of a spectator as he felt himself. A spectator with a guilty conscience. Between them they had first raised an accusatory finger at Darren Toller and then a gun. Cadence balled up the Kleenex in her hand and dabbed at her eyes.

He circled behind a large white marble statue of an angel so as not to disturb the Toller family and stepped toward her.

"Ms. Moran?"

"Detective Dupree."

She probably recognized his voice but there was something almost eerie in her identification, like she was some kind of human Caller ID.

"May I speak to you privately for a moment?" They moved two grave rows back from the crowd.

He kept his voice low. "We have undercover cars ready to follow you back to the house and take up position down the block. Officer Luis Ortega will be inside the house with you."

"Thank you. We saw your officers in the truck behind us on the way over."

Dupree paused. "The officers on your surveillance team were on motorcycles this morning."

CHAPTER 75

Nobody was going to try sneaking up on me with the kind of police escort Dupree gave us on the way home from the cemetery. We followed Dupree's car and Brodie said there were two more unmarked cars behind us. No sign of a small, light-colored pickup truck.

Dupree followed us inside, bringing with him a tall, thin officer, Luis Ortega, who wheezed when he spoke. Asthma, maybe. That gave me an idea. I called Juanita from the phone in the kitchen.

"How are you holding up over there?" I asked. Voices behind her sounded like they were chanting.

"You remember the longest one-syllable word in the English language?" she asked.

"Yep."

"It's a toss-up now. It could be 'prayer.' "

"They're praying?" The volume of chanting increased.

"For my recovery and for the salvation of my soul. For over two hours now."

"That's good, right?"

"Good for the soul, honey. Bad for the headache."

"Got a question for you, Juanita. That stink you smelled when the guy attacked you . . . fruity, right? Maybe smelled sweet, like something fermenting?"

"That's it. Sickly sweet and acrid at the same time."

"I think it could be from diabetes. Remember Mark Thurley in high school? We always thought he didn't wash, and it turned out his insulin wasn't regulated?"

"Of course. Diabetic ketoacidosis. God, you're right. That's exactly what it smelled like."

"Thanks. Go back to saving your soul. I'll be in touch."

I hung up and went to find Dupree in the living room. "Was there someone near me at the cemetery today, a man wearing corduroy pants?" I remembered the swish of corduroy wales as he walked. At the time, I had only thought that corduroy must be hot in hundred-degree weather.

"Yeah, I remember him," Brodie replied when Dupree didn't speak up. "Khaki shirt, corduroy pants. A young guy. He was standing right behind you."

"Did you get a good look at him?"

"Why?"

"He may be the guy we're looking for. Juanita and I think that smell coming from him is from diabetes, an insulin imbalance."

I explained about discovering my high school friend's diabetes. "That's what this guy smelled like today."

"There are lots of diabetics in the world," Dupree said. "What made you think this guy was suspicious?"

"When I first ran into him, he had a rake and plastic bag. Then he dropped them and joined the ceremony around the grave. It doesn't make any sense unless he was trying to get close to me. What did he look like?"

Dupree took notes while Brodie described the man he'd seen. "Heavy build. About five eleven. Brown hair long enough to curl under a baseball cap. Maybe nineteen, twenty."

"So we're looking for a nineteen-year-old diabetic with brown hair whose insulin is out of whack and who's driving a compact, light-colored pickup truck." Dupree used his cell phone to call his partner. "Check stolen trucks in the area for the last two weeks. Did it have a closed back on it?" His voice had angled back toward me with the last question.

Brodie answered for us. "A small truck, you know, a Japanese model, maybe Mitsubishi, cream colored. It had a closed bed with a tailgate — no camper shell, just something like a tarp or hard shell stretched across the bed. Arizona plates."

Dupree passed along the description, then hung up and gave us the news. "Two compact trucks stolen in the last couple of weeks. One was already recovered. The other was taken last Tuesday from the parking lot at the Tucson Mall. It belonged to an employee at Dillard's and he didn't discover it missing until the end of his shift. We'll put out an APB on it.

"Thanks, Mr. Brodie," Dupree continued. "Now you'd better get out of here if we want it to look like Ms. Moran is alone in the house."

Brodie picked up his car keys and approached me, placing two fingers under my chin to get my attention. "Take care, Cadence. I'm heading back to the office to see if I can ramrod through some of the evidence these guys have collected. We're going to get him. And don't forget, I'm just a phone call away."

I didn't say it out loud, but I wished that

he could stay. I'd been too close to evil today. Rubbed right up against it, smelled its fiery breath. I needed some arms around me now like I hadn't for a long time.

God, I hoped this identification was better than what I'd done for Darren Toller. I couldn't forgive myself if I got another innocent man killed.

CHAPTER 76

Nellis and Dupree took the stairs this time and were halfway across the office and back to their desks when Sergeant Richardson called out.

"We've got a good lead on Beatrice Mc-Dougall. The owner of a clothing store on Fourth Avenue says she sold her a dress yesterday."

The U of A was on a summertime schedule, so they didn't have to battle the usual herd of students trying to find parking or bicycle racks near the stores. Handmade-sandal shops and tarot card readers brushed up against designer jewelry stores and vegetarian restaurants. Fourth Avenue had started to shuck off its hippie image, but there were still enough rainbow-arched doorways and wandering homeless folks to remind shoppers about the genesis of the area.

The Hang Up wasn't so much a vintage

clothing store as it was a custom dress shop that used vintage fabrics. Dupree introduced himself to the clerk, a tall red-haired girl wearing a feathered hat, a black skirt, and a crinkled pink blouse.

"I understand you sold this girl a dress yesterday." He showed her the high school photo of Beatrice he'd taken from the Mc-Dougall house.

"She came in alone, but she kept watching the window, like she was waiting for someone."

"How did she seem to you? Was she nervous?"

She looked for the right word. "Not nervous. More excited-like. She took one look at these 'prom dress minis' we make" — she held out a confection of Lycra, ruffles, and sequins that Dupree thought would fit a Barbie doll — "and got this big grin on her face. Said she wanted it for a special occasion."

"Did she say what kind of occasion?"

"No, but she did say something funny. That normally the dress should be white, but she wanted hers to be either red or black. She wound up buying the red one." The tiny skirt hulaed in her hand.

"How did she pay?" Nellis interrupted.

"Credit card. The name on it was Mike

May. She said it was her father's card."

Nellis jotted down the name and took the offered credit card slip.

"A full week missing, she's got a credit card, and she's going shopping for a dress for a special occasion. Does that sound like any kind of kidnapping you've ever heard of before?" Nellis asked when they were back in the car.

"I'd say it's more evidence that she's part of this."

"But if she was watching for someone out the window, maybe the guy is still with her. Maybe she's afraid of him," Nellis said.

"Maybe. But what kidnapper gives his prisoner that much latitude? Trusts her not to call the cops once she's in a store and out of sight? And something else about that purchase. When she said 'normally, the dress should be white'?"

"Yeah, everything else in her closet was white."

"And what other kind of dress is normally white?" Dupree asked, glancing at his partner.

"Oh, shit. A wedding dress."

CHAPTER 77

A police escort, riding what sounded like a Japanese dirt bike, kept a discreet distance behind me all the way to Walt's, and I put in four hours before my aches and pains caught up with me. Between my hit-and-runs, the damage done to Juanita, and the deaths of Wanda Prentice and Darren Toller, I hadn't been there much in the last two weeks. Walt had been terrific about it, but I wasn't going to be paid for hours I didn't work. And I still had bills coming in.

Walt had left me a tune-up, a couple of lube and oil jobs, and a radiator replacement to do. I got all of it done but the radiator and promised to finish that the next day.

When I tapped up the driveway, the dirt bike was replaced by the sputter of a Moped behind me. It was too soon since the attack on Juanita and my nerves still jangled at each unexpected sound. Brodie's helmet-muffled voice put me at ease.

"Hey, Cade. I just missed you at the shop. Thought I'd come by and see if you wanted to go to lunch."

I let out a breath and changed my grip on Lucy from batter's swing to promenade. "Impeccable timing, sir. I've got chili and corn bread in the refrigerator from last night. Want me to warm up some of that?"

"Sounds good." He parked the bike near the honeysuckle bushes and followed me inside. I flipped the switch to turn on the cooler but there was no answering swoosh of cold air. Damn. I had hoped to make it through the summer before putting money into a new cooling system. I opened the backdoor and my bedroom window to get a draft going.

With the chili warming on the stove and the corn bread in the microwave, I wondered if it was too late to offer a cold salad for lunch instead.

Forgetting food for the moment, I turned to face Brodie in the kitchen. "Do me a favor?" I placed my fingertips alongside his mouth. "Smile."

I traced the graceful, relaxed arc as his lips curled up.

"Thanks." I went back to stirring the chili.

"You want to tell me what that was all about?"

"Just my own prejudice. Juanita insists that there are two kinds of people in this world: those who smile with their teeth and those who don't. I think there's a third, those who smile with their gums showing too." In truth, I preferred people who smiled with their voices instead.

"And does this translate to a specific character trait or increased sexuality?"

"Oh, it's probably as indicative as phrenology and horoscopes. I've just never trusted people who smiled with their gums. Sometimes even the tooth smilers are suspect."

"I'll remember that," he exaggerated with closed-lip pronunciation.

The doorbell rang. "Want me to answer it?" he whispered. "Or are you still supposed to look like you're here alone?"

"Your scooter shot that ruse all to hell. Go ahead."

He was back in a moment, with Detectives Dupree and Nellis in tow.

"We tried to find you at the Crime Lab," Nellis said to Brodie, "but your boss told us that you'd gone to the garage to see Ms. Moran. We've just come from there. Man, you always keep it this hot in here?"

"Cooler's out." Nellis ignored my reply.

"Your boss said you had some early results, Brodie. What can you tell us?" Dupree asked.

"I've got lots of news, but it's not all good. We got nothing off the metal button Cadence found in the driveway. There were two strands of hair caught on it and we tested them for DNA, but there's no match in CODIS."

Nellis started to interrupt, but Brodie stopped him. "Most important, though, is the DNA from the chewed gum at the McDougall house. It matches the DNA from the hair on the button in the driveway."

"The first real proof that the murders are connected," Dupree said. "Or at least James McDougall's murder and the attack on Juanita. Can you confirm that it was the same knife in both those attacks?"

"It's not take-it-to-court definitive, but the knives used in both attacks have the same cutting characteristics and the same shape and width. That goes for the knife that killed Mrs. Prentice too."

"Anybody have a chance to take a look at that burned-out van we got from Mount Lemmon?" Dupree asked. "If we can tie that to the murder, even if it doesn't have any prints on it . . ."

"Whose is it?" I asked.

"It's registered to a Gerald Pickett. A nineteen-year-old who knew James McDougall's daughter, Beatrice," Dupree replied.

"Where's Pickett now?" I asked.

"We're still tracking him down. He moved from the address on his driver's license."

"No prints on the van," I mused, not realizing I'd said it out loud.

"Wiped clean," Brodie said.

"Gas cap? Rearview mirror?"

"Cadence, I know how to do my job." He gave me a not so subtle jab with an elbow, but that wasn't enough to deter me.

"And not just the hood release. Check the radiator cap too. With these temperatures, the van might have overheated. Especially if I'm right about that antifreeze leak."

There was a pause that lasted long enough for me to believe that Brodie would take my suggestions, a pause almost long enough for an apology.

"I'll double-check it."

"Do you have any more news of the missing girl?" I asked.

"We've actually got two missing girls now. Priscilla Strout has disappeared too."

"When?"

"Right after you talked to her at the police station."

"But we know she didn't kill her grandmother . . ." I didn't understand why she would run away, right after I'd said I could prove she wasn't there when Mrs. Prentice was killed. But maybe they hadn't told her that.

"We don't know anything for sure," Dupree admitted. "But it's sure holding up the funeral plans for Mrs. Prentice. All those people who loved *Wanda's Story Hour* have contributed to a memorial fund, but with the next of kin missing . . ."

It sounded like that next of kin was still a suspect in their eyes. "Where's the McDougall house?" I asked, changing the topic.

"Near the intersection of Oracle and Wetmore," Nellis said, humoring me.

Way out on the northwest side of town. I had an idea. "Juanita and I were driving around out there a couple of weeks ago. I heard those chirps for blind person crosswalks. First time at that intersection. If they were putting in new lights and crosswalk alerts, maybe they also installed traffic cameras. I mean, I know it's a long shot, but maybe they got a picture of the killer's car in the neighborhood."

There was a pause while somebody scratched a note. "We'll look into it," Dupree said.

I nodded and went back to stirring the chili.

"Ms. Moran, your surveillance team will

be changing shifts in about an hour," Dupree said.

"And I've got to get back to the office," Brodie added.

I guess he had decided not to stay for lunch. Hope it wasn't my cooking that changed his mind. "I'll be fine, guys. Unless one of you knows how to fix a cranky old evaporative cooler, I'm going to give my cousin Kevin a call and see if he can come help me this afternoon. This is not a day to be without airco." I brushed damp bangs off my forehead in punctuation.

Come April, when the temperatures first top one hundred degrees in the desert, Tucson moves to a freon-based economy. Your social standing rises if you have an air-conditioned car, and your net worth improves if your house has real air-conditioning instead of a swamp box cooler. I had no car, and a dead evaporative cooler wasn't going to increase my sex appeal.

When they left, I called Kevin and asked for help in resurrecting the dead machine. I knew I could handle the mechanics of the repair myself, but my leg was still sore and unsteady enough that I didn't want to be climbing a ladder or working on the roof alone. He said he'd intended to take the afternoon off anyway, since Emily had a doctor's appointment and he'd need to pick the girls up from school. He'd get the girls and bring them over within the hour.

There was a tap on the open back door. "Ms. Moran? Officer Dolenz. I came around the back so no one would see me come up the front walk. My replacement should be here in just a few minutes. He phoned that he's on his way."

"Thanks, Officer. My cousin's on his way over too. But I think I'll close up this back door till he gets here." Ugh. It was going to feel like a Crock-Pot in here by the time Kevin arrived, but I didn't like the idea that it had been so easy for the officer to surprise me. I hadn't heard his approach at all.

"Good idea, ma'am. I'll stay until he gets here. And if you'll have somebody here inside with you, I'll tell the guys to just keep up the surveillance outside."

I thanked him again and shut the door behind him, unsure if I was imprisoning myself or keeping the bad guys out.

CHAPTER 78

It was only a half hour before I heard
Kevin's car in the driveway. He knocked
and called out, "The Bernadette and Teresa
Dulcey Express now arriving on Platform
Two!"

I opened the door to child squeals and a
bracketed hug around the hips as my nieces
caromed past me and into the house.

"I want to hear 'The Dump Truck Song'
again," Bernadette said.

"Ah, the joy of CDs. Put your earphones
on, honey. We don't want to drive the whole
neighborhood crazy," Kevin said. "Nice
fashion statement, Cadence."

He tugged at the gauze wrap around my
throat. I'd been tempted not to wear it at
home — it was already sauna hot without
the cooler — but decided to go through
with the charade.

"Yeah, it's all the rage right now."

Together, Kevin and I first checked the

fuse box for the cooler and the wiring at the switch. I couldn't be of much help with the color-coded wires, but Kevin thought everything looked okay there. Next place to check: the roof.

The swamp box cooler, sitting like a small metal shed on the roof, works by forcing air through a wet straw pad. Not exactly the elegance of the big refrigeration systems in use in most businesses and new homes in Arizona today, but somehow a more natural and pleasant way to cool off, I thought.

Kevin and I traipsed through the house and into the backyard. I located my collapsible ladder lying horizontally against the back fence and stretched it to its fullest length. It fit snug against the edge of the roof, buttressed by the small overhang that marked the back porch. I slung the tool belt around my hips and started up. Kevin held the bottom of the ladder until I reached the roof, then followed up behind me.

"Can I water your plants, Aunt Cadence?" Teresa called from the front yard.

The plants were probably parched in this heat. "Sure, honey. But stay there in the front yard where we can see you." Well, where your father can see you, anyway.

"Thanks for taking the time for this, Kev. What else is on your schedule today?" We crab-walked up the slope of the roof and started work at opposite sides of the metal box, removing screws to get to the inner workings of the cooler.

"It really is the Teresa and Bernadette Express, I wasn't kidding. We've got to pick up some incredibly important yarn and shells for a dream catcher they're weaving with Emily, then a ballet rehearsal for Bernadette and a Brownies meeting in the park for Teresa." Kevin knew how to smile with his voice.

We opened the damper and I reached inside. The straw pads were slick with moss and there was a drip from a loose connection at the water hose. "These pads aren't in great shape."

"Ah, here's the problem," Kevin said, reaching past me. He handed me a rubber snake.

"Broken fan belt on the blower. No wonder it quit. I've got another one in the garage. And some extra pads. Wouldn't hurt to change them as long as we're up here."

"No problem. I'll get the old ones out. When you get back with the new pads, just lift them overhead and I'll grab them from you. That should be easier than trying to climb with them."

I nodded and scooted on my butt back to

the edge of the roof, then felt left and right until I located the ladder.

Bernadette was still in the living room, singing along to some song that had more rhyme than reason. I opened the kitchen door that led to my small garage. It was hot and musty inside, but I found the new straw pads and a spare fan belt just where I thought I'd left them.

"How's the jasmine doing?" Kevin called down to his daughter. His wife had taught Teresa more plant names by the time she was seven than I knew at thirty-two.

"It's okay, Daddy. But the lavender needed some water." The hose scraped across the gravel and water splashed on the concrete path to the front door. I was glad Kevin had managed to successfully plant the jasmine for me after I'd dropped it the night of Juanita's attack. That plant would always remind me of how important my friendships were.

The roof creaked with Kevin's footsteps overhead. "You have any bleach, Cade? That'll help keep the moss down."

An ice cream truck tinkled a song somewhere in the neighborhood and a brace of jets from Davis-Monthan Air Force Base streaked overhead, trailing a whoosh of sound behind them like audio litter. Two car doors opened nearby.

I was turning to retrace my steps to the backyard when I heard the scream. Had Kevin dropped something? I hadn't heard anything slide. Had Teresa tripped and hurt herself? I rushed out the front door.

Kevin's footsteps stuttered to the front eaves. "Hey, get your hands off her!" He didn't go back toward the ladder. I felt the roof shudder as he launched himself into the front yard. Then a thumping crash and a groan.

"Kevin? Are you all right? Teresa?" I stood alone on the front porch holding the cooler pads, like Don Quixote's ineffectual armor, in front of me.

Teresa screamed again and I plunged across the yard in her direction. A smashing blow rocked my head from the side.

Someone grabbed my upper arm and shoved me headlong into the foot well of a small passenger car or truck. My cheekbone smashed into the gearshift and the door struck my ankle. Someone in the passenger seat pushed down on my back with both feet. I was bent and crushed into a space under the dashboard that was usually just big enough for a purse and a pair of knees.

There was no sound from Kevin. Was he dead? Unconscious? Teresa was on the seat just above me and battered at all of us with fists and feet.

"Hold her, Lolly."

Teresa's wails became muted, the engine started, and we raced away.

"Stop! Police!" It was a voice I didn't recognize and it sounded far away. One shot rang out, but there was no answering ping of metal to suggest he'd hit anything. A few moments later, I heard a siren wail to life behind us.

It got louder as we careened around a corner, tires chirping their pain. Two turns later, we screeched to a stop and the siren faded into the distance. There would be no rescue.

I heard duct tape rip, then my legs were bound together. Someone slapped tape across my mouth, then grabbed my wrists and did the same to them, tying them tightly behind me. A foul-sweet odor of rotting fruit filled the cab of the car. The engine started again.

I tried to scream but nothing came out. Blind, bound, and now mute. Terror froze my mind as well as my muscles.

In an effort to gauge where we were going, I tried to count the seconds between turns but quickly lost all sense of time and direction. What I was counting instead was my machine gun heartbeat.

Heartbeat. Heartbeat. Heartbeat.

Heartbreak.

I had failed to protect yet another one of Kevin's children. And this time we were both going to die.

CHAPTER 79

The steering wheel was a blur in his hands as they slalomed around the corner. Where the hell had that cop come from? If he'd known the woman had police protection so close he never would have tried to take her.

"C'mon, c'mon, c'mon," Lolly chanted beside him, willing the car to go faster. Willing him to find a way to escape.

They'd never outrun the cop. They had to find somewhere to hide. But where? The cop was only a block or two behind him.

It would be tricky, but it might work. He'd noticed these carports last time he'd been in the neighborhood. At several houses, the residents had affixed a bamboo or straw rolling shade to cover the front of the open ramada and protect their cars from the worst of the afternoon heat. He needed a house with an empty carport and a rolling shade, and he needed it now.

There! He squealed around the corner

and up the driveway. Then shut off the engine and shoved the driver's door open. He had only seconds left.

He yanked the cords that held the shade in place, releasing eight feet of woven bamboo to unroll and hiding the car from any view from the street.

Plastered against the front ramada post, he held his breath. The unmarked car raced past. The cop hadn't even looked this way.

CHAPTER 80

"This is going to make me go blind," Nellis said, scrunching closer to the computer screen. The photos taken by the red light camera at Oracle and Wetmore the day that James McDougall had been murdered had been sent electronically to the Homicide Unit. They were reviewing the pictures taken from ten to four o'clock that day, widening the estimated time of death the medical examiner had provided.

Nellis got up to close the blinds next to his desk. Dupree slouched in an armless chair behind him, and Detectives Hinds and Muller were reviewing the opposing camera angle at a computer across the room.

The detectives didn't know what they were looking for, so they didn't dare hurry through the grainy images. They'd asked for the camera angles that showed the best view of the northwest corner, since the McDougall house was only a little farther down the block. Each time a car or van turned down the street, Nellis paused on the image.

The time stamp on the photo showed 1:22 p.m. when the pale Econoline van turned left into the lane like a lethargic, elderly shark.

"Stop it there!" Dupree jumped from his chair. "Can you zoom in on it?"

Nellis clicked on the enlargement button and the image of the van filled the screen. "It's got the stolen tags on it," he confirmed.

"Can you tell who's driving?"

Nellis recentered the image and zoomed in again. Dupree exhaled in satisfaction. The man's profile was grainy but clear. It matched the MVD photo on Gerald Pickett's driver's license.

"Gotcha."

"Let's see if he comes out the same way." Nellis crawled through another seventeen minutes of photos before the Econoline appeared again at 1:39 p.m. "There he is."

The van faced east this time and turned right on Oracle without using its blinker.

"There. Can you see it?" Dupree's index finger hovered over the passenger window of the van. Her face was turned away. Long, straight blond hair flew out the open window like a pennant. "Beatrice McDougall is in the van."

Detective Hinds tapped Dupree on the shoulder. "That's not all," he said. "You've got to see this angle." They hustled across the room to the second computer terminal.

Dupree leaned in to see the image frozen on the screen: the Econoline van facing west, time stamp on the photo matching the van's 1:22 p.m. entry to the neighborhood.

Beatrice McDougall's smiling face was clear. Her arm stretched toward the unseen driver.

"Damn. She's been in on this all along."

"We've got trouble." Sergeant Richardson waved from his office doorway. Nellis and Dupree met him halfway across the room.

"He's taken Cadence Moran. And her seven-year-old niece."

"What the hell happened?" Dupree asked the officer who'd been guarding Cadence Moran. "We had men outside the house, and she said her cousin was coming over."

"The cousin did come over, sir. It's his seven-year-old daughter that's been taken, along with Ms. Moran," Officer Dolenz said. "Officer Travis was replacing me. He'd already shown up — parked down there at the end of the block — so I was checking the alley. Came running when I heard the gunfire."

Dupree turned to the second police officer. Pat Travis had only been on the force for a year, and the excitement of the chase had left his cheeks flushed with a ruddy glow. He held himself ramrod straight to deliver his report.

"What happened?" Dupree asked.

"I confirmed that Officer Dolenz would stay with the injured man and I gave pursuit, sir. Code three," Travis said. "I wasn't but a couple hundred yards behind them. Then they took one corner and disappeared! I patrolled a six-block grid until backup got there and we could organize a more thorough search. But the vehicle had slipped away by then."

"Did you get the license plate?"

"Yes, sir. Just a partial, but we called it in, along with a description of the truck."

The paramedics were still attending to Kevin Dulcey, who lay splayed in the gravel driveway. One medic held his neck still while another maneuvered a spinal board under him. Dulcey's younger daughter, Bernadette, clung to the leg of a female officer and never let her eyes leave her father's face.

"Is he okay to answer some questions?" Dupree asked the EMT. Blood oozed from Dulcey's forehead and his left leg canted sideways halfway down the shin. Kevin Dulcey didn't seem to notice.

"His vitals are okay," the paramedic answered. "Let me get an IV started. You'll only have time for a couple of questions before we take off. Got to get him to a trauma center fast."

Kevin wasn't willing to wait. He struggled, but the medic held him still. "They've got Teresa! You've got to find them!" The paramedic tightened the straps on the long board and started the IV.

"We'll get him, Mr. Dulcey. We have a description of the truck, and we've already got an APB out," Dupree replied.

"It was a small light-colored pickup. A man and a woman, I'm sure. I don't know why they grabbed Teresa. Maybe it was just to get Cade out of the house. That's when they hit her over the head and took her too."

"What did the man look like?" Dupree asked.

"Early twenties, maybe. Baseball cap. Hefty build. He looked strong." Dupree recognized the description as the same man he'd seen in the red light camera footage, behind the wheel of the Econoline van. Gerald Pickett.

"What about the woman?"

"She looked like a kid. Long blond hair, jeans, and a black T-shirt. She couldn't have been older than sixteen or so."

That was Beatrice McDougall, except that the black T-shirt and jeans were new additions to the all-white wardrobe they'd found at the house. "Get those descriptions added to the APB," he said, turning to Officer Dolenz. Dolenz nodded and moved back toward a squad car.

The ambulance crew aligned Dulcey's leg bone and moved him to a gurney. Bernadette, along with the female officer, accompanied him in the ambulance.

"We'll find them," Dupree said under his breath. It was more of a prayer than an order. "I promised Cadence she'd be safe."

CHAPTER 81

At the red light, Pickett glanced first at Beatrice in the passenger seat holding the little girl, then in the foot well on the passenger side, where the blind woman lay curled like a pillbug.

"Oh, Jesus, Lolly, what have we done? We've got to change cars again. Those cops saw us. And that guy on the roof."

"Why didn't you just kill her like you said you were going to?" Beatrice pushed her feet down on the blind woman's back.

"I got spooked by that guy on the roof. And the little girl was looking at me. I couldn't think."

His thoughts were a little more settled now. He'd timed it perfectly, leaving the bamboo-draped ramada just an instant after the pursuing cop had turned the far corner. But the police would have a description of them and the truck on the airwaves by now. They'd have to dump the truck in a hurry.

He turned off Country Club and into Winterhaven, the old central Tucson neighborhood famous for its lights and decorations at Christmastime. Traffic could get backed up for more than a mile when revelers came by to tour the lighted holiday displays by foot, by car, or by horse-drawn hayride. No worries about that in July.

Christmas Street itself arced as gracefully as an eyebrow, with Aleppo pines and palm trees spaced along the street like strangers in an elevator. The neighborhood's rolled curbs and green lawns put the world of car chases and police sirens a million miles away.

After a tour up and down the block, he selected a house set deep in the subdivision, with a mature palm tree, a shallow, shaded porch, and an RV parked alongside the garage. If his luck was holding, these folks would have taken off for someplace cool to avoid the screaming summertime temperatures, and he could take his pick of the RV or whatever was in the garage. It would be easier if he had the keys and some cash to go with them.

He unsheathed his hunting knife, told Beatrice to keep the woman and girl quiet, and approached the kitchen door. The knife had barely scratched the lock plate surface when a white-haired man in a polo shirt and khaki slacks opened the door.

"Hey, what do you think you're doing there?" The man's hair stood up in back. He blinked and rubbed his eyes but took a step back as if inviting the intruder in.

Staccato images flashed through Pickett's mind. Lolly grabbing the blade in Mrs. Prentice's kitchen doorway. Knife dance. Lolly's father asleep with his arm flung to the side. Knife dance. The dark-haired woman in her car in the driveway. Another slashing knife dance.

His arm seemed to operate independently from the rest of his body. He didn't even have to will it to raise and gather speed and power. The knife flashed — once, twice — and the old man fell against the pristine white stove. Pickett panted and looked down at the crumpled form at his feet, the last moments lost to a black reverie that left him dizzy. He sat down at the kitchen table for a moment and dropped his head between his knees. He couldn't risk passing out now. Just a little while longer. Keep his head clear. Then he could rest.

There was no noise from the interior of the house or from neighbors. He steadied himself and saw a Peg-Board beside the door, with labeled key rings. As much as he wanted to, he knew he shouldn't take the RV. Too easy to spot and too easy to stop. He reached for the keys to a Mercedes and backed out, wiping the area around the doorknob as he went.

Trying to slow his breathing and his swirling thoughts, he pulled the small pickup truck behind the RV. He didn't know how long it would go unnoticed, but if this man lived alone, it might give them enough of a head start.

"Let's leave these two here," he suggested to Beatrice as he maneuvered the truck through the narrow gap beside the RV.

"Only if you want to kill them both now," she said without hesitation. She took his hand, massaging the web of skin between his thumb and forefinger. "This — all of this — you did for us. So we could be together. Be a family. You've got to be the man now."

He nodded. Finish what you start. And don't leave loose ends lying around that can trip you up. But he couldn't face killing them right now.

When the garage door was open, he hustled the blind woman inside, throwing her into the open trunk of the Mercedes. The gauze bandage around her throat had come loose. There was no wound underneath. Hell, he hadn't even managed to do that right.

He'd keep the little girl up front with them. Easier to control the woman that way, and he could make sure they weren't working to get the tape off each other's wrists.

At the last moment, he decided to go back into the house and see what else he could pick up for the trip. He soft-stepped from room to room, in case anyone else was home. The house was quiet. There was a cold deli chicken in the refrigerator and a six-pack of Fresca. He set those aside. He opened a carton of orange juice and took two big gulps. There. He could already feel his system responding, his sugar level rising. He wiped where he'd touched the carton and put it back in the refrigerator. Then he tapped the homeowner with his boot until the man's hip was up and he could reach his wallet. Forty dollars. Enough to start with.

The best find of all was a little .38 Smith & Wesson in the bedside table.

It was time to get out of town, and now he knew where to go.

CHAPTER 82

I banged my shin on the bumper, then bashed my forehead against more metal and landed headfirst in the trunk. The trunk lid didn't brush my shoulder when it closed. Must be an SUV or a fairly old sedan. I had trailed my fingers across the lip of the lid as he shoved me inside and found the abbreviated peace symbol of a Mercedes logo.

Teresa's muffled cries poisoned the air. They must have taped or gagged her. I worked my tongue under the tape and rubbed my face against the trunk liner until my gag came loose.

"Teresa! I'm still here! Don't cry, honey, everything will be okay!" I lied.

A few minutes later, two car doors slammed shut and the engine started. A powerful *ratchety-ratchety* sound with a tinny metal top note, like all the nuts and bolts were trying to tear themselves loose and go flying off into space: the sound of a well-tuned diesel engine. There was a lot of carbon in that first exhaust after ignition; the car hadn't been driven recently or often.

There was a hard, dry rubber trunk liner instead of the plush nylon carpeting used today, and that would make the car an early 1970s vintage. That knowledge didn't help me, but it allowed me a moment's recognition that I hadn't given in to the panic. I was still thinking, processing. Maybe it would lead to an escape plan.

We reversed, then turned left and right in seemingly random patterns. I was thrown from one side to the other without warning and my terror mounted. The trunk was no darker than what I was used to, but the movement — the jostling — was like a bad dream of perpetually falling, never knowing when or what you were going to hit. You're powerless, it screamed. You have no control. You're going to die and there's nothing you can do to stop it. I couldn't hold back the tears.

CHAPTER 83

Brodie and Juanita Greene marched through the stairway door and approached Dupree's desk as he was hanging up the phone. The slash across Juanita's throat was still wrapped with gauze, but the bruises around her eyes were fading from black to yellow-green.

Nellis returned from Richardson's office and joined them.

Dupree nodded at Juanita, then asked Nellis, "Any news on the truck?" Nellis shook his head.

"I'm kicking myself for leaving Cadence alone," Brodie said.

"She had two cops out front and her cousin inside. It should have been enough," Dupree said.

"But it wasn't."

"We've got some news on the Econoline van," Juanita said. "It was burned pretty badly in spots, but the gas tank didn't explode, and both the engine compartment and the back part of the van were almost untouched. It was definitely the car that tried to run Cadence over."

"Specifically?"

"There are wood splinters that match her cane trapped in the undercarriage, and the right front fender shows the impact where the car hit her on her way to the laundry." She paused. "Cade was also right about the antifreeze leak, the suspension problem, and the radiator cap."

"I can't say for sure that we would have dusted there," Brodie said. "Maybe so, maybe not. But she was right. They'd wiped off everywhere else — even the hood release — but they forgot the radiator cap."

"Whose print is it?" Dupree asked.

"Beatrice McDougall's. It matches the prints from her room."

Dupree nodded. They couldn't prove when Beatrice had touched the radiator cap, but she was familiar enough with the car to be helping with repairs, and she was in the van when her father was killed. "Was there anything in the van to tie her directly to the Prentice killing?"

Brodie grimaced. "The metal canister in the van had come from Wanda Prentice's kitchen. There are three sets of prints on it

— Wanda Prentice's, Beatrice McDougall's, and one other we don't have a name for."

"That would be Mr. Pickett. His prints aren't on file."

"All three prints were covered in blood," Juanita added. "So we know both kids were there."

"Do we have some kind of Romeo and Juliet thing going on?" Brodie asked.

Dupree's shrug looked more like a shudder. "Only if Romeo and Juliet decided to waste everybody in Verona instead of killing themselves."

CHAPTER 84

I inched sideways until my bound hands connected with the side of the trunk. Was there a sharp edge someplace that I could use to cut the tape? Nothing. Damn Mercedes for their rounded corners and rubber-padded luxury.

Maybe I could reach the wiring for the taillights and disable it. I scootched backward until I found a rubber-coated wire about half the thickness of my little finger. I pulled until it came free. There, at least the car had a malfunction that the police could stop it for. I thought about using the taillights to send a signal but realized that a flashing turn signal or brake light would not attract much attention in daylight hours. And how many times, in my sighted days, had I followed some old car with its blinker turned on for ten miles? Back then I'd just thought the driver was forgetful, not evil.

Who was this driver? His voice sounded

half-man/half-boy. How could someone so young have so much hate inside him?

There was a hard lump under my left hip. I still had my tool belt on! Most of the tools had sprayed across the front yard as I was catapulted into the foot well of the car, but maybe I hadn't lost all of them. I twisted the belt so the buckle was behind me and clawed at the fastener until it came loose. Then rolling left and right, I left the belt on the floor of the trunk and rolled back with my hands on top of it. One pocket was flat and empty. In the other, snugged down into the corner, was a short-handled screwdriver, the handle and shaft together no more than the length of my middle finger. Good for close-in work, not much good when you needed leverage. All I needed was the tip.

The car accelerated and held that high rate of speed. We must be on the freeway. I palmed the screwdriver and started digging at the tape that kept my hands behind me. In no more than two minutes, I had loosened the torn edge and could grasp an inch of tape. I began unrolling it, tugging, then passing the loose end from one finger to the next. I broke free just as the car darted across several lanes and back again, sending me flying against the gas tank. I almost let out a roar of celebration but gritted my teeth and started work on my ankles.

When the next turn sent me careening to the left, I was jammed against the gas tank, with a crushed paper bag between my feet. I grabbed the bag, uncurled the top, and reached in. Maybe there would be something I could use.

I burbled a laugh of hysteria when I realized that I was holding a flashlight. Of all the useless tools I could find. I used to tease Juanita that her roadside emergency kit would include red wine, chocolates, and a paperback book. Mine would include WD-40 and maybe tortillas. I'd never asked for a flashlight.

What else was in there? A plastic tub of something that smelled like baby wipes. Extra batteries — for the flashlight, I presumed. And a slim plastic bottle with a bullet-shaped twist-open tip. What was it? What had our handy homeowner thought would be appropriate to leave in a paper bag in the trunk of his old Mercedes?

Only one way to find out. I took off the tip and sniffed at the open bottle. Just for confirmation, I put a drop on my finger and rubbed it. Yep. Elmer's glue. I had my own bottle at home, since I used Elmer's or rubber cement when drawing maps to someplace I'd never been before. Ten small drops on a page meant thirty paces. An X to the side of a line could mean a bench or a tree or a mailbox. I could follow the glue like a beacon.

I tucked the screwdriver and the glue into my jeans pocket, then lifted the corner of the trunk liner and hid my tool belt. I didn't want him to see the tool belt and realize that I might be armed. It was the only advantage I had.

Like that liquor store sign Juanita had told me about last month: "I'm not surrounded. I'm just free to attack in any direction!" I wasn't exactly optimistic, but at least I wasn't dead yet. And Teresa needed me.

CHAPTER 85

Dupree paced outside the counselor's office at Palo Verde High School, the door in front of him closed and locked. C'mon, c'mon. There was a killer loose out there. Smothered sobs leaked out across the linoleum. He knocked again, harder this time, and the door opened. The counselor, Mary Ellen Costova, ushered out a teary young woman whose red eyes and Kleenex attested to her freshman state of mind.

"It'll be okay, Julie. Go wash your face and go back to class." She patted the girl on the shoulder and turned to the detective.

"I'm sorry to keep you waiting," she said after Dupree introduced himself. Costova looked like a teenager herself, slim and blond with the wings of her hair caught up in silver combs. "This must be about Beatrice McDougall. It's been all over the news." Dupree took the metal guest chair at the side of her desk.

"What can you tell me about her time here?" Nellis was running down all the leads on the stolen truck, while Dupree was backtracking in hopes of finding another way to locate them.

"She was only here her freshman and sophomore years, then her family moved across town. I think her father said he preferred to homeschool her."

"Any reason for that? Did he dislike the school system, or was there a discipline problem?"

"Probably a little bit of both. He was a very conservative man — very religious — and felt that Beatrice needed more spiritual guidance than she would get here." Her delivery was straightforward, but Dupree got the impression that she hadn't agreed with McDougall.

"Isn't that what church services and Sunday school are for?"

"Mr. McDougall would have preferred religious instruction in all facets of education. He circulated a petition to have intelligent design taught as part of our science program." Now Dupree could definitely hear the distaste in her voice.

"What's the girl like? Is she in agreement with her father's choices?"

Costova glanced at the closed door.

"Hardly. She was very conservative in looks — no makeup, always wearing white — but there was something rebellious about her, almost malicious. Her life had been so cloistered. If I had to guess, I'd say she'd be one of those kids who really overreact when they finally get off their leash."

"So Mr. McDougall decided to home-school her?"

"Yes, but there was another reason too. He thought there were bad influences here and he wanted to get her away from them." A momentary flashback to Spider and his Bitsy, then Dupree refocused as the counselor continued. "Do you know the name Gerald Pickett?"

Dupree sat up straight.

"A good boy from a bad family. His father's in prison on an assault charge. The mother's a drunk, and his older brother has been in and out of trouble his whole life. Well, anyway, Gerald — and it's always Gerald, he never let anybody call him Gerry — fell head over heels in love with Beatrice. Worshipped her from afar. When Beatrice's father found out about it, he just about had the kid arrested."

"For what? Love's not a crime."

"There weren't any real charges, just a lot of shouting about how Gerald was a 'bad seed.' He wouldn't let him anywhere near his daughter. Tried to get the kid expelled."

"So what happened?"

"Gerald set out to prove him wrong. He found out about that new emancipation law that went into effect a few years ago and decided to divorce himself from his family when he was sixteen."

"Why didn't he just go into foster care or something?" Until the law had changed, anyone under the age of eighteen would automatically have gone into a foster care program if there were problems at home. With the new law, a sixteen-year-old could file to be emancipated from his family — considered an adult — if he could prove he had the social skills and financial support to live alone.

"We talked about that. He got a job at Home Depot and a small apartment. He proved to the judge that he could keep up his grades and take care of himself. He graduated last year with a B-minus average." She shrugged. "He was acting like an adult."

"And the relationship with Beatrice?"

"I don't know. Maybe it died out. Maybe they hid it for a while. I never heard anything more after Mr. McDougall took her out of school."

"You describe Pickett as a 'good boy.' Do you think he could be involved in something like killing Beatrice's father?"

"Well, he sure didn't have good role models to learn from. And I have seen violent behavior from him — like fighting — if someone was teasing him about Beatrice, but I don't know. He's got a moral compass, if that's what you're asking, but I don't know if it's pointed north."

She jotted a name and number on a piece of paper and handed it to him. "If you really want to find out about Gerald, go see Mr. Janetos, the history teacher. They were close."

Dupree leaned forward to take the paper, exposing the rough sketch he'd drawn of the counselor.

She glanced at the page and smiled in surprise. "It's only got a half dozen lines, but you made it look like me."

Dupree waved away the compliment. "It's just something I do to jog my memory." He closed the notebook, embarrassed for one of his portrait subjects to have seen the work. "I wonder if the father drove them together by trying to keep them apart," he said.

She shrugged. "Her life was so controlled — so mandated — by her father. Gerald

Pickett might have looked like the only way out."

In the parking lot, Dupree flipped down the visor and pointed the car west toward police headquarters. Now he was wondering if he'd done the same thing with Bitsy.

CHAPTER 86

Three screws held the trunk latch in place. Three Phillips head screws. And I had a regular screwdriver. I tried to notch it into the crossed indentations but it wouldn't hold for even a quarter turn. I cussed myself, remembering Turbo's teasing. "Just grow your fingernails into the shape of a Phillips head screwdriver," he'd said. "You'll have those Ferrari guys drooling all over you, Stick."

Sweat ran into my eyes and down my chest. I checked my watch, but it was stopped at three-ten. Must have taken a direct hit during the pummeling. I didn't know what time it was, but it seemed like two hours later when, my knuckles bloody and grossly swollen with repeated battering, the second screw came loose. If I could pivot the plate to the side, even with the one remaining screw holding it in place, I could relieve the pressure on the hook that held the trunk closed and slip it open. My breath was hot and shallow. The trunk was getting hotter and I felt like I was being kiln-fired. I scrabbled with both hands, biting my tongue in pain when I pulled two fingernails off. There, finally, a fresh breeze through the slit of open space. I held the top of the trunk in place so the driver couldn't see it rise up in his rearview mirror.

The car turned left and slowed measurably. We weren't on pavement anymore. A dirt road, but well maintained, not rutted and not too dusty. A rural lane? A long private driveway? No voices or traffic sounds in the distance.

The car stopped. Two doors opened, the suspension bouncing as bodies exited, then the doors closed. Nothing from Teresa. Was she still alive?

Suddenly the trunk lid was pulled from my hand and I felt sunshine and fresh air on my face. I lashed out with the short-handled screwdriver, connecting with flesh somewhere above me.

A scream. A young woman's voice, high-pitched with pain.

Someone slammed the trunk lid once on my wrists, pulled me forward by the hair, and smashed my face on the bumper. My nose erupted and blood flooded my mouth.

"That's not nice," the woman said. I batted ineffectually with throbbing wrists and hands. "Stop it or I'll hurt your little girl."

That was enough to freeze me. I heard Teresa's muted wails. It sounded like she was still taped up, but she could probably see what was happening.

"Lolly? Bea? Put this on your arm. I'll find something to wrap it up with." The young man's voice.

He retaped my hands, this time in front, and pulled me from the trunk. I leaned against the rear bumper of the Mercedes, trying to regain my balance and clear my head. Teresa ran to me and buried her head in my stomach. I reached around her with bound hands and held her close.

The girl I'd hurt kept sniffling and crying. He'd called her "Lolly" and "Bea." Was this Beatrice McDougall? It didn't look like she was a kidnap victim at all.

He pulled me by the elbow and I tripped down the weedy path behind him. Teresa's feet must have been untied as well, as she followed along with my shirttail wound around her hand. We crossed a clear, dusty area and I heard a fountain — two levels of cascading water — to my left. Dappled sunshine, then the full cool of a shaded entryway. The man knocked hard on a thin metal door — a trailer? The aluminum pop when the door opened a moment later confirmed it. The thick, waxy smell of air freshener and the peaty odor of cigars.

"Hey, Gerry. I thought you were too good to mix with the family criminals."

"It's Gerald . . . you know that. And I need help, Marty." He pushed me up two steps and into the trailer. A wave of body odor came off this new man, dueling with my captor's sickly sweet diabetic tang. "We need a place to stay. Not long. Just until the heat dies down."

"Can't help you," Marty replied. "Too many folks around here would see you."

"At least trade cars with us."

"Shit no. I don't have a car, and you're not getting your hands on the Harley."

"Please, Marty! We're talking about my life here."

"Yeah, I'm sure Mom and Dad would be real broke up about that. Maybe crime really does run in the family, after all. Tell you what," Marty continued, "you leave the little girl here. I can make good money off her, and I'll send you someplace safe. One of my buddies has a house he's not using near Casa Grande, about an hour from here. Not much there, but it's private."

I almost gagged at the idea of leaving Teresa with this man and froze when I thought of the ways she could be valuable to him. He sounded like part of my captor's family. A brother? An uncle? And which family? He'd introduced himself as Gerald. Was it Pickett, the nineteen-year-old who Dupree said had owned the burned-out Econoline van?

"It's a deal," Pickett said, pushing Teresa forward. "Get some bandages first so I can take care of Bea's arm."

Marty turned away. "So you got your girlfriend back too, huh?" Pickett's grasp on my arm loosened as he turned toward the voice.

I used the distraction to make a run for it. "Go, Teresa. Now!"

CHAPTER 87

Dupree sprang for the phone when it rang. Maybe this would be the call that would send them into action. He had to find Cadence Moran and the missing seven-year-old.

"August!" He barely recognized his wife's anguished voice. "It's Bitsy. A motorcycle accident. She's at TMC." It took precious moments to calm her enough to get the story.

Bitsy and Spider had been hit by a car, coming back from the grocery store. They didn't know the extent of the injuries yet. "I'll come get you," Dupree said. "We'll go to the hospital together."

He grabbed his coat, calling the news over his shoulder to Nellis. "I'll be on the cell phone if you hear anything!"

He picked up Gloria and still made it to Tucson Medical Center within a half hour. Bitsy was in the emergency room, loosely covered by a pale blue blanket and groggy with painkillers.

"Baby," was all he could say, cradling her head in his hands. Her teeth chattered like ghostly castanets.

"We've taken care of the dislocated shoulder, but there are at least five broken bones that will need to be immobilized," the doctor said.

"Any internal injuries?"

"We're taking her upstairs for a CAT scan and X-rays now."

"Where's Spider?" Bitsy asked, her voice an echo of the little girl he remembered.

"Hush, they're taking care of him." Spider had taken the brunt of the force when the car hit. His head injuries were extensive and he was in surgery for a collapsed lung.

Dupree held her closer against his chest. His baby. His life. Maybe not healthy, but alive.

He hoped the same was true of Cadence Moran.

CHAPTER 88

Lunging to my right, I broke loose of Pickett's hold and pushed through the doorway but tripped down the steep metal steps and landed in a garden bed planted just beside the front door. A six-foot bush with leathery, banana-shaped leaves broke my fall. I felt the crushed shrubbery with my bound hands as I lay there. The distinctive cockatiel shape of a bird-of-paradise blossom, and the sweet, strong smell of pineapple sage where I'd landed.

Teresa screamed, "Let me go! Let me go!" Her freedom hadn't lasted much longer than my own.

"Take the lady too," Pickett said, pulling me upright and shoving me back toward the trailer door. I prayed that trailer park Marty would take him up on the deal. I had to stay with Teresa.

"I can't get much money for her. Too old, and she looks like too much trouble. She's all yours," Marty said.

My captor was silent, and I knew he was weighing whether to kill me now or later. I looped my tied arms around Teresa. "I'm not going anywhere without her."

Marty was stronger than I had imagined. His fist smashed into my jaw, sending me sprawling in the dirt. One man picked up my hands and the other my feet, and they carried me across the yard like a deer carcass.

"I'll hold on to the little girl until you get her back in the trunk," Beatrice offered.

Now I knew for sure that we wouldn't be getting any help from that quarter.

"Pickett! It's not too late. Let me help you! Nobody else has to get hurt." No response from either of the men dumping me into the trunk.

Teresa's cries rent the air and my heart. "Teresa!" I couldn't manage any more reassurance. I had none left.

I drew a mental map. We'd traveled a little more than two hours since I'd been put in the trunk. If Casa Grande was an hour away, and if we hadn't been traveling in circles, that meant that we had gone north or east or west, not toward Mexico, since we hadn't stopped at any kind of border inspection station. If my sense of direction was right, we'd traveled north and were now in Phoenix and not the desert or smaller burgs that the other directions would have given us.

"Here's the address," Marty said. "Don't call me for a while. Wait for things to die down." I wished he hadn't used the word "die" in a sentence.

Pickett borrowed a Phillips head screwdriver from Marty, replaced the missing screws on the trunk latch, then slammed the lid shut again. Without my screwdriver, I had no hope of escape.

But I did have a plan. I gnawed at the duct tape on my wrists.

As we pulled away from the house, I eased the Elmer's glue from my pocket. I started at my wrist, marking an *L* or an *R* every time the car turned, then a drop of glue for each thirty breaths I took. I didn't know how fast the car was traveling, but when it reached and held a speed for a long period of time without turning, I dotted a wriggly line to indicate a freeway and speeds of seventy or more.

Semi trucks roared past us and once I heard powerful car engines revving in the distance. Ignore them! Count the breaths! Fifteen. Sixteen. Seventeen. Oh, Teresa, please be brave.

Concentrating on breathing kept me from thinking about other things. Things like not really believing that I could lead the police to Marty's house at all. Things like wondering what the police would think when they found my glue-studded body in a ditch.

CHAPTER 89

Dupree was waiting for Bitsy to return from X-ray when his cell phone rang. "We found the pickup truck," Nellis said without introduction. "The two hundred block of Christmas Street in Winterhaven."

"I'll be right there." Dupree turned to Gloria beside him. Her hair may have grayed just the tiniest bit more in the last hour. She worried a Kleenex between her hands, wet eyes focused on her lap. "Will you be okay here if I have to leave?"

She nodded, eyes mirroring his concern. "We'll be fine. Go."

He raced down the stairs to his unmarked car and sped across town.

Three police cars, an ambulance, and the coroner's van crowded the usually calm residential street. Afternoon shadows from the palm trees stretched long, creating jailhouse bars of shade across the yards.

"I told them not to touch anything in the house until you got here," Nellis said. He and Dupree donned latex gloves and approached the open kitchen door.

"Meet Mr. Whitman," Nellis said, gesturing to the dead body of the elderly man on the kitchen floor. "A neighbor came by to check on him when he didn't show up for his usual five o'clock sherry with her."

"Please tell me she didn't . . ." Dupree gestured to the bloody footprints that led away from the body.

"Yeah, the footprints are hers. She knelt down to see if he was still alive. At least she had the brains to go back to her house to phone it in."

"Anything taken?"

"His car. A '71 four-door black Mercedes sedan. They left the pickup truck hidden behind his RV. I've got the guys going over it now."

"Let's get the word out." And hope it's not too late.

CHAPTER 90

When we reached the Casa Grande house, Pickett hustled me straight from the car and into the bathroom. I heard grunts and muttered curses as he shoved furniture against the door on the outside; when I tried to open it, it wouldn't budge. I turned my attention to the small window. Security glass, woven with what felt like thin wire for reinforcement. I made no progress at all and retreated to the bathtub. I imagined that I could still hear Teresa's sobs in the air.

Twice, when Pickett or the girl shoved the furniture aside and came in to use the bathroom, I refused to turn my blind eyes away from them. I was done with pleading. "I will hunt you down and kill you," I promised Pickett. He didn't reply. The rotten-fruit reek of his piss was almost choking in the small room.

When I realized they weren't coming to feed me or allow me out, I propped myself up in the tub and used towels to cushion my shoulder and hip from the cold porcelain.

I'd heard distant traffic sounds when we arrived. We were close to a freeway or major thoroughfare. But I hadn't heard any friendly-neighbor televisions or radios during our transit from the car to the house. Screaming wouldn't do any good.

Darkness is my constant companion but not always my friend. I knew I wouldn't sleep tonight. I would keep my eyes wide open and pinch myself to stay awake, as if a state of alert readiness would make any difference at all.

When everything was quiet in the house, I groped around the walls and ceiling until I'd located and unscrewed all the lightbulbs. It wouldn't do much good — I knew the light from the other rooms would flood in when the door opened — but I wanted at least a moment when I could see as well as my captors did.

I stretched out on the floor across the doorway, doing sit-ups and leg lifts until I thought my muscles would snap. I chanted Juanita's animal groups in time with the reps to stay awake.

"A smack of jellyfish." I lifted my legs and held them.

"A parliament of owls." Again.

"A float of crocodiles."

"A descent of woodpeckers." My muscles burned.

"A cowardice of curs."

"A lamentation of swans."

I curled into a ball and wailed.

CHAPTER 91

Pickett's history teacher, Mr. Janetos, had not been at school and had not responded to Dupree's phone messages or the "Call me, URGENT" note he'd left on the teacher's front door. After checking on Bitsy, Dupree was back at the teacher's house before seven in the morning, pounding on the door.

"Sorry I didn't get back to you last night," Janetos said. "I had a killer headache. Migraines, you know." He was in his mid-forties and trim to the point of skinny, with a bristly mustache and Harry Potter glasses that rubbed against his eyebrows.

Dupree stifled the urge to tell him about another kind of killer, one on the loose with hostages that included a seven-year-old girl. And how much he'd rather be at the hospital with his daughter right now than standing in the cool morning air mouthing platitudes to a man who didn't even have the courtesy to call in sick yesterday so the school could schedule a substitute.

"Tell me about Gerald Pickett."

"I think he's a good kid, trying to find his way. It can't be easy. Do you know about his family?"

"Ms. Costova told me they were nothing to write home about."

"Unless you were writing a very sad letter. His brother, Marty, is only a couple of years older and belongs to a motorcycle gang. His father will be in prison for aggravated assault for another five years before the possibility of parole."

"I know about his emancipation. Were you the one who helped him with that?"

"I did. The one thing about Gerald is that he always follows through. Always does what he said he'd do. That's very grown-up behavior. I thought he'd be a good candidate for this emancipation law."

"Did he ever make any promises about following through with his attraction to Beatrice McDougall? Ever make any threats?"

"No, but we didn't really talk about that kind of thing."

"What stays most in your mind about him?" Dupree didn't feel like he had a real picture of the kid yet.

"It's all or nothing with him. We were

416

studying civil rights in class, and Gerald gave this paper about his grandfather."

"What about him?"

"Gerald claimed that the old man was the one who tried to make Rosa Parks stand up on the bus that day."

The black man in Dupree bristled, but the cop in him was interested. "Was it true?"

"I don't know, but that's what he had always been told. That was the legacy his family was proud of. It doesn't matter if it was true; he believed it. And he thought those same genes were part of him. He even has diabetes like his grandfather did."

"How serious is his diabetes?" Dupree asked. Cadence Moran had been right again.

"He's not insulin dependent. It's type 2 diabetes; he doesn't need shots. But he needs to control his exercise and diet or he could be in serious trouble."

Dupree jotted a reminder to canvass all the pharmacies in the city. Maybe they could track down Pickett through his diabetes-testing supplies.

"So what was it about this history paper he gave?"

"I think talking about his grandfather really underscored for him all the reasons that he wanted to leave his family. That was the day he came and asked me about the new emancipation law."

A boy who wanted to divorce his family and free himself from a legacy of criminal behavior and racial intolerance. Maybe prove he wasn't the "bad seed" he was accused of being. A boy who was organized and smart enough to use the legal system, to get a job and an apartment, and to graduate from high school without much adult supervision.

How does that boy become a murderer?

"We got some good tips on the Mercedes," the communications officer said two hours later. "Three callers said the car is parked behind a house in Casa Grande. They didn't see it until this morning." Dupree arranged for his Highway Patrol brethren to keep watch on the house until he and Nellis could get there to coordinate the takedown. Their ETA was thirty minutes.

They met the Highway Patrol car at the I-10 exit nearest the Casa Grande house and followed it west to the address where the Mercedes had been spotted. They stopped thirty or forty yards back from the building, hoping to keep the advantage of surprise.

It was a compact house, as deep as it was

wide, tucked into the shade of a massive cottonwood tree. The windows were barred, and a heavy wrought-iron screen covered the wooden front door. Nothing but sagebrush and knee-level prickly pear cactus for three hundred yards in any direction. Dupree sent officers around the back to cover that exit.

"Any sign of them?" he asked the senior Highway Patrol officer.

"We haven't seen or heard anything from inside. But with everything closed up like that, I'm not sure that we would hear them at all."

"Have we confirmed they're in there?"

"We only got word about the car a couple of hours ago. They may have parked it and left, but none of the neighbors saw them."

Only one way to find out. Dupree picked up the amplified megaphone and approached the house.

CHAPTER 92

Maybe we've made it, Pickett thought, settling into the big chair in the living room. Maybe this is where our new life starts, right here in Casa Grande. No more hiding in the shadows from Lolly's father. No more need to distance himself from his family. They could start over and be whatever they wanted to be. He arched his back against the deep leather chair but, too nervous to relax, his thoughts continued to roam.

All those little decisions — thousands upon thousands — that we make every day that later morph us into the person we become. Pet a dog or pull its ear? Wear blue today or red? Steal a pencil or give it back to the teacher? Turn right or turn left? Tell the truth and take the punishment or cross your fingers and hope for the best?

What was that first step he'd taken that led to becoming someone who could, without hesitation, plunge a knife into a beating heart? Maybe it wasn't a decision at all. Maybe Lolly's father had been right, and it was bred into his bones.

In any case, he had willingly followed Lolly's example: he'd learned to kill. And now he was the man everyone had always expected him to become.

The Casa Grande place wasn't as private as he'd hoped — there were houses visible in the distance on both sides — but he had pulled the car around back and drawn all the curtains.

He and Lolly had warmed canned soup last night and tried to gather their energies with sleep. Not that he got much rest at all. His dreams had turned to horror flicks — knives slashing, guns dripping blood, a voice shouting, "Stand up, God damn it! Stand up!" — and he'd awakened with a half-caught breath of terror at least a dozen times.

Lolly was even more skittish than he was, and he'd tried to cheer her up by celebrating with a bottle of Myers's Rum and some Coke he found tucked into the corner of a low cabinet. She'd pretended to party but only drank Coke, just like she should with a baby on the way.

What would that be like? Holding that perfect baby in his arms, a new person created by the love of two. Had his parents ever felt that way about him? Had they spent days planning his future? He didn't think so. He'd make things different for his new family.

Or maybe he was just passing along more of his family's bad blood — genes that determined his child would never be happy. Never succeed.

His insulin levels were going crazy. Flop sweat covered his face and chest and his pulse raced like it was nearing a finish line.

He knew they couldn't stay here for long. One more car change ought to do it. And maybe a name change to go with it. They probably knew his name by now, and certainly knew Lolly's real name. That's okay. New names to go with their new life.

He'd love to head south. They could lose themselves in Mexico, find a little thatched house on the beach and grow brown as coconuts watching their soon-to-be child play in the sand. But that road led through Pima and Santa Cruz counties, and there were far too many people looking for them there. Maybe head east. New Mexico or Texas. Lots of room there to build a new world together.

They should have left town right after he killed James McDougall. It would have meant leaving with nothing but his last measly paycheck and nineteen dollars from Mrs. Prentice's coffee can, but they would have been safer. Except that they would have been leaving a witness to their crimes alive.

"What are we going to do with the lady?" Beatrice asked, joining him in the leather chair and rubbing the back of his neck.

"Maybe we should let her go."

Why had it been so important to go after her, even after the cemetery when he learned she was blind? If he ended the woman's life, would it somehow erase all trace of his crimes? Could he go back to being the Gerald Pickett who had a future separate from his family's rotten roots?

"But she knows who we are," Beatrice crooned in his ear. "Finish what you start. That's what you always say."

Pickett shook his head. Everything had become so complicated.

He moved to the kitchen in search of something sugar filled and found an old can of peaches in heavy syrup. He opened it and ate half, willing his dizziness to disappear with every bite.

"You, in the house, the place is surrounded. Come out with your hands up."

The amplifier turned the voice tinny but

it was still clear. Pickett jerked at the sound and ran to the front window, peeking through a slit in the heavy curtains. His heart caught in his throat. Three Highway Patrol cars were angled like an open fan across the dusty front yard. The doors had been thrown open and cops crouched low behind them, guns raised and aimed at the house.

"Oh my God, oh my God," Beatrice keened.

"Quick, Lolly, get her out of the bathroom!"

Beatrice hustled back down the hall, shoving the blind woman with each step.

Pickett ran back to the kitchen and peered through the shuttered window above the sink. Two cops were off to the left, hunkered down behind a big creosote bush. It was too late now. This felt like something that had been destined generations ago. The decisions had already been made for him.

"Take this," he said to Beatrice, handing her his knife. "Hold it right up to her neck, tight. And stay real close to her." He slapped a quick two loops of duct tape around the blind woman's wrists.

Pickett opened the back door and yelled, "We're coming out. We've got a hostage. Don't try anything or we'll kill her!" He held the gun to one side of the woman's head, and Beatrice jittered the knife against her neck on the other side.

"You make one sound and they'll have brains on cactus all over the place," he told the blind woman, his voice shaking with false bravado.

They edged out the door and toward the black Mercedes. Radio static crackled as the officers in the back of the house alerted the rest of the team to the movement.

When they reached the car, Pickett told Beatrice to put the woman in the backseat, duck down by her feet, and stay low. He eased into the front seat, hoping that none of the shooters had a clean shot at him with the blind woman's head directly behind his.

He started the engine and the car took off like a jackrabbit across the open desert. In the rearview mirror, three officers scattered as they returned to their cars in pursuit.

The car scraped bottom as they sped through the thick sand of a shallow, dry arroyo. The steering wheel spun out of his hands, and Pickett thought they were going to get stuck, but the tires found hard-packed caliche at the last minute and they skittered up the other side of the wash.

He could see the freeway in the distance and headed northeast across the flat, dry land to intersect it, once crashing through a barbed-wire fence and dragging fifty feet of wire and metal posts with him until the car shook it off.

Sirens raged behind him, although he couldn't see them through the roiling dust he'd kicked up. Then, off to his right, two more cop cars, hoping to cut him off at an angle. He veered left, paralleling the distant freeway now instead of aiming straight at it. His heart thudded in panic.

The city of Casa Grande was behind him. No hope of getting back there and losing themselves in even that small town. But the Mercedes, while old, had been built for German autobahns; maybe he could try to outrun them. He glanced down at the dashboard. Fuck! Less than a quarter of a tank of gas. He'd have to do something soon. Beatrice was crying in the backseat, but the blind woman was quiet now.

"Hold on, Lolly. It'll be okay." He didn't believe it any more than she did.

Another barbed-wire fence. They crashed through like a bull on locoweed. What was this? A straight paved road, right in the middle of nowhere. Then he saw the wind sock, fluttering uselessly in the already hot air. A small airport.

He floored the gas pedal, pushing the old

426

Mercedes up to a hundred right down the middle of the runway. In the distance, heat waves radiated off two metal hangars. A dozen small planes were tied down on the tarmac to the left of the buildings. He aimed for those and screeched to a halt beside an old orange and white airplane that was just beginning to taxi out.

Pickett leapt from the car and tore open the door of the idling aircraft. He couldn't keep the gun steady against the pilot's head, but the guy was spooked enough not to notice.

"Hey, c'mon man, what are you doing?" the pilot said, hands raised reflexively in surrender.

"You're going to fly us out of here." He turned back to the Mercedes. "Hurry up, Lolly, get her in the plane." The flashing lights and sirens of the Highway Patrol vehicles raced down the runway toward them.

"We don't need her anymore. You said it yourself. She'll just slow us down."

"I never leave things undone, Lolly. I promised you that."

"I can't take all you folks," the pilot said, still maintaining a veneer of politeness although his face was white with fear. "We'll never get off the ground."

"The girls don't weigh much," Pickett said, helping Beatrice into the cockpit. He wormed his way into the rear compartment with her and then dragged the blind woman into the copilot's seat by her wrists. That way he could keep an eye — and a weapon — on both hostages.

"Shut the door," he told the pilot, who reached across his unwilling passenger to slam the right door shut. "Now go."

The pilot, a man of about fifty in a clean white T-shirt and khaki shorts, tried again to abort the takeoff. "We'll never make it past those cars on the runway. In this heat, with a heavy a load like this, we'll need a lot more runway than we've got."

"If we don't make it, I'm putting a bullet right through the back of your head." He knew he could do it. He'd already killed for Lolly, and she'd killed for him, for their new life together. One more death — two — what did it matter?

The man gulped and pushed in the throttle. The plane responded with a shudder and began a fast taxi roll to the northeast. At the end of the runway he slued the plane around and turned back toward the southwest for takeoff.

Two Highway Patrol cars had skidded to a halt and parked nose to nose, halfway down the mile-long runway.

"Go!" Pickett pulled back the hammer of the gun in punctuation, hoping that he looked more at ease with the weapon than he felt.

The pilot nodded, stood on the brakes, and revved the engine as high as it would go. When he released the brakes, the little plane shot forward like a racehorse and barreled toward the waiting police. "Sixty . . . seventy . . . we're not going to make it." The man's hands shook with the trembling of the yoke.

Pickett's eyes widened as the patrol cars filled the windscreen. With only feet to spare, the pilot jerked the yoke to his chest and the nose of the plane began to rise.

"Damn good thing those cops ducked," the pilot said.

CHAPTER 93

Dupree's Crown Vic had kept pace with the dark Mercedes, paralleling it across the creosote-studded desert until he saw the tiny airport up ahead and cut across at an angle to intercept the car.

It hadn't worked. He'd gone nose-down in a steep wash that he hadn't seen coming, the grille buried in the sand and the rear wheels airborne and spinning. The Mercedes raced on ahead.

"Get your cars across the runway!" he thundered into the radio. "We've got to keep them from taking off!"

Nellis grabbed the binoculars and they scrambled up onto the roof of the car. The airport was more than a quarter of a mile away, and heat waves danced across their vision, blurring and watering the image so that it looked like a dream.

"See anything?" Dupree asked.

"They're in the plane now. It's coming

this way."

Dupree grabbed the binoculars to see for himself. The orange and white plane was moving quickly toward the end of the runway. A half dozen Highway Patrol vehicles and two unmarked cars were arrayed like scattered sugar cubes midway down the tarmac.

The plane started rolling toward them.

"Oh, please God, no," was all Dupree could manage. He handed Nellis the lenses. "Did they make it?" he asked a moment later.

"Barely."

Dupree had one more question. "Rich, when they made a break for the car, or when they were getting into the plane, did you see the little girl?"

Nellis's silence gave him the answer he didn't want.

CHAPTER 94

I shuddered along with the plane as we streaked down the runway. By the sound of it, we were at a small airport, no control tower, unless the pilot was too scared to even try picking up the radio to announce his departure.

His voice was tight but still calm. I hoped he knew what he was doing. What had Kevin said about hot weather takeoffs? How much extra runway would you need for a small plane like this?

I gasped when the nose of the plane rose into the sky, willing it to go higher, faster, to make sure we didn't end up as a pile of smoldering spare parts at the end of the runway. We bumped into a sky full of summertime thermals, jostling the plane like a satanic fun house ride.

"My name's John," the pilot said. "John Anderson." I applauded his calm and his attempt to ease the tension of the standoff.

"I'll take you wherever you want to go, but you've got to put that gun away."

"Shut up and head south. We're going to Mexico."

The plane banked slightly to the left. "I'll take you south, but I wouldn't recommend Mexico. They've really beefed up the response to unidentified aircraft over the border. We have every chance of getting forced down by jet fighters, or just shot out of the sky. How about if I find some out-of-the-way landing strip and you all can take it from there?"

Keep him talking, Mr. Anderson.

"Lollipop, how you doing, honey?" The girl's breathing was rapid and strained.

"Lolly, you okay?" I felt Pickett lean toward her to say it this time. Again no response. "You hang in there."

I wondered if the girl was injured. Maybe afraid of flying? Or maybe the killings, the car chase, the sense of desperation had all become too much.

Suddenly the plane plunged down and to the right in a steep spiral. The sound of grunts and fists landing on soft flesh, the whine as the engine revved and the nose of the plane turned farther down.

"Gerald! He's going for your gun!" Beatrice shouted, coming out of her hyperventilated trance.

Two shots! The smell of cordite and blood. Moaning from beside me.

"What's happening?" I screamed.

The pilot gave a wet, gurgling breath.

I lunged sideways, my bound hands mapping the slumped shoulders of the pilot in the seat next to me. "Is he still alive? Pickett! Is the pilot still alive?"

From Pickett, a whistled intake of air through gritted teeth. From the pilot, nothing but a soft moan and a gush of blood from the chest.

The plane continued to spiral down.

"Hold him straight back in the seat," I ordered Pickett. I pushed the pilot's body back from his slumped position, knowing that if he let go of the yoke, the plane would at least return to horizontal flight instead of the death plunge the pilot had put us in. A moment later, the nose came up and the plane leveled off.

"I'm sorry, Bea. I'm so sorry. It wasn't supposed to end like this. I love you, Lollipop."

I gave silent thanks to whatever God there was that Teresa wasn't in the plane with us. And that this plane had dual controls like Kevin's did.

Flexing my knee, I foot-tapped around me

on the floor to trap the jittering rudders and gasped at the pain when the wound on my knee reopened. I placed my hands on the yoke and tried to swallow the bile that rose in my throat at the thought of what I had to do.

"Pickett, I'm going to need some help up here."

"Fuck you." A teenager's all-purpose snarled retort, and one of my favorites as well. Nice to know we had something in common.

"You help me right now or I let this plane fly itself."

Pickett leaned forward into the tiny space between me and the pilot, his breathing shallow and rank with his disease. Then he slumped into unconsciousness, head wedged between my shoulder and the side of the seat.

"Gerald! Wake up, wake up!" Beatrice wailed. Soon her cries descended into wordless ululations, broken by tears.

I explored Pickett with my bound hands and found a sticky, wet mass of clothing and torn flesh on his torso. He'd taken a bullet in the stomach.

Somehow, that didn't make the situation any better. A dying pilot, a gut-shot murderer, a catatonic teenager, and a blind lady in an airplane. It sounded like the setup to a very bad joke. God couldn't have made my last moments any more ridiculous if he'd tried.

"Pickett, get this tape off me!" I stretched my hands in his direction, but there was no response. I ripped the tape off with my teeth for a second time.

"Pickett!" I yelled again, jostling him with my elbow. I needed him awake and alert. "What does this dial say? This one right here." I pointed at the Plexiglas cover to the instrument panel. "Does it look like a watch, and the numbers go from zero to nine?" The plane felt familiar to me. If it wasn't exactly the same model of Cessna I'd practiced flying, it was at least a kissing cousin to it. Maybe a 172 if it had rear seats. I hoped I was pointing to the altimeter.

No response from Pickett, but Beatrice leaned over my shoulder. "It says four o'clock. And the one that looks like a second hand on a watch is stuck on zero."

Her response was almost childlike. I couldn't let her retreat any farther into physical and emotional withdrawal; I needed her eyes. But her description meant we were at four thousand feet. We might be okay for a little while.

"Beatrice! Look around, tell me if you see

any mountains anywhere." I hoped to hell she wasn't going to say yes. She took her time, leaning from one side of the plane to the other. Sweat ran between my breasts.

"The two tallest ones are one behind the other, way off over here" — she pointed past my right ear — "and there's a littler one behind us." I wondered if she'd ever flown before, if she understood the perspective I was asking for. In any case, I thought we'd be all right for the moment.

Pickett roused himself, leaning forward between the seats and fumbling around on the floor of the aircraft. A moment later, he jammed his newly recovered gun into my ribs. "South. We're going to Mexico," he grunted with pain.

"Sure thing, boss." I turned the plane to the right, having no idea at all where south was but hoping that he didn't either. Two minutes later, when I tried to turn back to the left, he jabbed me again. "Straight. Go straight."

If the gas tank on the plane had been full when we started, we could fly straight to Utah, east Texas, or the Pacific Ocean before we fell out of the sky. Or we could be shot by overzealous Homeland Security defenders as we crossed into Mexico.

Maybe I could keep us close to the cops

who were looking for us. I reached for the radio. Pickett lunged forward, smashing the gun on my outstretched fingers.

"What the fuck was that for?" I said. "The Border Patrol will shoot us down unless I radio who we are."

"No radio." He ripped the mike from the instrument panel.

We weren't going to make it. Sure, I could keep a plane flying straight and level, but, like the aviation-loving terrorists in Florida, I'd never learned to land one. Without help from a radioed Mayday — and even then I wasn't sure they could talk a blind person through a safe landing — as soon as we ran out of gas, we were going to crash into the empty desert like a hurled stone.

CHAPTER 95

The plane had been gone for almost a half hour.

"Did you get through to the Mexican Air Force?" Nellis asked.

"And Homeland Security and the federal aviation officials," Dupree said. "They all know that we're dealing with a hostage situation here."

"They also know it's a hijacking. And that makes it just as likely that they'll shoot them out of the sky."

Dupree knew that was true. In this post-9/11 world, the plane didn't have to cross international borders before it became a threat. Now Homeland Security was authorized to take the plane out before it crash-landed in a more urban environment or threatened a military facility.

"They could have gone seventy-five miles in any direction by now," Dupree said. "We've got patrol units spread out in case they've crash-landed." Two units had gone west on I-8 toward Yuma and California, and two others were streaking east on Highway 287. Traffic through Phoenix had hampered search efforts there, but the local television traffic copters had been enlisted to check the skies and less urban acreage to the north.

Military aircraft, on the lookout for the hijacked plane, covered the southern route. He knew they wouldn't last long if that was the direction they had gone.

CHAPTER 96

The heat in the cockpit increased, and sweat coursed down my face and neck. Fuck it. Our chances of getting out of this were slim, anyway. I apologized silently to Kevin and Emily. At least Teresa wouldn't die with us in the plane, but now there was no chance of finding her. I would be responsible for taking the life of yet another of their children. I was only glad that this time I would lose my life as well. I wouldn't have to witness the pain and sorrow I'd caused.

I wasn't going to take us any farther from the police than we had already gone. This little pocket of air — this hot, dry desert breath that tossed the plane like a toy, and the patch of ground underneath it — is where I would end it all.

I took a deep breath, settled into that karmic middle zone that Kevin called my autopilot, and began the slowest, most perfect two-minute turn of my life. Pickett's breath became shallow and irregular. He may have been losing consciousness again, but for whatever reason, he didn't detect my circling maneuver.

"Beatrice, are you okay back there?" I asked. The girl shifted into a new position but didn't reply.

I reached past Pickett and groped my way down the pilot's arm. No pulse. My stomach turned in horror. There was no way we were going to live through this.

I tried Pickett again. No response. With feather-light fingers, I waltzed across his thigh and down his forearm until I reached the gun that lay just inches below his unmoving fingers. I eased the gun toward me and shoved it under my right leg. I exhaled. At least we wouldn't die that way.

I nudged him again. This time harder. Nothing. I couldn't hear any breathing from him either, but the sound of the engine and the wind whipping past the plastic side windows may have muffled that. Unconscious or dead? I didn't care either way.

But I didn't know what his death would do to Beatrice. Catatonia or chaos? A lamentation of swans.

"Beatrice, cover your face with your arms, okay?"

I braced the steering yoke with my thigh,

gripped the barrel of the gun in both hands, and smashed the Plexiglas that overlaid the instrument panel. The first assault left a star pattern of cracks. I smashed again and again, grunting with every swing. Finally a sharp triangle of plastic fell away from the bottom center of the sheet. With slippery hands, I tore away the other pieces around it, sobbing with urgency, until I could locate the dials I wanted.

Great, I could reach the dials now but still not read them. I gripped the bezel around one dial with sweaty hands, but it wouldn't budge. Should I smash this second layer of glass to get to the instruments? I hefted the gun again. I wasn't sure if breaking the seal would affect the instruments that relied on static pressure.

Fuck it. Static pressure should be the last thing I was worried about. The accordion effect of plowing nose-first into hardened caliche at two hundred miles an hour was more likely. I tightened my grip on the gun and smashed the glass over every gauge and dial I could reach.

"Beatrice? I need your help up here." It was all I could do to keep my voice calm. Beatrice was my last resort. After an agonizing thirty seconds, she leaned over my right shoulder.

"You see this dial here?" I pointed at the altimeter. I located the raised edges of the bezel and cleaned away the remaining shards of glass. I needed a way to read the hash marks Kevin had described to me.

I leaned to the left, eased the bottle of Elmer's glue from my pocket, and handed it to her. "Try to line up right behind me, just like you were my eyes, and put a dot of glue right where the number one is. Then another dot for the number two. Go all the way around the dial." Her cheek, soft and warm, brushed mine as she reached past me. I focused on my perfect two-minute turn. I had to give the glue time to dry.

Bea finished her task with a sighed "There," and leaned back.

Blood had caked on my nose and lips from the damage done at Marty's house. It hurt too much to touch my nose; I knew it was broken. I settled for breathing through my mouth.

"Good job. But you've got more to do." I felt around to the next dial. "Do you see this one? Does it look like a speedometer? And it's got three colors on it? I'm not sure, maybe a green part and a white one —"

"And a yellow one," Bea filled in like a game show contestant battling for an un-wanted prize.

Good. The airspeed indicator. "Put a dot of glue right next to the number sixty, and the number eighty, and the number one hundred." If I kept the airspeed between those numbers I'd be able to keep the plane from stalling, I could use the flaps, and I might be somewhere near the proper landing approach speed.

We did the same for the vertical speed indicator, although I didn't know if I could monitor that one plus the altimeter at the same time.

Now for the directional heading. This one wouldn't matter as much if I didn't know where I was trying to land, but it would help keep me out of Mexican airspace. "Do you see a dial that has the shape of an airplane in the middle of it, and it's got the letters N, S, E, and W on it, like a compass?"

Beatrice took my hand and guided it to the right dial. The glass covering the dial was still intact and I smashed it with the lightest touch I could manage with the butt of the gun. "Okay, one drop of glue next to the N and two drops of glue next to the S." She did as she was told, and I felt the little airplane shape in the center of the dial shift direction to the west as I turned.

"One more thing. I want you to look out both windows as we're turning and tell me what you see. Are there any roads? Any hills? Do you see telephone poles or fences?"

She was quiet for a long time. When my fingers traced the same heading for a second time, I asked what she'd seen.

"There's a road down there. Kind of skinny and no cars on it."

"Does it look like a paved road?"

"Yes."

Okay, a paved road would be good. But aiming at something that small would be impossible for me to get right. I'd have to set it down on the desert floor and hope no saguaros or arroyos flipped the plane over as we landed.

"No fences? No telephone poles?"

"There are telephone poles along the road, but nowhere else." Okay, I'd have to avoid the road at all costs, then.

"Do you see any streams or little washes?"

"I don't see anything blue like water anywhere."

I had to smile. Kevin had told me about his first solo flying experience, when he got lost over a stretch of desert because he kept looking for "blue water" like the rivers shown on a map. In Arizona, most of the riverbeds are dry year-round, except during the monsoon floods of August when the arroyos are full of roiling brown water for at least a few hours.

"Okay, one more thing. Do you see any big saguaro cactus down there?"

"Lady?"

"Hmmm?"

"I'm sorry I smashed your hands. And, ummm, I'm sorry I told him to kill you."

I couldn't afford the luxury of reflection right now, either to damn her or offer penance. "What about the cactus?"

"It's mostly just little bushes. But I see some saguaros too."

I nodded. We'd just have to take our chances. If my sense of direction and Beatrice's description of the mountains were right, we were probably someplace east of Casa Grande. The Tortilla Mountains would be ahead of us and Picacho Peak to the south. I dropped to one thousand feet — much too low for the surrounding peaks of the Tortillas, but I thought they were far enough away.

"Beatrice? I'm going to keep turning the plane around real slow. When we get lined up with the road, you tap me on the shoulder, okay?" There was a hesitant tap when the directional indicator showed us going due south. I turned the plane sharply to the east to get out of the way of those telephone poles and began our descent.

Two minutes later, I put the flaps halfway down and decreased speed. The air in the cockpit was as hot and stale as an old devil's breath. The altimeter said seven hundred feet. I swiped at the sweat dripping into my eyes.

"Beatrice, can you get Pickett — Gerald — into the rear seat with you?" I put my palm on his forehead and pushed him back.

"You'll have to fasten his seat belt for him." I waited until I heard the belt buckle snick shut. She'd started crying again.

In my eyes, Beatrice was as guilty as Pickett. Egging him on to kill me, restraining Teresa for the motorcycle man. But the murders and chases had taken a toll on her. She was retreating to a childlike world of safety and security to avoid the pain. She'd become another child I was responsible for.

"Get your own seat belt on . . . curl up and cover your head with your arms."

Two hundred feet.

I hadn't heard her seat belt close, but couldn't wait any longer. I pushed the flaps all the way down, increased backpressure on the yoke to reduce speed, and settled in for what I hoped would be a landing and not a crash. Thank God this plane didn't have retractable wheels. I'd never learned that with Kevin.

One hundred feet.

"Head down! Put your arms over your head!" There wasn't time for more. The stall-warning siren shrieked as the reduced speed and angle of the plane weren't enough to keep the air flowing under the wings. We dropped like a boulder.

CHAPTER 97

Where the hell had they gone? Dupree gnawed on the cuticle around his thumb, willing the radio to spark to life with the answer. "Check in for me?" Dupree asked the senior Highway Patrol officer at the scene. They'd coordinated the search through the Highway Patrol dispatcher. The officer nodded and picked up his mike.

"Four-seven, Casa Grande. Any sign of our plane?"

"Copy, four-seven. I'll check," the dispatcher answered.

Big rigs hummed down the highway in the distance, and a car-size tumbleweed rolled lazily against the barbed-wire fence the Mercedes had carried across the desert then discarded at the last moment.

"Negative, four-seven," came the reply at last. "But we have two citizen calls into 911 from the Eloy area, about a plane flying erratically. No confirmation that it's the plane you're looking for."

"Thanks, Casa Grande. Four-seven out."

"Let's go," he said, but Dupree was already strapping himself into the seat.

CHAPTER 98

The altimeter read fifty feet and the stall warning continued to scream. With palsied fingers, I checked it again. If I was off by even one hash mark on the dial, we'd plunge into the desert sand like a cannonball.

I held my breath.

Then, five seconds before I expected it, the wheels bounced heavily in contact with the ground, and something smashed into the passenger window behind me. I cut off the gas, slammed on the brakes, and held the yoke as steady as I could. We raced forward over uneven ground, dipping and slashing at the vegetation around us. Then a sudden impact on the right wing, probably a saguaro, grabbed the plane and spun us around like a square dancer. We came to rest with one wing on the ground and one big grin inside.

A gust of wind caught the edge of the door. It beat a staccato metal-on-metal tattoo against the fuselage, in cadence with my racing heart.

It sounded like applause.

CHAPTER 99

The radio crackled to life. "We've got them in sight! East of I-10 near the Picacho Reservoir!"

Dupree and Nellis had been southbound in the Highway Patrol vehicle but turned at the Eloy exit and headed back north, spotting the plane shimmering like a mirage in the desert off to his right.

They skidded to a stop two hundred yards away, and Dupree motioned the other cars to go no closer. The plane was canted at a forty-five-degree angle, its right wing sheared off midspan by what used to be a thirty-foot saguaro.

He keyed the amplifier in the car. "You in the plane. Come out with your hands up!"

The passenger door was open and rattled against the cabin of the plane. Dupree drew his gun in preparation for the arrest. He'd seen Pickett and Beatrice McDougall racing from the Casa Grande house to the Mercedes, using Cadence as a human shield. Those three, plus the hijacked pilot, would be on board. Did he have another hostage standoff here? And where was the little girl?

When he reached the plane, he saw Cadence Moran in the copilot's seat and grinned. She waved distractedly, as though she'd seen his smile, then reached behind herself to a slouched figure in the rear compartment.

The other officers approached at a run, guns drawn. He flattened himself against the side of the plane and called in, "Ms. Moran? Are you all right?"

"Detective Dupree? Is that you?" Her voice was shaky.

He holstered his gun and moved to the open door. "It's me."

Signaling Nellis around to the other side, Dupree leaned into the cockpit. "Is he still alive?" he asked when Nellis placed two fingers against Pickett's neck. The response was a shake of the head.

"That's the pilot, John Anderson, beside me. Is he okay?" Cadence asked.

"No, he didn't make it, either." Dupree didn't know if the gun had been the pilot's or Pickett's, but Anderson's chest was bright with blood and it looked like he'd lost two fingers to the blast as he fought for control of the weapon.

Dupree held Cadence Moran under the arms and lifted her down from the plane. Her fingers were bleeding where the nails had torn off, her wrists were covered with bruises, and her nose was bloody and broken. "Where's Teresa?"

"They've still got her. Pickett left her with a man named Marty. He could be his brother or uncle or something." Dupree had already reviewed Marty Pickett's rap sheet and knew that he wasn't living at the last address he'd listed with the parole office.

"We've got to go get her! Ask Beatrice. She can take us there."

Dupree handed Moran off to an officer on his left and climbed into the cockpit to check on Beatrice McDougall in the back-seat. She still had a pulse, but she'd been tossed by the landing and must have cracked her head against the side window. A bloody smear coursed down the Plexiglas, and the right side of her head was creased with a four-inch red gash. Beatrice McDougall wasn't going to be of any immediate help in finding the little girl.

Dupree and Nellis escorted Moran away from the plane and settled her into the back of the unmarked car. Dupree pulled two bottles of water from the trunk.

"Are you really okay?" he asked, handing her a bottle.

"Sort of. How did you find us?"

"Somebody radioed in that a small plane was flying erratically and losing altitude." He smiled when he said it.

"Erratically, my ass. I was just waggling my wings to get your attention."

"What can you tell us about Marty Pickett's house?" Nellis asked from behind Dupree. It was the first time he'd sounded like her help would be welcome.

She rolled up her left sleeve and traced the raised white bumps that lined the inside of her arm like the beaded skin of a Gila Monster.

"We have a map."

CHAPTER 100

Cadence explained the system. The dots of glue started at her wrist and ended halfway across her biceps. "One dot for every thirty breaths, and I'd guess one breath every five seconds. So that means each dot is about two and a half minutes."

They drove back to the Casa Grande house where they'd started the chase. From there, Cadence's directions to turn left and right led them to a freeway exit ramp.

"This exit would have been for southbound traffic," Nellis said. "We'll cross back over for the entrance ramp we need to head north toward Phoenix."

"We were at freeway speeds for a long time up to here," Cadence said. She counted the raised glue on her arm. "Eighteen dots — about forty-five minutes. No stopping during that time, like for lights, and no sharp corners like intersections."

"Assuming that Pickett didn't want to attract any attention, he'd probably go the speed limit, so that's seventy-five miles an hour," Dupree said.

"Yeah, but within forty-five minutes you're going to hit Phoenix traffic, and there are sections through the city with lower speed limits. That'll screw up the calculations."

"Let's try it at the posted speed limit for the time Cadence says." They drove in silence, Cadence counting to herself as they ticked off the miles.

Nellis pulled off to the shoulder once the freeway had cut through the main congestion of the city of Phoenix. "We've got three different freeways you could have taken here and still not felt a major change of direction or speed."

"Can you remember anything else about this section of the trip?" Dupree asked.

Cadence closed her eyes as if it could increase her concentration. "We paralleled some train tracks for quite a while here. I heard the train whistle, and it kept pace with us."

"That rules out I-17 to Flagstaff," Nellis said. "But it still leaves us with either I-10 toward Blythe or northwest on Highway 60. They both parallel railroad tracks. Is there anything else?"

Cadence counted the dots again. "About

five or ten minutes farther on, I heard race car engines. Not like go-karts or kids having a sideshow, I mean real race engines. Meaty, growling, like NASCAR engines or something. I guess I was concentrating so hard on counting breaths that I forgot it."

"PIR!" Nellis said. Phoenix International Raceway was just off I-10 in Avondale. He started the car again and headed west. Fifteen minutes later they exited the freeway where Cadence told them to and jogged left and right through an old subdivision to an area where the houses were scruffier and farther apart.

"Okay, we're looking for a long driveway on the right. Not paved, but definitely smooth. I think he was in a mobile home and it had a shaded front porch. He had a motorcycle and there was a fountain not far away."

The first two driveways they turned into yielded nothing. Nellis drove through overhanging mesquite trees and pulled the car to a stop at the end of the third driveway.

"Does this one seem familiar?"

"I don't . . . I don't . . . Wait a minute. I don't remember tree branches brushing the roof of the car. This isn't it."

"Would you even have heard them from the trunk?" Dupree asked. "There's a metal

460

shed here that might have sounded like a trailer. We'll check it out."

He and Nellis circled around the rusted metal toolshed, guns drawn and held down by their legs. No signs of life, either at the storage shed or the bigger residential house a hundred yards away.

The shed was unlocked. The detectives bracketed the door and opened it with a slam. "Police! Come out with your hands up!"

No response. Dupree chanced a glance inside. A snow cone of pea gravel on the floor. Rusted rakes, a shovel, and a posthole digger leaned against the wall. No sign that Marty or his prisoner had ever been here.

By the sixth driveway, the panic was rising in Moran's voice. "We've got to go back to the freeway. We screwed up somewhere. Hurry!"

"We're close, Cadence. I can feel it." Dupree believed in her glue system and her calculations.

The seventh driveway led into a small mobile home park with a dilapidated swayback trailer at the end of the court. As they idled in the turnaround area in front of the trailer, Moran rolled down the car window.

"Two tiers of falling water, the fountain sounds right. Is there a bird-of-paradise by the front door? And a pineapple sage?"

"It's not much of a fountain. More like a big metal birdbath. And I've got no idea what that second plant looks like, but there's a bird-of-paradise," Dupree said.

"Use your nose. Does it smell like pineapples?"

Dupree got out of the car and, glancing at the mobile homes on each side to see if his movements were being detected, walked up to the front door and inhaled deeply. Pineapple: the smell of the islands. When he got back to the car, Nellis was hanging up the radio mike.

"The owner is listed as Anton Gregory. He's a biker, and he's got a record. Maybe Marty is staying with him or renting the place."

Dupree motioned the officers from the two patrol cars following them to fan out on either side of the trailer. He and Nellis approached the front door and knocked hard on the metal siding. "Police!"

A muffled greeting from inside, like that of an old dog left too long by himself. He didn't bark.

Dupree returned to the car and opened the back door for Moran. She snagged her foot in a red shop rag on the ground and bent down to pick it up. She held the cloth to her face and breathed in. "This is it."

"There's no one here. We'll leave officers to watch for him, and put an APB out."

Moran turned her head left and right, then pointed back to the entrance to the long driveway.

"There. That way. Maybe five hundred yards. Marty said he drove a Harley, and that's a Harley."

Dupree could hear it now, too. The junkyard-dog-grab-you-by-the-balls thunder of modified Harley pipes, revving up and moving away to the south. He motioned to the cops in the last car. "Let's go! Nellis, you stay here with the other car in case he circles back!"

He threw himself into the patrol car's backseat and they took off, spitting sand and gravel as they turned. The bike was moving south, about a quarter mile ahead of them now. It looked like the rider was alone, but from this angle Dupree couldn't tell if he had a little girl straddling the gas tank in front of him and clutching his chest.

They accelerated, moving past sixty . . . then seventy. Dangerous speeds on a thin rural road.

"Watch out!" The motorcycle slued left, trying to avoid an old pickup truck nosing out of a driveway on the right. The front wheel jigged from side to side, the rider overcorrecting in his panic.

Dupree gasped as the bike slid sideways, the rider's leg caught between asphalt and metal.

The patrol car screeched to a halt beside the downed motorcycle and Dupree ran to the man on the ground. He was as big as a buffalo, greasy hair to his shoulders, and tattoos like dark lace across his chest and arms. His left arm was bent at an impossible angle but his right hand was still on the gas. Dupree shut the bike down.

"Where is she? Where's the little girl?"

"Back at the trailer, man." Marty Pickett let his head fall back to the pavement.

Nellis used a tire iron from the patrol car to lever open the trailer door. He was the first one inside, but Moran pushed past the other officers to join him.

"Teresa!"

A buried, swaddled sound and thumping came from the bedroom. Wrenching open the narrow closet door, Nellis unlocked the makeshift cage that made up the bottom third of the space. Teresa's hands, feet, and mouth were bound with duct tape and her eyes were wide with terror, but she seemed otherwise unharmed.

"He said my new daddy was coming to get me," Dupree overheard her tell Cadence Moran in the back of the police car. Even the blind woman's strong arms couldn't stop her trembling.

He waited until the paramedics arrived and they were moving the girl into an ambulance.

"How'd you know it was Marty Pickett's Harley?" he asked Moran.

"That cloth smelled like him so I knew we were in the right place. I was just hoping it was the right Harley out there." She paused for a swig of water. "But I'm glad I finally found a use for my cousin's Guidelines for Being Able to Move Away From Home."

Dupree pretended that he knew what she meant.

CHAPTER 101

That night, when I was back in Tucson with an ice bag on my packed nose and cooling salve on my bruises, I celebrated with all the people who were important to me, and one who wasn't important anymore.

Juanita and Brodie flanked me on the couch, but Teresa and Bernadette were the ones who wouldn't leave my side. I cuddled and cooed until I felt like a mother mourning dove, and Emily snapped pictures as they kissed me.

Kevin had his broken leg propped up on the coffee table and had switched from beer to champagne in celebration. I was celebrating too, with the coldest glass of water I'd ever tasted.

My mother was there, eschewing the champagne for the bottle of gin she'd brought over for herself. "You never should have gotten involved, Cadence. You put my grandniece's life in jeopardy. I would never have forgiven you if something had happened to her."

We could all share in the blame for this one. Not just Gerald Pickett, a young man so desperate to shed his own skin that he would not only kill, but also be killed, in the process. So ready to prove his love that what he demonstrated was hate. And not just Beatrice McDougall, evil as she was. There were others to be added to the list.

Dupree and Nellis came in late, when the party had settled into self-congratulatory murmurs and recounted tales, not all of them true. My mind was already editing my performance: erasing the shakes and terrors, and cranking up the volume on the escape. As usual in the retelling: the hero of my own story.

Funny that we take credit, snatching it before it can get away, but we accept blame, holding it close only when no other arms reach for it.

Dupree, with his sweet gospel voice, probably already knew about handling blame and loss, but I didn't know how he would deal with the death of Darren Toller. Toller was as much an innocent victim as my Teresa, or Wanda Prentice.

Dupree and Nellis told us about the rat maze investigation that had led, too late, to

Gerald Pickett. About Priscilla Strout's extracurricular sex and petty thefts, and a pharmacist named Stephanos who stole money from both insurance companies and the elderly. About an anonymous young girl in a ghost town, whose family would never know that she was gone.

Darren Toller was part of that confusion, and that was my fault. I'd sent the police down that path and it had cost Darren Toller his life.

"Do you have proof that Pickett was behind it all?" I asked Dupree.

"His prints match what you and Juanita found on Mrs. Prentice's front window, and the Bible Gum cards at McDougall's house. Once the DNA testing is done, I'm sure that will match too."

Plenty of proof. Too late.

"But we found a partial print from Beatrice McDougall on Pickett's knife too. It was made when Wanda Prentice's blood was still wet. Beatrice is responsible for at least one of these killings herself." Dupree paused. "She's pregnant, you know. That's why she and Gerald had to get away. They couldn't let her father know."

Beatrice was going to have a chance to disprove her father's "bad seed" philosophy, after all. But she'd be doing it from a jail cell, watching from afar as someone else raised her child.

"There's no proof she participated in her father's death, but she's being charged with the murders of Wanda Prentice and the pilot and the man in Winterhaven. The county attorney wants to try her as an adult," Dupree said.

How strange that her father wouldn't treat her as an adult, but the state would.

Dupree said his good-byes, telling us he was anxious to get back to the hospital and his daughter. He told us about the motorcycle accident and said her boyfriend was going to make it but would never be the same man he'd been before. "Did I tell you they only had fresh vegetables and skim milk in that bag of groceries they were carrying? I may have to give Spider a little more credit in the future." I heard commitment in Dupree's voice, and maybe the desire to right a wrong he never thought he'd have the chance to correct.

"Did you find Priscilla Strout yet?" Brodie asked.

Nellis gave a sour laugh. "Yeah. She didn't want to split her inheritance with Arlen, so she got Randy Owner to drive her up to Las Vegas to get a divorce. And Owner, who thought we were on to his Corvette thefts again, was happy to get out of town."

Nellis asked me to close my eyes — the ultimate redundancy — then placed a wrapped package in my hands. I tore off the tissue paper to find a pair of sequined cat's-eye glasses. "New sunglasses," he explained. "You see better than some sighted people I know, so I thought your sunglasses should be flashier."

Given where we'd started, I took that as a compliment.

Brodie excused himself and went out to the car to get what he called my "homecoming present." The screen door slapped behind him when he returned, and my homecoming present announced herself with a sharp bark.

"This is Haley. She's a ten-week-old Lab and retriever mix and a washout from the Seeing Eye dog program 'cause she's deaf. I thought she could use a friend."

A deaf dog and a blind woman? It sounded like we'd both be learning some new tricks. "I think we were made for each other."

Brodie was the last to leave, promising with a scratch behind Haley's ear and a kiss on my cheek that he'd be back with coffee and Krispy Kreme doughnuts in the morning.

Haley dozed on my lap and I tested the

silence. It had a hollow, empty ache to it, the way the air can feel when a loud bell stops ringing. I ran my fingers through the puppy's feather-light hair.

Blame was the bitter brew at our communal trough, and I drank deeply. It didn't matter whether we were blind or sighted. Intuitive or scientific. None of us got it right. We followed the trail but failed to solve it in time. We dug through evidence but didn't discover anything. We proved but could not prevent. We even learned the killer's name but may never really understand what made him kill. Like a desert tarantula, he left no footprints in his passage.

All of it, all of it — too little, too late.

I'd done my best, and someday soon that would give me solace.

But the wind was picking up. And I swear I could hear the leaves of the Fault Tree rustling.

ABOUT THE AUTHOR

Although **Louise Ure** spent thirty years in advertising, she draws most deeply from her other passions — racing a 1966 Shelby Mustang and flying a plane — to bring *The Fault Tree* to life. Her first novel, *Forcing Amaryllis,* won the Shamus Award for Best First Novel. Born in Arizona, Louise now lives in San Francisco.

Please visit the author's Web site at
www.louiseure.com.

The employees of Thorndike Press hope you have enjoyed this Large Print book. All our Thorndike and Wheeler Large Print titles are designed for easy reading, and all our books are made to last. Other Thorndike Press Large Print books are available at your library, through selected bookstores, or directly from us.

For information about titles, please call:
 (800) 223-1244

or visit our Web site at:
 http://gale.cengage.com/thorndike

To share your comments, please write:
 Publisher
 Thorndike Press
 295 Kennedy Memorial Drive
 Waterville, ME 04901